THE WICKENHAM
MURDERS

THE WICKENHAM
MURDERS

Amy Myers

This first world edition published in Great Britain 2004 by
SEVERN HOUSE PUBLISHERS LTD of
9–15 High Street, Sutton, Surrey SM1 1DF.
This first world edition published in the USA 2004 by
SEVERN HOUSE PUBLISHERS INC of
595 Madison Avenue, New York, N.Y. 10022.

British Library Cataloguing in Publication Data

Myers,   Amy,   1938-
    The Wickenham murders
    1.   Private investigators - England - Kent - Fiction
    2.   Fathers and daughters - Fiction
    3.   Detective and mystery stories
    I.   Title
    823.9'14 [F]

    ISBN 0-7278-6116-6

Typeset by Palimpsest Book Production Ltd.,
Polmont, Stirlingshire, Scotland.
Printed and bound in Great Britain by
MPG Books Ltd., Bodmin, Cornwall.

Author's Note

I would like to thank Edwin Buckhalter of Severn House and his publishing director, Amanda Stewart, for their support for this novel from its very early stages, and their equally splendid team for seeing it through so efficiently to publication – in particular Hugo Cox for his eagle editorial eye. My agent, Dorothy Lumley of Dorian Literary Agency, also has my usual gratitude for her unerring instinct in picking the wheat from the chaff in my work.

In the path from the dawning of an idea to a novel's completion lie many pitfalls and I am very grateful to those who have done their best to help me avoid them: in particular my thanks go to Nick Claxton, Head of Forensics at LGC, Teddington, and his colleagues; to Suzanne Smith; to Martin Kender; to Allan Jamieson, Director of The Forensic Institute, Edinburgh; to the Royal Observatory at Greenwich; to Marian Anderson, to Clifford Long and to Valerie Barnard. If I have blundered into unseen pitfalls, it is through no fault of theirs.

A.M.

Chapter One

Georgia Marsh closed the front door and peered into her father's study. Good, he was up and she could hear the familiar squeak of his wheelchair. He was not at his computer desk, though. Not so good. She entered cautiously, for she liked to know what she was in for. Now that they lived in adjoining homes instead of together, this was usually easier to gauge.

He was still at his breakfast table (shared with a few piles of books and papers obviously brushed impatiently aside) and was bent over an open spread of the *Daily Telegraph*. He must have sensed her behind him.

'Georgia!' came a triumphant roar. 'Marsh & Daughter are in business again.'

She whipped off her coat and hurried in to find out the worst. 'We're never out of it, Peter.'

It was always 'Peter' at work; the role of father was left behind at the office door – at his wish as well as hers. It made each other's company more bearable outside office hours if the slanging matches that went on within them could be distanced – in theory, at least. The system worked, more or less.

Her comment was true enough. There was always some article to write, some interesting line of inquiry to follow up, some book to finish or proof-read, some phone call to be made to DI Mike Gilroy (poor chap). Straight-faced, she'd suggested once that the Stour, Peter's former Kent police area, should lay on a scrambler phone to his home for secure speedy access. It was sourly refused, with no sign of a grin on the DI's face. In Peter's endearing mind, the right to ask well-earned favours went on for ever; after all, it was only nine years since he'd had to retire because of the shooting incident that had paralysed him.

'What's set your nose twitching this time?' She peered curiously over his shoulder but no obvious headline leapt out at her.

'Fee fi fo fum, I smell the sniff of a stink here.' He jabbed his finger down on a four-line paragraph under 'News in Brief'. 'Remember Wickenham? Up on the North Downs somewhere towards Gravesend. I *said* it was a sad sort of village, didn't I?'

'Can't place it. Yes, I can.' A vague memory returned. 'Donkey's years ago though.'

'It may be donkey's years ago – after all, these two legs were operating then,' Peter replied without rancour, 'but you must remember it. I'd had a case in Dartford, and you came to meet me for some reason. We stopped at Wickenham for tea.'

The memory was becoming more vivid now. 'A sprawling village trying not to be a dormitory town for London,' she recalled. 'Oh, and a funny old cream-tea place with stale cakes. What about Wickenham, anyway?' Annoyingly Peter was now keeping his fist over the relevant paragraph.

'Skeleton discovered in denehole.'

'Is that all?' The deneholes of the chalky north of Kent were a notorious danger for inquisitive boys and unwary walkers in the woodland areas. Their long vertical shafts, often with old treads in the walls for descent to the tunnels spreading out below, were an enticement for the adventurous, especially since their age was shrouded in mystery. Were they ancient mines, or hidey-holes, or more modern burrowings for the lime kilns of the nineteenth century? Whichever, the story didn't seem to merit Peter's excitement.

'Come off it, Georgia,' he said impatiently. 'Not like you to be so blinkered. How can we know if that's all? It could be the remains of a Saxon king, it could be Lord Lucan's, it could be the door to the greatest challenge we've ever had. You remember I said at the time there were unanswered questions in the Wickenham air.'

'Did you?' She frowned, annoyed that still nothing much came to mind, even though a shared 'nose' was the very basis of their partnership.

Research was chiefly her department, writing was chiefly his, and they divided the phoning and Internet work between them. Peter had his adapted car for transport, but his own forays into the outside world so far as business was concerned were cunningly crafted affairs in which the role of wheelchair-bound author was carefully exploited. You, Georgia, are my eyes and my legs, he would grandly declare – unless he decided to become involved himself.

On the whole Marsh & Daughter made a good team. Most importantly, she and her father shared an instinct for unfinished business, sometimes in a story, but usually in the atmosphere of a place. This was what gripped them both. She was never sure whether this instinct was inborn or developed over the years. Perhaps it was both. In his former career Peter had always been drawn to a particular kind of case, which the then Detective Sergeant Gilroy termed as 'having his name on it', and it invariably turned out to hark back to the past for its resolution.

'Fingerprints left on Time,' is how Peter and she described it. Nothing harsh, nothing tangible, just the imprint of traumatic events on the places where they had happened, especially those that had had no closure. After all, he would pontificate, ghosts were thought to be a form of fingerprints on Time, as they haunted the localities where they had lived. It was an illogical contradiction that although Peter scoffed at the idea of visible ghosts, they both believed wholeheartedly in the fingerprint theory. It was no different from entering a house or pub for the first time and sensing a happy or unhappy atmosphere. It could stem from the present or from the past, but it was there. Georgia had been sceptical at first, and then once she'd visited Montségur in south-west France, site of the massacre of the Cathars in the thirteenth century. That had convinced her. The passage of thousands of tourists and pilgrims had failed to expunge the air of tragedy there.

Wickenham might not be a Montségur, but Kent was an interesting county in which the all too evident signs of modernity, with its fast-rail Channel link and motorways cutting their scars through its middle, obscured the slumbering past, which every so often would rise up and remind the world of its presence. The recent discovery of the Bronze Age Ringlemere Cup was one such example.

Their own village, Haden Shaw, not far from Canterbury, and, as was Wickenham, on the Kentish North Downs, had an atmosphere about it that reminded her daily that with every step she took she was walking on the lives of the past. It was all the more annoying therefore that she couldn't remember Wickenham more clearly. 'So whose is the skeleton? Is that the mystery?'

'Not necessarily. In fact probably not at all,' he said complacently. 'Remember the Ada Proctor case? It came back to me while we were there and your mother looked it up when we got back.'

Always 'your mother', never Elena. It was his way of distancing her in his mind. The fact that her mother had done the looking up probably explained why Georgia had half blotted out the memory. Those had been the nightmare years, which now seemed another country, a land she and Peter did not visit any more, even though it still lay deeply buried within them. It was the tacitly acknowledged spur that drove the work of Marsh & Daughter, while Elena Marsh was now Elena Pardoe and living in France with husband number 2.

'Yes,' Georgia replied loudly.

'I thought you would.'

'The doctor's daughter.' She scrabbled in her memory. 'Found strangled in a field early one Friday morning in the 1930s or so.'

4

'1929, to be precise.'

'Sexually assaulted.'

'Wrong. Not proven. Some clothing missing, torn and disarranged, plenty of signs of a fierce struggle – possible sexual attack, but no forensic evidence to prove anything other than strangulation.'

'But that was why –' Georgia was getting involved now '– the prosecution argued that wasn't important. She was a mature woman, well built, and was too strong for her attacker to succeed in his first aim. She must have fought him off, and he grabbed her from behind to stop her screaming.'

'Hardly important in the middle of a lonely field at night. I remember thinking that when I first read about the case. I've got it here somewhere.' Peter picked up his book claw contraption, which was always close at hand, and hoicked off the shelf, catching it in his free hand with a deftness born of long experience. 'John Mitchison, *Village Murders*, 1972. It's the only published account to my knowledge, and it stuck in my mind. Think, Georgia. You must see the glaring question.'

'Why was she in a field at that time of night with anyone whose company she hadn't carefully chosen? Didn't they say her attacker was a slight lad, medium height?'

'Yes. Young Davy Todd. Ah, Margaret –' he turned to greet his carer-cum-housekeeper – 'the restorative coffee and biscuits.'

'No. The restorative coffee and an apple,' she informed him tartly. Margaret was the sanest person Georgia had ever met. She had to be to cope with Peter's moods. She had been the village doctor's receptionist until she fell out with his computer. Fortunately for the Marshes, this had co-incided with Elena's departure, and her six hours daily kept Peter's life in order. Or relative order.

'You'd think, being a cripple, I could have something I liked,' Peter complained bitterly.

'Tell yourself you like apples.' Margaret was clearly in

no mood for negotiation and Peter had the art of judging this down to a fine art.

'Davy Todd –' Peter turned to Georgia after this ritual was concluded and Margaret retreated victorious – 'was the Proctors' young gardener. The evidence against him was circumstantial but strong, and Dr Proctor gave reluctant testimony that Ada was always hobnobbing with Davy. He was arrested, tried, found guilty and hanged for murder in April 1930. He was twenty years old in 1929. And she was thirty-seven.'

Only three years older than she was, Georgia instantly thought. 'Any doubt about the verdict, Peter?'

'That, Georgia darling, is what I keep a daughter for. It seemed to me such an unlikely murder, especially since it took place on Hallowe'en, hardly a time for canoodling in the open. So it's your job to find out if Ada Proctor and Davy Todd are still leaving fingerprints over the village.'

'We don't know anyone is,' she pointed out. 'It's years since we've been there. Whatever it was you sensed may have disappeared ages ago.'

'So what? If the ghost of Anne Boleyn stepped out from behind that fireplace, you wouldn't say push off, you're too late to be interesting, would you?'

'I'm not sure what I'd say,' Georgia answered fairly. 'I might run for my life, or I might ask her whether she knows her daughter, Good Queen Bess, became a twenty-first-century media celeb. There was another historical documentary on TV last night. Did you see it?'

'Don't change the subject. Wickenham.' Peter jabbed his finger on the paper. 'It needs Marsh & Daughter.'

'Cut the rhetoric,' she suggested politely.

'You're unusually crochety this morning, Georgia. Where's your sense of mystery, of endeavour, of adventure?'

'Still asleep on my pillow,' she retorted. 'A somewhat disturbed night. Someone was playing a tape of "The Emperor" very loudly at 3 a.m. It's all very well for you, this house is on a corner, it's just me that suffers.' It was the usual badinage. They both knew why he did it.

Ada Proctor had refused to go away during the two weeks that had passed since their first discussions of the case, but they were very little further forward. Before Ada had stepped into their lives, they had been working on an interesting case in East Anglia – another skeleton in fact, so why should it be Ada's murder that persistently thrust itself before her? Probably it was because of the lack of progress, Georgia convinced herself. Peter simply cast her a look when she expressed this view to him, however, and she knew why. They both remembered that when they had met in Wickenham that day she hadn't been alone.

It wasn't just Elena that had drawn a veil over Wickenham for them both. Zac had been with her. No wonder she'd done her best to forget the day – just as she had her brief (if exciting, she granted him that) marriage. Only that couldn't be entirely forgotten since Zac, once out of prison, kept turning up like a bright new penny – usually without any of the latter. A more incompetent criminal than Zac Taylor she couldn't imagine, save that he had succeeded in fooling her for three years.

If Ada Proctor had been a fool in encouraging Davy Todd, Georgia was scarcely in a position to throw stones. Indeed, Marsh & Daughter wasn't in a position to throw anything at present, owing to lack of information. She could find nothing in the local press about Davy Todd after the date of his hanging. The 1930s were before the days of pressure for investigation of doubtful verdicts – though nothing Georgia had so far read suggested this one was. There hadn't even been an appeal.

The greatest disappointment was that their trawl of the National Archives/Public Record Office website had revealed that the records of the trial were scanty.

'No appeal, and no transcript of course so far back,' Peter had reported gloomily. The practice of printed shorthand notes had come to an end in 1912, and there clearly hadn't been enough public interest in the case for the Treasury Solicitors and Director of Public Prosecutions to keep full records. 'Poor old Davy was hardly a Roger Casement treason trial,' Peter continued. 'There's a listing in the Calendar of Depositions and another under Indictments, but I doubt if they would tell us anything that we don't know already. Only jury summonses, the charges, gaol deliveries and so on, and the results of the original trial and appeals. With luck the coroner's report inquest documents might be there.'

'Any lists of exhibits attached?'

'Yes, you can pop up to Kew to see what's there. I couldn't see anything dramatic mentioned in the *Times* report that needed cross-checking.'

This was the one bright spot, since the law reports in the press were much fuller in the days of Ada Proctor than they were now, and some years ago Peter had splashed out on the microfiche of *The Times* for the first ninety years of the twentieth century plus the CDs for more recent years.

Davy Todd had been charged on 1 November 1929, the inquest was on Monday the 4th, and the funeral the following day. He was committed for trial at the Old Bailey on the 7th, and the trial was held early in February. All very quick by today's standards but fairly normal for those days. The trial only lasted two days, but *The Times* provided a few paragraphs of verbatim evidence.

'Here –' Peter waved a printed sheet at her – 'is the voice of Davy Todd, give or take an assumption that the *Times* reporter wouldn't or couldn't reproduce the Kentish dialect for his readers.'

'Read it to me,' Georgia asked. Local dialect past and present was one of Peter's specialties and he liked nothing more than speaking it. This was his moment and he took it.

'This is from his cross-examination,' Peter began. '"Question: That night you'd arranged to meet Miss Proctor, hadn't you?" "No, it were de next night," says Davy. "We'd been going to go dat night, being All Hallow's Eve, see, but she said she were going to Lunnon and didn't know what time she'd be acoming back. So it were de next night we fixed on and I went to see my Mary dat night instead. I were glad o'dat. Den I did see Miss Proctor dat night walking up lane to de fields, I were surprised and I said dat to Mary, I did. I did.'"

A chill ran through Georgia. Peter was good – too good. It might of course be a problem to listen to Davy's words across the decades. Too much of it, without knowing the background and understanding where and how it had sprung from, could be dangerous. It could influence them too much too soon.

Peter realized this as much as she did, for he said, 'Just one more extract for now. Here he's under real pressure, I'd say. Question: "You liked Miss Proctor, didn't you?" Answer: "That I did." Then the crown counsel pushed on: "You liked her very much, didn't you? You wanted to touch her, kiss her." Answer: "No, I don't dare. She was doctor's daughter." Question: "Dare? So you did want to touch her." Answer: "I never wanted to. Not never."'

'What about Ada?' Georgia managed to say. 'She isn't here to speak for herself.'

'You'll find something,' Peter said airily, 'when you go to Wickenham.'

When, she noted, not if. Wickenham was the next hurdle to face – and preferably without the shadow of Zac trotting along beside her. She needed objectivity. At the moment Peter was far more certain than she was that either the Proctor case or the skeleton merited a full investigation by Marsh & Daughter. So far all she'd discovered about Ada's life was an obituary notice recording the death of Dr Edward Proctor of Wickenham in 1935, and some further ferreting by Peter on the Internet had produced the death of Winifred Proctor, presumably his wife, some ten years earlier. The presumption was therefore that, as well as helping in the surgery and perhaps in the dispensary, Ada had kept house for her father, an inevitable role common to so many women who had been left without potential mates after the appalling slaughter of World War I.

Her face, photocopied from a newspaper report, and propped up above Peter's computer, stared out at them with all the defiance and mystery that a cloche hat could provide.

'Mask the hat and what do you see?' Peter asked.

'Someone who'd take a first at Oxford if she'd been born thirty years later,' Georgia replied promptly. It was a face not unlike her own, at least in its length and relative thinness, though since Ada's hair was straight and short, and her own longer hair was drawn back and held at the nape of her neck, it was hardly a true comparison.

'Yes. Would you say she was passionate?'

'Hard to tell.' Georgia frowned. The grey fuzz of the photocopy from a bad original hid personality. 'I would say yes, but that doesn't necessarily mean sexually. Firm about what she believes in.'

'It could be important, Georgia. Nothing we've read so far explains what she could have been doing in Crown Lea so late at night except meeting Davy Todd. Her father testified he'd seen her in the house at nine thirty when he retired for the night – don't you love that phrase, Georgia, I think I'll start using it – and she was killed between nine and eleven, a reasonably wide time span. Let's assume it's roughly accurate, especially since the body was found early next morning, not too long after the event. Had she been strangled where she was found? We don't know. Not reported. Had she been dragged there? And most important, if it wasn't Davy Todd whom she was meeting that night, who was it? She looks a sensible woman, which means whoever it was, she must have either wanted sex with him or thought it wasn't on the agenda. And even Davy admits they had originally arranged to meet then.'

'That brings us back to where we began. If she had developed a mad passion for their young gardener, she could have invented a more hospitable trysting place than a field in the middle of the night.' It was checkmate again. Love in a muddy field at the end of October? Surely even if she really fancied Davy she could have found somewhere more comfortable.

'His defence is that he was with his girlfriend Mary Elgin at her home until eleven thirty or so,' Peter pointed out, 'and she confirmed it on oath, although of course no one believed her. She said her father had come home and found them together, but he flatly denied it, so it was clear – to the jury anyway – that she was lying to protect him. There's an interesting point, though. Two witnesses testified they saw Davy returning home in a dishevelled state, with blood on his face, and this was at about eleven forty-five, after the dance ended. That might have helped corroborate his story but, as Mary's father denied it, it was assumed Davy had been busy murdering Ada and was coming home late. If we accept that Ada was indeed dead by eleven, what was Davy doing for those forty-five minutes?'

'Panicking?' Georgia offered.

'Then why not run away, or go straight back home?'

'Hoping to escape notice?'

'Weak. And another thing, one witness, their maid, testified Ada had been excited that evening because she was meeting someone later. It was a big secret and her father was not to know. Would Ada have told anyone at all if it were Davy she was meeting? I doubt it. Certainly not their maid. On the other hand, another witness said Ada was a prim and proper woman who would never have gone out late with anybody she didn't know and trust – and she trusted Davy Todd, according to her father's evidence.'

At that point the telephone interrupted them and Peter snatched it up irritably, then suddenly the voice changed to Peter Purr mode. 'Good to hear from you, Mike.'

He listened attentively, then purred his grateful thanks.

'Was Mike growling, groaning or grinning?' Georgia asked. DI Mike Gilroy's grins were detectable over the phone, but they were rare, even though she suspected there were more on the inside than he let the outside world see. She wondered if his wife Helen saw a different Mike. On the few times she had met them together, there was no sign of it, but she sometimes played with a fantasy of Mike indulging in silly Christmas games with a paper hat on his head.

'I can't think why you have this notion that Mike thinks I'm a pain in the neck. He was delighted to contact Darenth Area for me.'

'So what's the news on the denehole skeleton?'

'It was discovered when some kids were climbing down it. Strictly against orders of course. The denehole had collapsed, leaving part of the shaft intact but a bell-shaped hole at the foot. The skeleton was underneath a pile of debris that had collected over the years. The coroner's asked for a forensic report, and the interim news is it's that of an adult male aged roughly between thirty and forty; it had been there some time and had fractured bones consistent with a fall. You know, Georgia, I'm beginning to sniff that this skeleton is the path we should follow.'

'Any clues on identification?' She refused to share his excitement yet.

'Few shreds of clothing, and a bag of other stuff to go through that might or might not be connected. Nothing exciting yet, but you can bet your bottom euro there will be. Let's go for it, shall we, even if it's nameless at present.'

Just a body, Georgia thought. And now it's been found, he's unlikely even to be identified, whatever Peter so confidently predicted. Even if the lab could get a DNA profile from the bones, there'd probably be nothing to match it against on the National DNA Database. This perversely convinced her that Wickenham should be a Marsh project, even though the Ada Proctor trail was calling far more loudly to her than this unidentified skeleton. She knew it was the reason that drove Peter on too – and that therefore the die was cast.

'Do you see another book in this,' she asked bluntly, 'or just an article?' Peter had recently sent in their current script on a murder case from the 1940s, and he hated being without a project.

'Of course. But Wickenham itself is summoning us, my darling,' he said virtuously. 'Something there needs laying to rest.'

Chapter Two

There was little sign that anything in Wickenham needed laying to rest. It had all the appearance of a thriving community, near enough to London for commuting but with no sense that the village emptied itself between rush hours. Georgia decided to stroll around the streets before checking in at the Green Man, where she had booked a room for the night. Even for a woman, a pub was a good place to stay, but first she needed to acclimatize herself to the feel of the village. First impressions might not be correct, but they could be invaluable for that very reason.

Sniffing round villages was a whole branch of archaeology in itself. There was the physical archaeology: the old village was spread chiefly along one main street, with some splendid medieval and Tudor houses, with a green of rising ground at its heart. With golden leaves beginning to fall, and the gentle September sun, it was a peaceful sight, and not one that suggested hidden turmoil, either past or present. Statelier Georgian and Victorian buildings flanked the older buildings, and on the outskirts of the village came the twentieth century's proud additions, spruced up by a council estate and smaller newer private estates. She had the impression that a lot more had been built since she and Peter had come here. Replacing Green Belt country or not, the estates were a great deal neater and tidier than the usual sixties' and seventies' sprawl.

The mental archaeology interested her even more. Today, most villages had layers within layers in their communities; the old villagers whose families had lived there for

14

generation after generation, incomers who had lived in the village long enough to integrate fully, and incomers who had usually come more recently and who commuted and/or had no interest in the village as such. Old loyalties fought new blood, old ways met new attitudes and these would play their part if she and Peter had been right about Wickenham licking its wounds.

The Green Man pub was in the centre of the village. There was at least one other pub in Wickenham, the Red Dragon, not to mention the former manor house, Wickenham Manor, now a posh 'country' hotel. Opposite the pub was the Green, around which were grouped some fine Tudor brick cottages and one or two shops such as Todds' butcher's shop. On the flatter part of the Green cricket had once been played, according to her guidebook. It was not large enough for a modern pitch, however, and the game had gravitated further up the road to a field next to the football pitch, both belonging to the Wickenham Manor estate. She knew this since a poster on the village notice board on the pub wall had announced the formation of a group to protest against the sale of these fields. Judging by the passion such matters aroused in their own village, Haden Shaw, she guessed this would be a hotly fought issue, so perhaps Wickenham's peaceful appearance was indeed only superficial.

The Green was obviously now for show and for dogs. Not that any dogs' mess would be tolerated on this spick and span grass. This seemed a village that prided itself on its appearance. If there was an underclass, she decided, it was being kept firmly in its place or perhaps it only roamed at night. Staying in the pub, she would surely find out as she began the slow process of skimming away appearance layer by layer until she felt she could sense the soul of the village. Wickenham is a pleasant place to live, haven't we done well, was the message it was successfully putting over, whether consciously or not.

On impulse, she decided to walk further along the road from the pub to the end of the Green, for it was there that she remembered visiting that cream-tea place. Was the rather crabby owner still churning out yesterday's stale walnut layer cake in her beautiful garden? Funny she should suddenly remember that garden. Perhaps it had stuck in her mind because she recalled thinking that so much love had gone into tending it that there was clearly none left over for the owner's teashop work.

At first she walked right by the cottage, not recognizing it, and it was only when she saw the baker's shop beyond it and remembered the teashop's precise location that she returned to it. There were no teas offered here now. Perhaps new bylaws had put paid to it, but more likely it had been the owner's age. This was a smart private house now, with fancy new shutters and leaded panes. Clematis was being carefully trained to begin a steady climb upwards. A brightly painted cartwheel adorned one wall, and the cottage flowers and roses that had filled the original garden had given way to one bullied into shape with bedding plants. Roses there were, but they were modern hybrid roses, which any self-respecting bee would ignore. This was not the cottage garden she remembered.

O crabby old lady, why do you suppose
You mistreated your cakes and loved only your rose?

Careful, Georgia, she warned herself. She was here to do a job, not to compose doggerel on bygone teashops. It was time she began her research routine. She had a set plan for this now. She would check in to a pub late morning, and immediately come down for a preliminary skirmish with the owner or manager or barman, then stay on for a bar lunch to absorb local colour.

The Green Man, although an old building, had obviously undergone a lot of transformation over the years. It had travelled along the path of practical comfort too far for the clock to be turned back, as fashions changed, to quaint beams and nookery. Nevertheless it had a pleasant

16

atmosphere, and she felt encouraged that it might still be the meeting point for all layers of the community.

'What you here for then? Holiday?' The man behind the bar produced her half of shandy with as much aplomb as if it were the finest claret of his cellar.

He was the owner, rather than manager, she guessed from his relaxed 'I'm a welcoming barman' attitude.

'Work, I'm afraid.'

He couldn't be more than forty, Georgia estimated. Much too young to know anything about Ada Proctor.

'What work's there in Wickenham on a Wednesday?'

'I do research for writers.' She knew from experience the word 'journalist' couldn't be relied on to help her. Some would reward it with an instant glint, seeing publicity and money in the offing; others shied away. 'Research for writers' distanced it nicely. Few would know what it involved, and indeed she had no clear definition herself. She thought at first he wouldn't pick up on this, but at last he did.

'Research, eh?'

'Into Wickenham's history.'

'Oh. Bet you didn't know the Mighty Mynn played his first single-wicket cricket match here?'

She didn't and he hadn't, unless Harrietsham was a false claimant.

'How interesting,' she rewarded him. 'Do you play?'

'Me? Nah. You have to have lived here for fifty years to get on the team. I've only clocked up ten.'

'I'm looking into a murder that took place here in 1929.' This must be safe enough. There would be few toes to tread on here.

'Too early for me. We've had a few more since then, I reckon.'

'The skeleton in the denehole, you mean? Does the village think that's murder? Seems more like accident.'

'Don't know nothing about that.'

Georgia was afraid she'd gone a step too far, and he

would clam up, but he didn't. He went on to talk of a pub fight five years earlier, not at the Green Man of course, he hastened to assure her, and a carpenter who went mad and slaughtered his family eight or nine years back. Neither could have been the reason that Peter's nose had twitched, since they were both after the time of their first visit. Her own nose, she realized, had failed to come to life as yet. Was Ada Proctor a good line of inquiry or not? So far she hadn't a clue. There had, after all, been two other murders to which she'd found passing references in the local press. A girl in her twenties had been found dead on the outskirts of the village in the late 1950s, and a local farmer had been shot by a neighbour in the 1970s in a love triangle. She concluded that Ada Proctor had at least to be eliminated as the cause of Wickenham's 'unfinished business' before she began on anyone else, including the skeleton. She now felt a personal involvement with that face, and would not let it down without good reason.

The bar was beginning to fill up with lunchtime regulars, so she took her jacket potato into a corner, together with another shandy, and prepared to look like part of the woodwork.

Drinkers' body language could tell you a lot about a village. The sideways lounger with the elbow on the bar, the drinkers who squarely faced the bar, both elbows firmly on it, the mates' circle, taking up mid-floor position, the regular on the regular's stool, and the passers-through and pensioners who humbly retreated to the tables. There were few of the first sort here today, since they tended to be the commuters or the weekend visitors, but the others were well represented.

The telephone directory had revealed no Elgins but plenty of Todds living in the area, including the butcher. However it was a common name and, though she had patiently tried each one, all of them had denied any connection with Davy Todd. Nevertheless, bearing in mind that the murder was well over seventy years earlier, and memories could be short as well as long where murder was concerned, she had not yet given up hope. She had timed this visit to Wickenham carefully, for the local paper had announced a display of old postcards in the village hall this week, organized by a Mr Jim Hardbent. This was her afternoon assignment, and one of which she had high hopes.

The village hall was tucked behind the Green on a new road in a large site of its own, complete with car park. A modern building, it had Lottery money written all over it. The exhibition was in a side room and, since the whole hall had an empty feel to it, she was relieved to find that there was a solitary man sitting at a table.

She decided to 'do' the exhibition first, marvelling that one village could produce so many different postcards, and thanking her lucky stars that the majority of these stemmed from the heyday of the village postcard, the early twentieth century. She took her time, trying to gain atmosphere as well as information and to build up some idea of what the village must have looked like in Ada Proctor's time. That done, she approached the 'curator'.

'Would you be Mr Hardbent?' she asked. She could hardly believe her luck, if so. No young collector, but a tanned and bearded middle-aged to elderly man who had probably lived here all his life and would know the background to each and every one of these postcards.

'That's me.'

'Is there one of the old doctor's house, pre-Second World War?' she asked. 'I'm interested in the Ada Proctor murder.'

'Are you now?' He eyed her carefully. Bluff countryman he might look, but his eyes were sharp. 'Now what would your interest in that be?'

'Davy Todd,' she replied promptly.

He nodded. 'And why's that?'

At least he had heard of him. One up for Davy. 'I investigate old murder cases.'

'Funny job for a woman. What's the point of it? Gruesome, I call that.'

'If you were the victim's family you might not want to feel your loved one had just disappeared into anonymity. And if the murderer's family felt an injustice had been done they too might welcome an investigation.' She felt she'd put this unusually awkwardly and received her just deserts.

'Let 'em rest in peace, say I.'

'If they can. I don't know whether this applies to Ada Proctor or not, but I want to find out more. If there's nothing, I'll go away. If there is, I'll hunt down as much as I can until I reach the facts about what really happened.'

He thought this over, and gave a reluctant nod, to her relief. 'I'll show you. You missed it.' He took her to one of the stands and pointed out a postcard of a rather nondescript late-Victorian villa. 'Taken about 1910, that was. The Firs, it was called.'

'And who owns it now?' She couldn't recall seeing it.

'Pulled down for development years ago. Flying bomb fell on it.'

Without her asking – though she was aware she was being judged – he took her round the rest of the exhibition, explaining in such detail where and what everything was that the village began to blow into life in her imagination.

'That's Wickenham Manor.' He pointed out a large classical eighteenth-century house, surrounded by gardens. 'Hasn't changed much, for all it's a hotel now. Grounds were even bigger before the war, they had to sell off some. No such person as Squire Bloomfield any longer, though the family's still in the village and they own the hotel.'

'Would they know anything about the Proctor murder?'

'Might do. Tell 'em I sent you.' A pause. 'You're not from round here, are you?'

'No. I come from the other side of the Medway. One of the enemy to you,' she told him gravely. The ancient division of Man of Kent and Kentish Man still seemed to make a difference, so she always trod carefully.

'Got no murders of your own to look into?' He was

replying in kind, not necessarily offputtingly, she considered, but she was still under the microscope.

'It's this one interests me. It seems so –' she sought for the right word – 'unlikely.'

'Why's that then?'

Time to prove herself again, but Georgia was used to that, and gave him a straight answer. 'From the newspaper reports Ada doesn't seem the type of woman to fall for a gardener, especially one nearly half her age, so what were they doing out there together – if they were?'

'We don't know, do we? What folks are like, I mean.' There was a pause, and then he added, 'You need Bert Todd in the almshouse. You'll find him there – if he's not in the Green Man.'

'I telephoned him, but he said he wasn't related to Davy.' She remembered the call vividly. It had been the shortest one she'd made. He'd just said, 'No, I ain't', and put the phone down.

'He would, wouldn't he? Nobody wants an uncle who was hung for murder. You could try and talk him round. Tell him Jim Hardbent sent you.'

'Thank you.' Georgia was really grateful. A door-opener at last, and she wouldn't abuse it. 'How would you feel if my father and I – we work together – think there's a case for writing a book about the Proctor murder?' Stick to specifics. Jim Hardbent wasn't going to appreciate talk of Wickenham's having the wrong sort of 'sniff'.

A long pause now, which she didn't understand, was relieved when he finally answered, 'I daresay I'll read it. If it's done right.'

How to interpret that? He was waiting for her reaction, so she wasn't out of the wood yet.

She plunged in: 'These postcards of yours. They tell the truth, don't they, even though it's the truth of a hundred years ago. We're standing looking at them from a distance, not judging, yet making our own decisions about them. That's what my father's and my books do. Okay?'

Yet another pause, then: 'My dad used to talk about that case,' he reflected. 'He was at school with Davy Todd.'

'Was he?' She pounced eagerly on this. 'What sort of boy was Davy? Did your dad know Ada too?'

'Davy was a funny one, Dad said, only he never said why. And Ada, well, she was the doctor's daughter. They didn't mix. There was a lot of talk, Dad used to say, that Davy wasn't the only one she went with.'

'He didn't deny they had arranged a meeting, but according to the trial report said it was for the following night. Even so, why would she have been daft enough to choose to go into the fields with him?'

'He was the gardener. She couldn't carry on with him under her dad's nose, could she? Had to do her courting elsewhere. That wasn't the first time she'd been in the fields with Davy or one of the others, so Dad said.'

Here we go. She was getting nearer the heart of it now. 'She didn't look like someone with a train of lovers, in the pictures I've seen.'

'Never do, do they?' Jim added darkly.

Greatly cheered that there might indeed be more to discover about Ada, she decided to explore the churchyard. Ada's father would surely have chosen to bury her here; the only question was whether the grave would be here at St Nicholas or in the new cemetery she had passed on the way in to Wickenham. The church was on one corner of the Wickenham estate between the Green Man and the drive up to the hotel, and its churchyard was reasonably large. From a glance at the first tombstones she saw, she was in the right place. The name Hardbent was prominent on several of them, confirming her theory that Jim had been born in Wickenham. It took her some time to find the cluster of graves for the Proctors. Ada's parents were here, and several more forebears. Ada lay next to her parents, with a simple headstone: 'Ada Proctor, 1892–1929. Dear Daughter to Edward and Winifred. Rest in Peace.' The grave was neglected and overgrown, though not decaying, and she wondered who had ministered to it after her father's death. The Todds?

She returned to the pub with a new impetus. She would leave the Bloomfields for the moment, but that evening she introduced herself to Bert Todd. He wasn't hard to find in the Green Man bar. A nut of a man, occupying a corner stool that had 'regular' written all over it, and indeed she remembered seeing him there at lunchtime too.

'Ah. Jim said you'd be here asking questions. I don't like nosy women,' was his encouraging opening.

'Nor do I,' she returned. 'I'm interested, not nosy. That's different. Can I buy you a pint?'

'That's all right by me, but the answer's the same. I don't talk.'

'Fair enough.' Georgia fetched the pint and placed it before him. 'I can understand,' she told him, as she perched on the next stool. 'You assume your uncle was guilty, so obviously you don't want to talk about it.'

He spluttered into his beer, taken aback. 'I just don't talk. See?'

'Suppose he wasn't guilty. I'm not saying he was innocent, because I don't know if he was. But I want to know more about the case.'

'Look, missis, I don't come to the pub to waste time arguing with a blessed woman – I got one at home for that.' She laughed and he cheered up. 'No disrespect, mind.'

'No offence taken.'

'Look, I'll tell you,' he offered nobly. 'I dunno if Uncle Davy was guilty or innocent, but you couldn't blame the poor devil if he did do it. There he was, twenty years old, good-looking lad from his pictures, led on by the lady at the house. A teaser was Ada Proctor. Any fellow would do. Married, young, old, all the same to her. Mind you, according to what my granny said, she wasn't right in the head. Lost her fiancé in the Great War and went for anything in trousers after that.'

'Is there anyone in the village old enough to remember Davy or the Proctors? I'd like to talk to everyone I can.'

'The old doctor died not long after Miss Ada, and she was his only child, so that's them gone. As for Davy, I reckon Cousin Ned and me are the only ones who'd know about him. From our dads, that is. Ned would only have been two when Davy took a header, but Ned's family weren't living here then. I was born that year, 1930.'

'And no Elgins left?'

He took a swig of his pint. 'Not that I can think of. There's people that might remember, but not know, if you take my meaning.'

By the time she reached her room that evening, she was ready to crash out, but forced herself to make notes on what she'd achieved that day. She'd made a good start, she told herself, looking at the scribbled results, though she had a slight niggle of doubt that she might be missing something here. Tomorrow she'd work the notes up on to the laptop for Peter's benefit, she reassured herself, and any queries would surface then.

It must all come back to Ada Proctor. Was she Woman A or Woman B, the obedient reserved daughter or the sex-crazy rebel? Or both? Now there was a thought. It was all very well listening to Bert's story but hearsay and gossip could distort. Furthermore he was a Todd and the family might well have passed down an unflattering picture of Ada. Georgia was uncomfortably aware that she didn't usually focus so much on one person or aspect of a case until much further forward than she was with Wickenham. Ada was different, she told herself, or was it that she, Georgia, wanted her to be so? Ada was in her thirties, single, living with and working for her father. Ada had lost her fiancé in the war. Was she, Georgia wondered, seeing comparisons here? Had Ada balanced her life on a tightrope, unable to leave the past totally behind, and unable to move forward because of its shadows?

Georgia shivered. She had her own shadows, and Zac

was only one of them. Shadows had to be faced. Had Ada
done so, or had she hidden away in her role as doctor's
daughter and assistant? Or had she rebelled by taking
lovers?

Get a grip, Georgia, she ordered herself. You, my girl,
are raving. Ada was probably precisely what she seemed
in the trial reports, a dutiful daughter who had turned to
other means than marriage to fulfil her life. As for herself,
fortunately the shadows were only temporary visitors.

The next morning Georgia tucked into her researcher's
treat of a full English breakfast, and considered her options
with a clear mind. She decided to head back to the postcard exhibition for another look and to firm up on Jim's
co-operation. She was aware that this couldn't yet be taken
for granted, and this, she realized, was the reason for her
niggle of doubt. She sensed he was still reserving judgement on her, so why give her his co-operation so comparatively quickly? Whatever the reason, he wasn't going to
provide help out of the kindness of his heart; she had to
earn it.

Before that, however, she decided to find the spot where
Ada had died. The field called Crown Lea lay at the end
of a byway, a grassy lane leading off the main road which
she remembered seeing on the far side of the village from
Wickenham Manor, near the old teashop. She took the map
with her, and found the footpath that Ada must have taken
– *in the dark!* It was one thing walking up a byway in broad
daylight, quite another to walk along a footpath over a field
at night-time. Even a torch wouldn't make it a comfortable
walk. By daylight this field looked innocuous, full of the
stubble of recently harvested corn. There was nothing to
mark where Ada had died, nothing but the wind to erase
the present and help reconstruct the past.

Eventually Georgia gave up the attempt. If Ada had left
fingerprints, they weren't here. She needed to know more,
much more before this field would begin to make sense.
Frustrated, she returned to the village hall and the at least

part-known quantity of Jim Hardbent. She found him busy talking to a group of visitors to the exhibition, but eventually she secured his attention, and managed to her great satisfaction to end up with another tour and a vague mention of possible documents that he might or might not have. Nevertheless there was something here she wasn't catching.

'There's a skeleton been found down a denehole,' he mentioned. 'Did you hear about that?' He might have sounded casual, but it was a definite prod.

'Yes.' Guiltily, Georgia remembered Peter's conviction that the skeleton would prove to be the more important trail, yet here she was, getting blinkered by Ada. 'Do you know of any missing people in Wickenham?'

This sounded a broad question even to her, and Jim stared at her as though she'd taken leave of her senses.

'Depends what time of year and when. This was a hop area, Georgia. You know about hops?'

'Yes, stupid of me,' she told him cheerfully, acknowledging her own idiocy. Every year in September, hundreds of pickers would have descended on villages such as Wickenham. The casuals, who travelled from village to village looking for seasonal work, would come together with the pickers from London, who saw it as their annual holiday, and local pickers from neighbouring villages. In addition, every vagrant for miles around would see a chance of earning some cash. If one of them fell down a denehole, who would know – or care?

'Maybe' she suggested, 'this skeleton was a victim of murder as well?'

Jim chuckled. 'You got murder on the brain, you have. We're just an ordinary village here. Big on rumours and gossip. Short on facts. Here, come and look at this.'

He took her to the board dedicated to postcards of the church. 'That's the old vicarage.' He pointed to one she'd passed over yesterday; it was of an ivy-clad, gabled Victorian house, which looked ordinary enough. 'Now that,' Jim announced with satisfaction, 'is where dark doings went on, so they say.'

'Really?' Georgia grinned as Jim laughed at her eagerness.

'Old vicar died of poison, some said by accident, most said he was done in.'

'About the same time as Ada Proctor?' It was a wild guess and it was wrong.

'Nope. During the second war, it was.'

Her hopes fell. Still, it was interesting. She reminded herself that red herrings should be a later indulgence, and that Ada Proctor must come first. 'I'm grateful for your help, Jim. I really am, especially as there are no Proctors or Elgins left in the village.'

'That what old Toddie told you, did he?' Jim guffawed. 'He's right in his way; all the Proctors are gone, and Vi and Emmy Elgin both married, so Elgin wasn't their name. They're gone too, but they've family still here.'

'Why didn't Bert *tell* me?' Georgia was exasperated, even though she should have been used to village ways by now. At least she had unlocked some of Jim's reserve though.

'Did it on purpose. You don't know much about Wickenham, see. The Elgins and the Todds never spoke – and still don't. The old feud goes on. They was at it way back in the nineteenth century and the murder started it up again, so I heard. The only reason the Todds didn't leave the village is that the Elgins would have had the last laugh. It's been quiet recently, but it could flare up again any day. My dad always said that the feud could have been why Mary Elgin's dad refused to back up Mary's alibi for Davy. Dad said it was only natural for Mary to lie about Davy being with her, but why make up the bit about her dad, unless it were true?' He was watching her intently as though, for all his words, he felt a personal stake in this too. Or was it Wickenham rather than Ada Proctor that was his core concern?

'You're right, Jim.' It was a slender straw to cling to. 'Where can I find the Elgin family?'

'Well, Mary Beaumont is in a retirement house up on the Downs.'

'And she was who?'

'Mary Elgin of course.' Jim gloated, clearly delighted to be flooring her. 'Davy Todd's sweetheart.'

'Still alive?' she said faintly.

'That's right. She was only seventeen or so at the time of the murder. Later she lived in a cottage near the Green, doing cream teas after old Beaumont hopped it.'

Oh crabby old lady, who loved only her rose. Georgia felt a shiver of excitement. Now she knew why her father had smelled unfinished business in the atmosphere at Wickenham. Or was the shiver one of apprehension too? Peter never failed to warn her that the fingerprints on Time were alive, and that fingers could strangle as well as caress. Take care, Georgia, take care.

Chapter Three

A s she drove up The Street, Georgia saw Luke's car parked outside her father's house, and drew up behind it. Haden Shaw, high up on the Downs, had no main through road, which meant parking was easy. How long it would remain so, she didn't care to consider. It was a sleepy village – or appeared so to the outsider – and the façade of the compact terraced Georgian red-brick houses that lined the street conveyed a warmth and security that made her thankful to scuttle inside this haven each time she returned home.

Usually. Today she was torn between pleasure and annoyance that Peter was jumping the gun by summoning his publisher before she had even reported home. Unusually for these days, their editor Luke Frost owned the firm, which operated from the village of South Malling, near Maidstone. Luke also played another role in her life. He wanted to marry her, and there were many times when she was in favour of the idea. Something always held her back, however, the something that had Zac written all over it. She no longer loved him, but that didn't make that shadow stop dogging her. Particularly when it turned into reality from time to time – and there he was again, his grin, his look of innocence, his charm, his genuine warmhearted-ness, his manipulativeness and – oh hell! *Forget* him, Georgia. She loved Luke, she loved her work. She walked tall.

She hastily dumped her overnight bag in number 4, her own home, and hurried round to number 2 before too much damage was done in the way of commitment to a project that might or might not turn out to have substance.

As soon as she walked in, Luke came into the hall to greet her, and the look on his face told her that books were not the reason he was here. What she constantly feared must have happened again.

'Where is he?' she asked sharply.

'Margaret's put him to bed, but he's not happy.'

Right on cue she heard Peter's howl from his bedroom on the ground floor at the rear of the cottage. 'Georgia!'

She hurried to the ground-floor bedroom, somewhat cheered by the strength of the protest. Her father was sitting up in bed, glaring towards her, but he looked a frail old man, not the lion she worked with.

'What is it, Dad?' she asked gently, sitting down at his side. 'The usual one?'

'Yes.'

So it hadn't been the shooting incident that had brought this attack on. It was Rick, her younger brother by three years, and the cause of the other shadow over her life. Rick had disappeared in France on a walking holiday ten years ago, and ever since, even before Peter was shot and para-lysed a year later, in a drugs set-up with a Customs & Excise team, which had gone badly wrong, he had period-ically suffered these terrible nightmares. They began during the night but their effects usually lasted throughout the day, leaving him shaking, white and perspiring, a man in the grip of a mental fever. There'd been no trace of Rick. He'd simply vanished. He'd gone alone; he didn't come back. I'll send you a postcard, he said, but it never came, and nor did he.

'That bloody denehole caused it,' Peter muttered. 'Suppose Rick—'

'No, Dad,' Georgia said firmly. 'We've been there.' They had, and her mother too. It had been the nightmares followed by the shooting a year later that had led to her mother leaving – her own way of coping, Georgia acknowledged when she was being charitable. Together, she and her father had climbed back, attempting through Marsh & Daughter to bring closure to the unfinished business of others, since they could not achieve it for themselves. Onwards, not back, but the abyss remained below, waiting for the weak moment. For Georgia, it clutched at her unexpectedly. The very word 'missing' might set it off. Anything. She regained sure ground quickly – until the next time. With her father it was worse, for it was the terror that struck by night. It came less often now, but when it did it was terrifying, both for him and for her.

'I saw him in that hole, trying to climb up. A hand, a face—'

'No, Dad,' she cut in firmly. '*This* denehole has an answer. And we'll find it.'

Peter managed to shrug, as though he never doubted it. Seeing Luke in the doorway helped. 'After your contract, are you?' he roared.

'No. You are,' Luke replied calmly. 'We publishers are callous folk. You know that. We're slavedrivers, counting out our pennies while you minions build our pyramids for us.'

Georgia was grateful for Luke's comforting, sturdy presence. He'd been here and she hadn't, even though it was through no fault of hers.

'That bloody woman won't even let me have a drink,' Peter complained. 'Carers, they call them. What a word for a control freak.'

'Of course you can have a drink, Dad,' Georgia replied, seeing signs of approaching normality, or at least a step towards it. 'Cocoa?'

A snort reassured her. 'Whisky.'

'A glass of red wine,' she compromised.

'Done. Damn you, daughter.'

'I'll get it,' Luke volunteered. 'One for you, Georgia?'

'Mug of tea for me, please.'

'Tell me what happened,' Peter said immediately, as

Luke tactfully vanished into the kitchen. Luke was *always* tactful. And undemanding into the bargain. Georgia was uneasily aware that half the time she took him for granted, forty-five per cent of the time she relished every moment she was with him. Four per cent of the time, however, she fluctuated between irritation that anyone could be so good to her and a maniacal desire to seize him in holy matrimony on the spot. And the last one per cent was Zac.

'I'm going back tomorrow, Dad. I just wanted to report in.'

'Good. Glad you remembered who's boss.'

She ignored this. 'Mary Elgin is still alive.'

'Ha!' He leaned back against the pillows, with great satisfaction. 'So the unfinished business could be there.'

'Not proven yet, but I do sense you're right. There are unanswered questions, at any rate, such as why her father refused to back up her story that Davy was with her at the time of the crime. Was he the upright citizen telling the truth of the matter or betraying his daughter deliberately because there was a feud between the two families?'

'A feud, eh? You have done well,' Peter gloated.

'There's an interesting lack of agreement as to what Ada was like, but the consensus seems to be that she was a sex-starved or nympho spinster who enticed Davy Todd out to the field. When he got carried away with the rough stuff she panicked, and he strangled her to keep her quiet.'

'Proof?'

'None, save what we know from the press reports. I'm going to see Mary Elgin tomorrow, unannounced in the hope that no one has forewarned her that I've been asking questions. That way she won't have time to think up a good story if she has any need to. She's in her nineties, though, so I'll have to take care the way I do it.'

'You do that kind of thing well. What's your opinion so far?'

At that moment Luke came back with the drinks. 'Anything in this Ada Proctor case?' he asked casually.

'Could be.' So Peter had wasted no time in preparing the ground with Luke. Great. Georgia was not amused. Luke the publisher was a bloodhound, bearing little resemblance to Luke the lover. Now she'd be under pressure to produce the goods, and would have to take care not to see hobgoblins where only shadows of Time existed.

'Because of the unlikelihood of the doctor's daughter creeping out at ten at night to meet the gardener in a field?' Luke enquired.

'No. Because of the tea place. Dad –' Georgia turned to Peter – 'you remember we walked into the front parlour, which was full of tables, but decided to go into her back garden, which was full of flowers, plus the odd bench. Then the cakes were stale.'

He frowned in concentration. 'I don't remember the cakes. I remember the old woman though. She took a fancy to you.'

'*What?*' This startled her, since, apart from the crabbiness, she remembered nothing about the old lady.

'Maybe not a fancy, but she kept staring at you, and I wondered why. Odd how things come back.'

'Well, that old woman was Mary Elgin, or Mary Beaumont by then. That's what must have sparked you off about Wickenham.'

Peter sighed with satisfaction. There was already some colour coming back into his face. 'I knew I was right. "Scarborough Fair", skeletons, Mary Elgin. Remember, Georgia?'

She did. Half-recalled incidents, snatches of music in the air, faces without a name. This was how it worked at first, by impressions. Then the jumble had to be turned into hard fact, so that it would pass Luke's eagle eye. Simon and Garfunkel's 'Scarborough Fair' had been Rick's favourite song as a child, an odd choice when 'Nellie the Elephant' was still a more accessible alternative. Now they never played the song, and if its haunting strains floated over from the radio it was switched off. It rang in their heads, so there was no need of reminders. Peter was using their private shorthand to tell her not to forget those first elusive fingerprints. Tomorrow she would return to Wickenham to learn more about Mary Elgin's lost love, Davy Todd.

'What about the denehole?' Peter's voice floated querulously after her as she and Luke prepared to leave, once he had grudgingly admitted he might like some supper later. Margaret always left a dinner that he could reheat in the microwave, a system he vastly preferred to being dependent on his daughter. How, he asked when they had originally fixed their guidelines for operating as Marsh & Daughter, could he yell abuse in working hours at someone to whom he was beholden for survival outside of them? The flaw in this argument was that he had no compunction in yelling at Margaret either, but that, he informed Georgia, was between him and his carer.

'Nothing. Mild curiosity in the village, that's all. There doesn't seem to be any speculation as to whose it might have been. None of your "Ah, now, me proud beauty, I allus said the squire's dead body would turn up one day." Most people assume it was a vagrant from hop-picking days.'

'You didn't do a damn thing about it, did you?' Peter accused her. 'So set on your precious Ada.'

'I did,' she said defensively.

'The denehole, girl. *Please*,' he added belatedly. 'Ever occur to you they might be connected?'

'No,' she whipped back. 'Because there's not a shred of evidence apart from the fact that the skeleton was probably there within a range of a hundred years or so.'

'Oh, yes there is. I had a phone call from Mike yesterday evening. *He* believes in keeping an open mind,' Peter added innocently. 'From the tree roots growing above, and soil analysis, it looks as if the body was in there before the chamber collapsed, and though they didn't know when that was, they've managed to date the skeleton to within fifteen years with the additional help of one or two objects lying near it.' A pause for effect. '1919 to 34. There are the usual disclaimers and provisos of course that you can never be a hundred per cent certain in such cases, especially since it's theoretically possible the body was deliberately placed there together with misleading artefacts *after* the chamber collapsed. Nevertheless, it's a good hypothetical range to start on, don't you think?'

'So hypothetically he probably murdered Ada and jumped in the denehole in remorse,' Georgia shot back at him.

'Any better theory?' Peter glared at her. 'It might interest you to know I attacked the Internet after you left yesterday evening.'

'So that's what brought this on.' She should have guessed it. 'You've been deneholing on the Web.'

'Someone had to do it.'

'Okay. What did you find out?'

'According to the website of an enthusiast, one Jonas Ticklememore—'

'I don't believe that for a start—'

'—the Wickenham denehole shaft was about three feet in diameter and fifteen feet deep down to the original chamber, and it had foot-treads all the way down. So if it was an accident our chap was unlucky not to have been able to break his fall one way or another, and if it was suicide it seems an uncertain method to choose. Furthermore –' he paused impressively – 'the chamber was still known to be intact in 1925.'

'So what does that tell us?'

'Assuming our upper limit of 1934 is roughly correct, our fifteen-year period is down to nine.' Peter beamed, and colour began to creep back into his face. 'I rest my case. The skeleton is the trail to follow, probably connecting with the Ada Proctor murder. I'll ring Mike again.'

'Not tonight you won't,' Georgia said gently. 'Rest. Okay? A little light television, supper and dreamless sleep is the plan for you.' She kissed him and he sighed.

'I suppose I'm lucky to have you.'

'You're a grudging old curmudgeon,' she informed him affectionately.

Luke put an arm round her as she closed the door to her father's bedroom, relieved that he was back in fighting mode. 'Trembly?' he asked, as they walked back to her house.

'A bit. I'm sorry I wasn't here. How long . . . ?'

'Margaret rang me since you were away and she had to get home. I came over immediately. Before dinner,' Luke added pointedly.

'Funny thing. I haven't eaten either. Pub or freezer?'

'Freezer.'

'I can't be seduced tonight, Luke. I'm off early tomorrow.'

'Nobody asked you, my fair maid.'

She laughed. 'Still freezer?'

'Certainly.' He followed her with alacrity into the kitchen of number 4, and peered over her shoulder as she extracted some home-made bolognese sauce and fresh (if frozen) pasta. To these she added some early salad leaves from the garden, and together with cheese and the scrag end of a bunch of grapes they sufficed for a reasonable dinner.

'You, Georgia,' Luke remarked later, 'are a remarkable woman – in fact, incomparable.'

'Thank you, kind sir. Not even comparable to a summer's day?'

'Not summer. Infinitely more beautiful. To me, you are spring, the sharp edge of hope.'

Georgia was ridiculously pleased. 'Is this the claret talking?' was all she could find to say.

'Since I'm being sent home shortly, it's only whispering. But as you are not in the mood for love, let us return to business. What do you reckon about Wickenham? Is there going to be a book in it? It sounds flimsy to me.'

'And probably so did a book about Timothy Evans' innocence when Ludovic Kennedy proposed writing *Ten Rillington Place* about serial killer Christie.'

'You're hooked, aren't you?'

'On the way, but not far enough along to mind if it all leads to nothing. It could just make an interesting article, but nothing more substantial.'

'But you don't really think so. A tale of injustice, avenging a lost sweetheart. It's a good theme, if there's enough for a book, but it's not usually the kind you go for. Look at *The Penstow Triangle* or *The Forest Gate Murder*. This one seems too simple.'

Georgia reflected on this. *The Penstow Triangle* had concerned a small village tucked away on the Cornish Moors, where the aftermath of a family secret dug out by persevering family researchers led to murder. She could still remember the powerful brooding sense of disgrace and shame that the family had retained, over what was now a small matter of a child born out of wedlock. And still it had lingered. A simple seed had sown the crime, and, oh, how the complications had multiplied as the years had passed.

'You know the annoying thing about you, Luke?'

'Is that there isn't one.'

'Is that you're often right.' This was poor compensation for his calm acceptance of her lack of response to his overture, but it was all she could offer. 'I think the Wickenham story just might be more complicated than it seems.' She grinned at him. 'My usual madness, I expect.'

'Not madness at all. Just Georgian enthusiasm.'

She kissed him lightly. 'You're very understanding.'

'Do that again, and I'll marry you. How about that?'

Back on an even keel. 'Some day. Some day.' And some day perhaps she would, shadows notwithstanding.

'Georgia, you'll be careful, won't you?'

'Of what? Mary Elgin's feelings?'

'No. What you might stir up.'

'Mud. That's all,' she reassured him.

Marsh & Daughter had stirred up plenty of mud in its seven years of existence. It had been Luke in fact who had inadvertently sparked this off. She had been working part-time in a bookshop, which dealt both in new books, particularly of local interest, and in second-hand books. Luke had called in with his list one day when she was deep in discussion with the owner about the latest hoard of books she had acquired from an elderly collector in Sussex. One of them was a mid-nineteenth-century account of the Savage case, the murder of a middle-aged woman in the Kentish Weald, and Luke had immediately seized on it. That, he had said, was something he'd like to get into – the human side of history, both its tragedies and its entertainments, not just the books on the towns and villages he was publishing at present.

When she had reached home that night, which for a time after her divorce and then her mother's departure had been her father's house, she found him worse than usual, dull-eyed and turned in upon himself in despair. No job, no son, no wife. But he did have a daughter. Determined to arouse a spark of interest, Georgia began to tell him about the Savage case. He tried to cut her off impatiently – of course he knew all about it. It had never been solved, she pointed out, hoping he would be roused enough to begin speculating on what had happened.

'It should have been solved,' was all he had muttered.

'Your kind of case,' she had ventured. 'Mike Gilroy was always saying that some case or other had your fingerprints stuck all over it before you even got there.'

He had shot a look at her. 'And yours,' he had pointed out. 'Don't forget that beach your mother and I took you to once when you were about eight, and you began to cry, saying you didn't like it? It was the beach where Maisie Wilson had been found murdered, but of course I never told you that.'

'Fingerprints on Time,' Georgia had said, and suddenly they had been in the middle of a discussion that went on half the night, a discussion that sprang from Luke Frost's desire to publish a new line of books, and then led to Marsh

& Daughter. The business was born, she had moved to the house next door to allow room for Peter's office (and her own foreseen need for personal space), and now they had published five such studies, each taking a different case. The last one, on London mysteries, differed in that it covered several cases. On the publication day of the third book four years ago, she and Luke had, to their slight mutual surprise, become lovers. She'd been so used to thinking of Luke as a friendly regular fixture in her working life that she had been completely overwhelmed when he peeled off the professional face and became Luke the passionate, not entirely predictable lover. Did she too wear such a mask? Possibly, though she wasn't aware of doing so.

Georgia thought about those working masks, and about stirring up mud while wearing them, as she drove to Wickenham the next day. It was raining and all too easy to think in those terms. She always pooh-poohed the idea of danger to Luke, for the living fingerprints theory was between herself and her father, and did not intrude into the written word. In the cases Marsh & Daughter had undertaken so far, the danger potential had not been put to the test, but that didn't mean it didn't exist. There had been no evidence of strong emotions so far in Wickenham, merely mild interest, but the big test might now be coming – not least because she was aware that the quest for the truth about Ada Proctor already contained a personal element over and above Marsh & Daughter's basic driving force.

She was later than she had intended because she had decided to wait to check that her father was okay before leaving. Once this clearance had been obtained from Margaret she set off. 'The Fleet of Two' was what her father called their cars, since she, as well as he, had a modern Alfa Romeo 147, not because she had any desire to create a business style, but because she liked the car. His was the two-door hatchback model, modified to his needs. Before the shooting, Peter had had two classic cars. They had gone now of course but his interest hadn't, and piles of car magazines littered the house. Show me the car, and I'll show you the man, he would declare grandly on occasion.

Her excitement mounted as she arrived at the retirement home where Mary Beaumont lived. Four Winds (what an encouraging name for the frail) was on a slope of the North Downs overlooking the village, a nice spot but lonely (and certainly windy despite the rain). As a hotel it might have been ideal, but for old people living apart from the community it seemed hardly that.

The house was a Victorian monstrosity made bearable by huge rhododendron bushes and wisteria growing up the wall. The staff seemed welcoming enough, which was a good sign, but it was dark inside the entrance hall.

'Mary's in her room,' she was told.

No dignifying the elderly with 'Mrs Beaumont' here. 'Which is?' Georgia enquired.

To her surprise the girl actually took her to the room rather than jerking a thumb. Another good sign.

'Is she . . .' Georgia broke off, not knowing whether she would find someone hale and hearty or an Alzheimer's victim.

It was obviously a familiar question, for the girl cut in: 'It's one of her good days. Quite perky she was this morning.'

The door was flung open without ceremony. 'Here we are, Mary. Visitor for you.'

At first Georgia could see no one. Then slowly a heap of brightly coloured shawls in a large armchair by the window moved and Mary Elgin peered out at her.

'You've come then,' she snapped before Georgia could even deliver her prepared introduction. 'You've taken your time, I must say.'

Oh crabby old lady . . . Georgia thought with relief. No Alzheimer's here.

A sharp pair of blue eyes stared out of the lined sunken

face, but her thin hair once released from its cocoon of shawls had a bright diamonte-studded blue bow adorning it, and the blouse was a jazzy red. No hiding from the world here.

'I had to go home to see my father last night,' Georgia explained.

'Last night? It was years ago I saw you. I ain't lost my marbles yet, young woman.'

Oh boy, Georgia thought, heart sinking. And this was one of the good days.

'I've been in here nine years and it were before that,' Mary Elgin continued.

'What was?'

'When you came. I knew you'd be back. I knew it.'

'Came where?' Georgia asked carefully. Surely she could not mean—

'To my teashop of course. Where do you think? Buckingham Palace?'

'But you can't remember me. I only came—'

'Ah, that got you, didn't it?' Mary said with quiet satisfaction. 'I knew you were the one. I knew you'd be back. You and that man . . .'

'My father.'

'Yes. I knew it.'

Georgia refused to believe it. This must surely be Jim Hardbent's doing, and it had become confused in Mary Elgin's mind. 'Did Jim telephone you last night?'

'No Jim rang me. No one else neither. They never do.' Mary's eyes fixed her with a piercing gaze. 'I have the sight, young woman. Of course I knew you were the one.'

'The sight?' Georgia hesitated. 'You mean you can foretell the future?'

'Not so clear as my mum, but I saw you all right. Mum was a true Romany. Should never have stayed in Wickenham, but that's what love does for you. I should know. She belonged to the woods, to the roads, a travelling woman.'

'Davy Todd,' Georgia said abruptly. 'That's why you knew I'd be coming.'

'There you see. You know. Why did it take you so long?' she asked querulously.

'I've only just . . .' Georgia was going to say 'learned about you', but that wouldn't be the right phrase, 'understood,' she amended.

'And what do you understand, my lovely?'

'I understand – ' emotion battled with the need for honesty – 'that you think Davy was innocent.'

'Think, lady? I know he was. Davy was with me that night.'

'Your father denied it.'

'I've nothing to say against my dad.'

'Then—' Where was this going? Georgia couldn't make it out.

'Lady,' Mary interrupted, 'I have something to say against the world.'

'What is that, Mrs Beaumont?' Georgia asked gently.

'For hanging my Davy. Now you've bothered to turn up at last, I'll tell you what really happened, so pin back your lugholes and listen. It was the night of the Hallowe'en dance. Thursday. Mum and Dad wanted to go, so I agreed to mind the little 'uns. Davy came over to join me, though of course they didn't know that. Davy was a gentle soul. Loved his work, loved nature. Green-fingered was Davy. He knew a Dartford warbler when he saw one, and the rarest orchid, together with every plant on God's earth. What with me being interested in plants like Mum was, we got on well – she knew all the healing plants, so Mum didn't mind Davy too much. Dad would have liked him too if he hadn't been a Todd. The Todds and the Elgins didn't get on, see.'

'What was the reason for that?'

'Went way back. All because some Todd ran off with an Elgin's wife. Or maybe an Elgin did the running. Don't matter anyway. So me and Davy took what chances we could for being alone. About ten o'clock Davy said he'd better be going, and as he got up he saw something out of the window. "That looks like Miss Ada," he said, "going up the lane to Crown Lea. Funny that." "Why?" I asks. "Because that's where we're going tomorrow night." "We?" I says indignantly. Davy was mine. "Me and her." Davy caught sight of my face, which must have been a picture. "You can come too if you like. Miss Ada won't mind. She wants to listen to nightingales, and I said I'd show her the badgers too." '

'I don't remember any reason for the meeting being given in the press reports,' Georgia said. This was a new angle altogether. Badgers and nightingales were unlikely, but no more so than the idea of Ada and Davy going there for lovemaking.

'It weren't there. Davy's lawyer said it didn't matter what they was to do the following night. It was this night that was important, so he shouldn't go on about it; the more he talked about a meeting being arranged the more it would prove that there was something between them.'

Mary was right; Davy's confirmation that he was expecting to see Ada on the Friday night hadn't sounded good. He should have stuck to what his lawyers said – or should he? Georgia shook herself impatiently. Surely that one was up for Davy? He spoke the truth; if he had been guilty he'd have followed his lawyers to the letter.

'So what happened then?' Georgia held her breath, aware that there was a hint, just a hint that Davy could indeed have been innocent.

'I told him I didn't mind, and I didn't. Miss Ada was an old woman to my mind. So I told him he was welcome to her, knowing I had his heart. Well, we were so busy talking about it, we didn't hear Dad coming back early from the dance. When we did, Davy rushed out of the back door but Dad saw him and dashed after him. I went out too, and we all had a battle royal, him saying Davy was up to no good with me – he was wrong there,' Mary added complacently. 'Very good it was, I can tell you. So, anyway, I was saying

I was going to marry him, Dad saying he'd see me dead first, Davy saying no he wouldn't and he was going to marry me. And on it went turning into a bit of a punch-up. It was past eleven thirty when he let Davy go home. I had such a walloping after that for being out with a Todd and bringing dishonour on the family.'

'Why didn't all this come out at the trial? You only said your father had seen you with him.'

'My dad denied it and told me I'd be a goner if I said at the trial Davy had been in his house, so I said I met him outside. I was only a kid.'

'But why—'

'Don't I blame my dad? You're young, missy. And so was I. Mum explained it to me. Dad was an Elgin and he felt it really badly that I'd let the family down by courting a Todd. It was family honour involved, and there's no gainsaying that. I hated my dad, honour or no honour. Next year, Mum went back to her own folk. Never saw her again, save once, when she was passing through. Dad killed himself after she left.'

Georgia shuddered. 'But you still wouldn't say anything against your father.'

'Nothing would bring Davy back and I was born an Elgin. I owes the family something now it's too late for Davy.'

'And now?'

'I'm ninety-two, and you came back. So I know it's the time to speak out. I'll be meeting Davy soon and I need to look him in the eye.'

Georgia battled with emotion versus common sense. Emotional pressure was being piled on her, and perhaps Mary Elgin with her gimlet blue eyes was well aware of it.

'So what happened after that evening?' she asked quietly.

'Next morning we heard Miss Ada had been killed, and the police went after Davy since he'd been seen going home all dishevelled with blood on his face. Of course, that was because of the fight with Dad. I said Davy had been with me outside the house but no one would believe it. Everyone in the village apart from Mum and Dad knew we were courting, so of course I'd say that. Dad just denied anyone had been with me that evening, and they believed him because they wanted to. Dr Proctor was popular and Ada was his daughter; they wanted a scalp.'

'I'm interested in this appointment with Ada for the following night. Did you believe what Davy said about the nightingales or did Miss Proctor have an eye for the young men?'

'I wouldn't know about that.' She shut her lips primly.

'Ada had a fiancé who was killed in the First World War,' Georgia prompted her.

'That's right. Mr Guy, son of Major Randolph at the big house.'

'Wickenham Manor?'

'Nah. Another one, don't remember the name. Hazel something. He was a bad 'un was Mr Guy. They were engaged but he was carrying on with other ladies, and once he eloped with an heiress, so they say, only he was stopped just before he got a ring on her finger. Then he came crawling back to Miss Ada, like he always did. Except after the war. He never came back from that. Missing, believed killed. Broke the Randolphs' hearts, they sold up and moved away.'

'Is that why Ada Proctor never married? She was waiting, just in case he did come back.'

'So they said.'

Georgia hesitated then decided to ask her question: 'If Davy didn't kill Ada, who do you think did?'

'Some of them hoppers used to hang around after the season ended in the hope of more work. How would I know? Anyway, that's your job. It could have been anyone.'

So it could, Georgia reflected gloomily, as she drove away from Four Winds. It could have been anybody who saw a woman walking alone in the fields at that time of night and decided to take full advantage, not reckoning with Ada's strong physique. But that brought her full circle. Either Ada had a strong reason for being there alone or she knew her attacker. Had she mistaken the night of the appointment with Davy? No, that was definitely out. She wouldn't have arranged to meet him *in* the field; she'd probably have arranged to meet him at the end of the lane, the gate into the field. It had been dark, for heaven's sake. Even if it had been a moonlit night, it was unlikely anyone would have been lingering in the fields in the hope of a solitary woman wandering by. More likely she was followed from the road by someone – like Davy. Oh damn, she cursed softly. Everything led back to him – except for Mary Elgin.

The M20 was crowded for midday, and she pondered whether to turn off to South Malling to seduce Luke out to a quick sandwich. She decided against it. She would, she thought with pleasure, be seeing him tonight anyway. He'd offered to take Peter and her out to dinner and tonight, who knew, the course of true love might run smooth. She mulled this happy thought over, until the image of Mary's face came back to her. Crabby, hopeful, tired, all in one. True love for her had stopped with Davy Todd, Georgia suspected. Whatever Bill Beaumont had been like, it would have been hard to live up to a Davy Todd enshrined in her memory as a tragically lost Romeo.

Star-crossed lovers indeed, but in this case it had been the feuding parent who had died, and Juliet lived on to her crabby old age. Dear heaven, if she lost Luke, would she become like that? Was it sheer selfishness on her part to assume that love would merely wait around for her to make up her mind?

Get real, she ordered herself sharply. Relationships can't be forced by logic. They work themselves out – unless fate takes a vicious hand as it had done with Davy Todd. She was aware that she was now thinking of Davy as well as of his supposed victim. Now that she had scratched the surface of Wickenham's past, she was becoming as sure as

Peter that something or someone had disturbed its peace. Was it Davy or Ada who had lain their fingerprints on this village's history? Or both? Or, as she once again guiltily recalled, the skeleton?

Chapter Four

She found Peter in the garden, enjoying the golden September sunshine, which provided valuable thinking time and space. Whenever he'd had an overdose of the Internet, he would either retire to the window overlooking the one and only street of any size in Haden Shaw or, if the weather was good enough, whizz down the ramp from the conservatory doors into the garden.

He listened to her account of her visit to Mary Elgin with unusual patience for him, from which she deduced that however fruitful a day he had had on the Net, he wouldn't be satisfied until he'd 'placed' Mary Elgin there too.

'Badgers!' he snorted in disgust, when she had finished. 'Did you discover who Ada Proctor *was*, Georgia? Nature lover, string of human lovers, dried-up spinster mourning her lost sweetheart?'

'That's chauvinistic typecasting,' Georgia pointed out. 'Long out of date. She might have been mourning her lost lover, but still have been leading a happy fulfilling life. Anyway, I've only had one interview with anyone who actually knew her. Give me a chance.'

'So Mary Elgin has the sight,' continued Peter as though she had not spoken. 'Pity she can't use it to see who framed her Davy.'

'If anyone did,' Georgia reminded him. 'And although her story was credible she'd had a long time to think it up.'

'What was your instinct?'

'It's worth looking further into.'

'The fingerprints are there?'

48

'Yes.'

'Good.' Peter leaned back, placed his hands comfortably over his stomach and pronounced: 'They'll vanish of course.'

She knew that. The further they delved the more they risked the original fingerprints being overlain by the reality of the present. Everyday events would blot out the intangible threads they struggled to connect. That's why it was so important that their initial impressions had to be captured, just as those on entering a crime scene had to be faithfully recorded.

'But it's worth a cup of tea,' Peter finished hopefully.

Georgia seconded that. She brought the tray into the garden, looking with affection at her father, who was lying back, eyes closed, with his face tilted upwards to the sinking sun. Not for long. 'So you've fallen for the old Romeo and Juliet line, have you?' The eyes shot open suspiciously.

'Rubbish,' Georgia retorted guiltily, conscious of a grain of truth in his accusation. 'There was no hard evidence against Davy, only circumstantial.'

'There was the blood on his face.'

'She was strangled,' Georgia pointed out. 'How could he get blood on him? She must have had a torch. She looks a powerful woman, so why didn't she clock him one if he began to get fresh? Or is that the supposed reason for the blood?'

'The Crown claimed Ada scratched his face in her own defence.'

'How?' Georgia pounced. 'This was 1929. It was the end of October and she was in the middle of the fields. No lady would ever go out without her gloves, particularly at that time of the year. Did she have time to take them off before scratching his face, do you think?'

'Gloves,' growled Peter. 'You have a point,' he admitted grudgingly. 'You should check that exhibits list. No mention of them in the *Times* evidence, or a torch come to that, yet there were, if I recall rightly, mentions of her handbag and shoes. Court shoes. Hardly badger-hunting gear, are they?'

'People only had old clothes and new then, not vast ranges of casual wear.'

'But don't court shoes have high heels?'

'Yes and if,' Georgia admitted, 'she was going to meet a lover, she might have worn them, field trek or not. But,' she concluded triumphantly, 'lover or not, she wouldn't have worn them for Davy. He must have been used to seeing her in gardening boots. She'd have dressed up perhaps, but not to that extent.'

'Accepted. Unfortunately for Davy, however, he had been cutting the last of the lavender that day and his jacket was covered with bits of dried flower seed. There was some on Ada's coat too, which the defence couldn't explain, since her father testified that she had been wearing her best and not her gardening coat. The prosecution went to town on this. When tackled with this, Davy suddenly "remembered" that he *had* seen her when she came back from London. She'd popped outside to ask him to roll the lawn next day. Weak.'

'So weak, it could be true,' Georgia pointed out. 'But that best coat doesn't sound like a canoodle with Davy, any more than the court shoes do.'

'If we tentatively agree we've heard a little of Davy Todd's story, where,' Peter complained, 'is Ada's? Absent.'

'The victim's usually is.'

'No, it's not. It's usually lurking somewhere, whether in letters, in diaries, or just in memories of people who've known the victim.'

'She's beginning to whisper.' Georgia concentrated. 'We've agreed that even though she'd been in London, she would surely have changed those court shoes for walking across a field unless—'

'She was meeting not just a bit of rough in the form of Davy Todd, but someone she really fancied,' Peter finished for her with relish.

He had a pleased smile on his face. 'Don't tell me,'

Georgia groaned, following his thoughts through years of experience. 'You can't be thinking—'

'Why not?' Peter asked belligerently. 'You tell me that Ada lost her lover, this Guy Randolph, in the Great War, missing believed killed. There's no hard evidence about any other lover, only hearsay.'

'That doesn't mean there isn't one,' Georgia whipped back. Time to slow down Peter's stampede towards that denehole. She would concede there might be a link, but only when there was evidence to point the way.

'It doesn't rule out this Guy Randolph's return either.'

'You're just hoping for a "Jack's Return Home", like the old melodramas. Is Guy Randolph mentioned in the *Times* reports?'

'No.'

'So where was he?'

'In the denehole,' Peter finished with relish.

Reluctantly Georgia laughed. 'Don't you think you are rather ahead of the facts? You have a skeleton with no identification on him as to who he was or when exactly he was put there. You might just as easily work on the thesis that Guy Randolph killed Ada and then did a runner on the next train out.'

'We'll find evidence, I'm sure.'

'Aren't you forever insisting we should proceed *from* evidence to theory not from theory *to* evidence?'

'I am, and I'm breaking my own rule. I frequently do,' he announced with dignity. 'After all, fingerprints on Time are a sort of theory in themselves. You admit that.'

'I'm only prepared to admit,' Georgia continued doggedly, 'that Guy Randolph should be a line to be investigated and if there's no evidence he should be ruled out as a possible murderer, who then fled back into his former status of missing person. Without proof to the contrary, the denehole has to be a tangent.'

'Why?'

She'd play her ace. 'If this missing Guy was in your

denehole and he murdered Ada, who murdered him?'

Her ace was capped. 'So what? Now we're looking for two murderers.'

Sometimes Peter went too far. It was high time to drag him back to reality. Even theories – or new lines of inquiry, as she preferred to think of them – needed a plan of investigation. Her job.

'Look,' she said as patiently as she could manage, 'we have three choices if Davy is innocent. Choice One: Ada made a mistake in the day, went for her walk across the fields expecting to meet Davy, but instead met a chance attacker whom she fought off for a while. Then this stranger succeeded in strangling her to keep her quiet and made his escape – or, if you must, he accidentally fell down a denehole. Choice Two: you're right and Guy Randolph is mixed up in this somewhere. Choice Three: someone else killed her for some specific reason as yet unknown.'

'I'll take Number Two, Randolph and the denehole,' Peter said promptly. 'You can take A. N. Other. Tally ho, daughter, follow me.' He whirled his chair round, heading back to his beloved bookshelves, where he made a beeline for the row of Kelly's Directories to Kent. 'The invaluable Kellys await us.' He stretched out both hands and brought down the heavy 1901 edition. 'Here we are. Thank heavens for class distinctions in those days. Only the wealthy and professional folk of the village get special mention. Here they are. We need another look at this. Major Stewart Randolph, Hazelwood House, Wickenham. That must be it. Can't be two Major Randolphs in a village that size.'

Georgia remembered Jim Hardbent showing her a postcard of it. A brick nineteenth-century mansion, at the other end of the village from the Manor, on the other side of the road from where, according to Jim Hardbent, the Proctors had lived. That figured. The boy next door syndrome.

'So let's look at the 1938 edition.' No putting the first volume back, she noticed. It was usually Georgia's or Margaret's job to round up stray books at the end of the day. Sometimes she suspected Peter imagined house gnomes popped in during the night to tidy up after him.

'No,' Peter said, after checking this too. 'Hazelwood House is listed, but a Mrs Hubert Wilson is the owner. Let's try 1929.' A pause while he manoeuvred the next book in front of him. 'Mrs Wilson here too. So the Randolphs wouldn't have been here at the time of the murder as this volume presumably reflects the 1928 position.'

'They left after Guy went missing in the war. Unhappy memories.'

'If Guy Randolph did come back from the dead,' Peter mused, 'he would have returned to Wickenham and found his family gone, then. Either he made inquiries and followed their trail or . . .'

Their eyes met. 'You don't stand a chance,' Georgia said firmly.

'Oh, come on. Even Mike Gilroy needs help on this skeleton.'

'No, he doesn't and, anyway, it's up to Darenth Area not the Stour. It's too old to be a police case, now the missing persons' list has been checked. He's already said you don't stand a chance of a DNA search, quite rightly pointing out there's no lead on a possible match. Nor do we know there were any signs on that skeleton that the poor chap was murdered.'

Peter surrendered. 'You win – for the moment. Anyway, the Randolphs were obviously quite well established. I'll try an Internet family search request for info. When are you off to Wickenham again?'

'No time like the present. Tomorrow anyway. I might stay a day or two. Okay?'

'Splendid. And make sure you come back with Ada's voice.'

Luke was a wonderful antidote to an overdose of Peter, Georgia thought, as she drove back to his South Malling home, watching the tail lights of his car. He had plenty of professional push of his own, not to mention the occasional short fuse, but he presented the calm tones of reason, especially when Peter had enthused over the Guy Randolph theory this evening. Despite that, it had been an enjoyable dinner in Canterbury. Peter had been delivered to his bed, and Luke had suggested she come back for the night en route to Wickenham. She had leapt at the chance. To hell with the washing and ironing. She'd catch up later. Peace after the storm was Luke. How would she react to peace all the time? she wondered. Would she long for the storm? That was her dread, and she pushed it from her.

Luke lived in a rambling Edwardian house in the grounds of which were the offices of Frost & Co. It was no small local publishing venture, but a list that could compete even in these competitive times with the big conglomerates in publishing. It had three specialties: real crime, the military history-cum-memoir, and the Kentish history-cum-guide book series. Georgia was interested in all three.

'I always breathe the smell of common sense here,' she said gratefully, as he unlocked the door of the offices to show her the latest advance copies.

'Wishful thinking. All you can smell is laminated book jackets and the smell of being away from Haden Shaw.'

'That's what adds up to common sense.'

'Is this new book going to work out?' Luke asked bluntly. 'I still have my doubts after listening to Peter this evening.'

'Too early to tell.'

'Too early for a contract, you mean.'

'Never too early for that,' she said wrily. A lot of money disappeared in trails that led nowhere, although she didn't yet see the Wickenham murders as being one of them. When her father complained about the lack of voice, she knew all he was implying was that there was no case yet to write about, only snatches from out of the past, guesses that might add up to a path forward, but that as yet Ada herself, the core of the problem, remained elusive.

This was nothing new. Most of their cases had a point

at which they changed from isolated snatches of information into a definite trail. Waiting for this, as they were now, was the worst possible time for both Peter and herself. Unless that turning point came soon, they knew they would be left with the unsolved, intangible nothingness that spelled Rick. That was the spur that drove them on.

Luke, however, carted none of their kind of baggage. Baggage of a different sort, certainly, as did everybody, but not the intangible mess that leaves a sickness in the stomach. Luke was five years older than her, and his baggage consisted of a marriage in his youth, which had ended in a row that sent his wife storming off to meet her lover only to crash her car en route. She had died, and Georgia suspected Luke blamed himself for her death, regardless of the fact that it had been his wife who brought about the separation. His baggage had turned him into a workaholic – only alleviated by his care for Peter and, she thought, herself. Was that good? She could never decide, but in bed that night with his arms around her it didn't seem to matter one jot.

'So tell me why this one grabs you,' Luke said at breakfast the following morning.

'Mary Elgin and the sight,' Georgia answered promptly. That had really shaken her, and she was glad Luke had chosen the objective light of morning to press her on it.

'That might be a trick she pulls on everyone.'

'I have to take that chance. The unfinished-business atmosphere stems from her, I'm sure of it.'

'It's really getting to you. You were talking about Davy Todd in your sleep.'

'Was I?' She had had no idea of course. Living alone, one was free to sing the Hallelujah Chorus in one's sleep without knowing anything about it. To be called to account, even in the nicest possible caring way, was unnerving. What else might she speak of while her soul was absent in sleep? One handed more to a lover than just the physical; one put one's inner self in trust. Is that what she wanted? The thought was both comforting and scary, too much for today. Tomorrow she must think about it. Yes, tomorrow. Today, there were things to do.

Rather than stay at the pub, she had chosen a pleasant-looking bed and breakfast called Country Stop, which by coincidence she realized must be somewhere near where Hazelwood House had stood, with the Proctor home almost opposite. It was only after she had settled in and asked the owner her name that she discovered it was Todd, and her heart sank. She supposed in a village the odds against such coincidences were greatly reduced, but nevertheless it could be a hindrance.

'Are you related to Bert Todd?' she asked.

'Uncle. Olly's uncle that is. My husband. He's the butcher.'

So that was why this B and B did evening meals. Lucy Todd was about fifty, and despite a mask of professional efficiency looked flurried, as if her mind was always on the next job. It probably was. Georgia didn't envy anyone running a B and B. She wondered if she'd would be making a mistake in nailing her colours to the Todd masthead by staying here, but she could hardly retreat now. Anyway, no one would be bothered by it, save perhaps those elusive Elgin people if she ever caught up with them. Furthermore, so far as she could see, it was the only B and B actually in the village. The others were at farms on the outskirts, which was not what she wanted.

Georgia passed a conventional remark about its being good to see thriving shops in this day and age.

'Not for much longer,' was the gloomy and unexpected reply. 'Not if they have their way.'

'Who?'

'Them. Supermarket on our doorstep we'll have, though they're bribing us with housing as well. Do they care about that? They do not. It's the supermarket cash they want.'

'Who?' Georgia was lost.

'The blasted Bloomfields. Selling off the Manor and its land, aren't they? Kept that very quiet, they did. You'd think they'd have enough cash from running that ritzy hotel, but, no, they want to sell to a supermarket.'

Enlightenment came. 'Ah, the football field.'

'And the cricket field. Next door to each other, they are. Generations have played on these fields. And now they're going to sell them for retail development.' The last word came out in utter disgust.

'Don't the sports clubs have a lease?'

'Never bothered with them. Why should they? The Bloomfields have let them play there time out of mind with no trouble at all. Well, they won't have the cheek to stay in this village any longer. They'll be living on their ill-gotten gains.'

'Has planning permission been granted for the development?'

'Got it years ago, when they expanded the hotel and made it a company. We had a dozy parish council then, who never realized it affected the sports fields. It probably thought Class A1 retail use was some sort of ice-cream stall. Anyway, the estate wasn't for sale then; so the Bloomfields must have sweet-talked someone. Most of the village thought the fields belonged to the village anyway.'

'What a shame. This seems such a happy village,' Georgia lied brightly.

'Does it now? Maybe it does to those who don't have to live here. You ask my husband.'

Georgia leapt at this suggestion. 'I'd like to in fact. I'm interested in the Davy Todd case, and he might perhaps be able to help.'

As she had guessed, Lucy had either never heard of Davy or was very cagey on the Todds' behalf. 'I'll have a word with him,' was all she replied, with no great enthusiasm.

The said word must have been duly spoken, however, for after dinner that evening, Oliver Todd emerged from their private sanctum. He was a tall, lean man, far from the stereotype of a jolly butcher, and, judging by the photos and books around, was a cricket enthusiast, as were two teenage boys, presumably their sons, who, from the era of the photos, must now be grown men. Oliver nodded politely to her, but there was a distinct wariness here, she felt. Time to take the initiative.

'I spoke to your uncle Bert a day or two ago about the Ada Proctor case in 1929. Poor Davy Todd was hung for it, but I'm convinced there's more to it,' she said earnestly. 'So much doesn't add up, there's a good chance he's innocent.' Georgia decided there was no harm in putting herself over as a somewhat dotty but harmless researcher with a fixation on proving Davy's conviction was wrong.

'I wouldn't know about that,' Oliver replied easily. 'Uncle Bert knows more about it than me. We don't talk much, you see. It was a long time ago.' There was a kindly note in his voice, but his eyes didn't look at all kind. There wasn't much giving here.

'I'm not a sensationalist,' she replied quietly. 'You needn't worry about that.'

'I don't, m'dear.'

The stonewall approach, and Georgia might not have got any further had not Lucy intervened. 'There's no harm in letting her see our photos, Olly. After all, we don't want –' she hesitated – 'her getting the wrong idea because we didn't do what we could.'

There was a hidden subtext here but, whatever it was, Oliver grudgingly gave way. 'I don't know any more than Uncle Bert can tell you,' he repeated. 'No one said anything, see? I didn't find out myself till I was over twenty and reckoned old enough to know. But I suppose you can see the pictures.'

Lucy promptly flew out of the room and returned with an album. Georgia began to suspect that Lucy was as eager as she was to enter hitherto forbidden territory, especially since she flicked the pages so speedily to find one of Davy. It suggested it wasn't the first time she'd pored over it.

So this was Davy Todd, albeit only when he must have been about ten years old. Georgia studied the snapshot closely. He was sitting on a stone bridge with several other members of the family, judging by the caption underneath the photo, and had a schoolboy grin on a cheeky-looking face. Such photos were always terrifying. These were cheerful young innocents, not knowing what lay ahead for them. In many cases from the last century this would be death in the First or Second World Wars. For Davy it had been at the end of a rope for a murder he probably didn't commit. *Probably*. Georgia caught at the word her thoughts had produced and realized she was upgrading the likelihood of his innocence, at least in her own mind.

She swallowed, and glanced up to see that Oliver Todd's eyes were still wary. It would be up to her how far she got with this search for the past. He wasn't vouchsafing any more information to her, even though she suspected he could if he so wished. Tomorrow, however, she would meet the Bloomfields, who had reluctantly agreed to see her, as Jim Hardbent had suggested it, and she was pinning her hopes on them. Drinks at 6 p.m. It all sounded very formal, although she supposed this was an unfair judgement since Trevor must be at the Wickenham Manor Hotel working all day.

The following morning Georgia walked up to the hotel for coffee, trying to gauge what it must have been like as a private home, and what role it had played in the village in the 1920s. She decided that she wouldn't have liked to live there. Once upon a time the whole of Wickenham would have centred on this house and indeed, with the sale of the land for development, the wheel could be said to be turning full circle. The marble pillars of the entrance hall combined with the dull blue of the carpeting gave a grand but unwelcoming effect, and whatever atmosphere the house had possessed as a private home had long since gone. It did not bode well for her visit to the Bloomfields that evening.

Trevor and Julia Bloomfield now lived in a large modern mock-Georgian home set back from the road nearly opposite the entrance to the Wickenham estate. They were in their late fifties, she estimated, as they exchanged small talk on her arrival, prompt at 6 p.m. This house, however, with its bricked forecourt set within screening bushes, dark green carpet throughout, and display of expensive vases and antiques, spoke of the comfort the Manor no longer suggested.

Trevor was not the bland businessman Georgia had expected, but a tanned, grey-haired charmer who looked as though he worked out in the hotel gym every day. Both he and his wife Julia spoke of cash confidence, though Georgia was aware this verdict was unfair for a first meeting. To complement his polish, his wife was an elegant blonde (with help), who seemed to have worn her hostess's smile so long it stayed in place automatically. Her eyes did not obey the smile, however. Indeed they displayed no curiosity at all in their visitor, merely a resigned determination to play her role. Georgia had been put down as a duty to fit in between sundown and dinner.

'So you're a writer, Georgia.' Trevor Bloomfield handed her the glass of white wine she had requested, and Julia pushed a bowl of Japanese crackers towards her. Georgia rather liked these, so this became a minor point in their favour. Otherwise her jury was out on how she reacted to them.

'Yes, I write with my father. He does most of the actual writing and I do the research.'

'I've read one of your books,' Trevor said, sounding genuinely interested. 'The case in Forest Gate.'

Georgia murmured something appropriate, and he continued: 'So what can we do for you on the Proctor case?'

'Everything revolves round the Manor – and its lord. I thought if anyone was able to help me with records, memories and so forth it would be you.'

'We are hardly seen as public benefactors at present,'

Trevor said drily. 'We're more like Public Enemy Number One, to all the sports fans here. No one cares much that the Bloomfields are selling their interest in the hotel and the estate but when the question of these two fields becoming a supermarket came up, it was a different matter. So much for the beloved old squire tradition.' He laughed. 'You don't take enough free gruel round to the poor cottagers, Julia.'

'Most of them are richer than we are,' she rejoined sourly. 'I offered to let the kids in the village come in to blackberry on the estate a few weeks ago. And how many came, do you suppose?'

'None?' Georgia fed her the correct line, but personally if she were a village kid she'd steer well clear of this steely eyed witch and her offerings.

'Nearly right. Half a dozen old folks from the almshouses. Don't talk to me about being Lady Bountiful.'

Georgia dutifully laughed. 'I hope they made you a pie as a thank you.'

'They don't know the meaning of the word. Anyway, Trevor,' Julia continued, 'some people approve of the supermarket. Not that it matters a damn anyway since we already have permission and the sale will be going through soon. The Todd faction is against it, naturally enough, since it owns quite a few of the village stores, but that means the Elgins are for it. Especially since some of them are builders, who can see a chance of business coming their way.'

'Elgins?' Georgia picked up quickly. 'I've only met Mary Elgin.' Keep the conversation flowing. The more people speak the more they tell you, was her experience, whether they mean to or not.

'There you are, you see. She's Mary Beaumont, but she's still thought of as an Elgin.'

'To you, too?' Georgia asked curiously. 'You must still be very involved in village affairs.'

'The Manor might not be a manor any more,' Trevor answered, 'but the hotel needs local employees, and so, bang, we're saddled with village feuds. They all want work, they all want custom, though, and I made it clear they won't get it unless I can rely on there being no feuds waged at Wickenham Manor.'

'The Ada Proctor case seems to have been affected by the Todd–Elgin feud.' Georgia brought the conversation firmly back to her own needs. 'Would you have any records, do you think? Was your family involved at the time?'

'I don't see how it could have been. My grandfather was Squire then, so I suppose he must have been involved at some level. But then there was another war and that would have wiped the slate of village memory clean. I seem to remember a family photo of Grandfather with the old doctor standing by his Austin. I suppose he must have known Ada too.'

From the lack of interest on his face, Georgia began to realize she wasn't going to get very far. Hopes of being invited to trawl through the Wickenham Manor archives receded, but in that case she had nothing to lose and so decided to plunge straight in with both heavy feet.

'I've heard rumours that Ada had lovers other than Davy – if indeed he was one. She was engaged to a Guy Randolph during the war, but after his death there seem to have been others. Would you – I know it's a long shot – have any idea whom?'

'Randolph?' Trevor queried sharply.

'Do you know anything about him?'

'There were Randolphs who were chums of my grandparents, I believe. I only know of them because there were pictures in the family album. That was Major Stewart Randolph, but this Guy might have been a son perhaps. Another drink?'

Georgia accepted, knowing this was a signal it would be time to go once she had finished it. There was a distinct frostiness in the air now, which puzzled her. 'Your grandfather never spoke of Guy Randolph returning after the war years, did he? He was missing, believed killed.'

'I wouldn't know.'

'Or village rumours of other lovers?' Hell, she thought, I'm blowing this with a vengeance.

Trevor didn't even bother to reply, but surprisingly Julia did. For the first time she was displaying positive interest. 'More than just rumours.'

'Darling?' Trevor was having a hard time concealing his impatience now.

Julia ignored it. Somehow Georgia had struck a nerve. 'My mother told me about it. There was some kind of link between my grandmother's servants and the Manor's. This is all hearsay of course, and I might not have remembered it correctly.'

'Hearsay can be jolly interesting.' Georgia urged her on, in her researcher's earnest voice, as Julia shot a triumphant 'so what?' glance at Trevor. 'It can't do any harm now everyone's dead, and could just do some good.'

'Trevor,' Julia continued airily, 'I'm sure your father told me that John Sadler was having an affair with Ada. That's why I remembered what my mother had said. He was still here when I first met you.'

Trevor shrugged dismissively. 'John Sadler was my grandfather's trusted steward, running the estate, *and* he was married with two small children. It seems very unlikely he would have a fling with the doctor's daughter.'

To Georgia's relief, Julia persisted. 'Yes, but my mother said that Ada was good friends with Rose Sadler. She might have used that as a cover for a relationship with John.'

'Are the Sadlers still in the Wickenham District?' Georgia ignored the thundercloud on Trevor's face.

'Not that I'm aware of. I don't remember any Sadler on our pensions list.'

A pensions' list? This sounded good. 'I suppose none of the Manor servants you mentioned would still be alive?' Georgia asked hopefully.

She'd been addressing Julia but Trevor broke in once more. No doubt about it now. The gentleman was actively hostile. 'No. There was only one living in then and she died years ago.'

'Her daughter's still alive,' Julia said helpfully. 'She runs the W.I. here. Alice White. Trevor, you don't remember what happened to the Sadlers, do you?' She was bearing down hard on him, and he could hardly refuse to answer, though he looked as though he'd like to.

'I remember John being around in the early sixties, but I have no idea whether he dropped dead or left the district.'

'I suppose the Manor archives wouldn't have anything on them?' Georgia asked brightly.

'There are none,' Trevor whipped back with evident relief. 'My late grandmother occupied herself with sorting out such records as might be of interest to the country archive office, and destroying the rest. Regrettable, but in those days, there was not such a passion for disinterring the past.'

He appeared politeness itself as he showed her to the door, but nevertheless she knew his last remark had been aimed straight at her. She found it odd that he was so reluctant to talk about what must now be a mere matter of history. Perhaps he was one of those men who are fine so long as one sticks to the path they have preordained for you, but who refuse to go the extra inch, let alone mile. Then she remembered Jim Hardbent's similar reluctance to talk too freely about Wickenham's past. So far, and no more. There was still a barrier she had to either crash through or gently raise the latch. The message she was getting was that Wickenham looked after its own affairs, and that applied from the Squire down. Or, with her opinion of Trevor Bloomfield, from the Squire *up*.

Now Georgia was left only with the maid's daughter as a possible lead, she realized, as she walked back to Country Stop for dinner. The thought of going straight back to Todd territory was suddenly unappealing, however, so she decided to take another walk to Crown Lea field. Fresh air might clear her brain. Two hundred years ago or so, she reflected, as she walked up the lane into the field, there would have been a memorial erected on the spot where Ada died. Today withering flowers would mark such a murder. For Ada's there was nothing. No family, no friend, no record to resurrect the living woman.

The stile into the Lea was broken down, and she leapt the ditch, remembering – like Ada – that she was wearing the wrong shoes for this kind of terrain. Nor did she have the Ordnance Survey map with her. Ahead to her left were grass-covered downs. To her right, woodland. That must be where the denehole lay. When she was suitably clad she must go to see it, so that she could at least describe the scene to Peter.

And then she saw a man walking a dog coming towards her from the woods. Just an average normal sort of man on a routine mission. Apparently. But who could tell?

'Good evening,' she said, as he approached.

He glanced at her as though her solitary stationary self must mean she was intending to pounce on him, and he passed with evident relief. Had Ada seen someone she recognized coming towards her despite the dark? The sun was beginning to sink fast now, and it was nearing the time of year when Ada Proctor had died. Had she felt fear or excitement? Only seventy-five years separated them. If Ada were beside her now, would she like her, or not? It was not so fanciful to imagine one could stretch out a hand in the darkness and lightly touch the past.

Chapter Five

'Did you see *The Times* this morning? – Oops, sorry, haven't cleared away.' Lucy Todd dived at the table, which still bore the remains of its previous occupant's full English breakfast.

If anything was needed to make up her mind about her own order, that was it. 'I'll have the grapefruit and toast, please,' Georgia decided. 'And tea.'

'I've got real coffee.' Lucy was clearly surprised, and Georgia didn't know whether she should be flattered or merely amused that she had been set down as a coffee drinker. Sometimes she was, but today she wanted tea. Coffee would wind her up too much at a time when she was letting impressions seep into her rather than grabbing at them.

'Tomorrow perhaps,' Georgia announced to a speedily retreating back. 'No, I haven't seen a paper yet.' Obviously. She was only just up.

'We've made the front page with the protest meeting.' A grapefruit was whisked from kitchen to table.

A misunderstanding here, then. Not the national *Times,* but probably the *Gravesend Times,* which covered Wickenham. Equally important in people's lives, but the focus was narrower. Last week's edition had carried a mention of public opposition to the sale of the sports fields and that feelings were running high. Georgia had gathered that the council had refused to revoke the planning permission and that this protest meeting was being hastily called to organize some sort of appeal to the Secretary of State for the Department of the Environment. She wondered how this news was being taken by the Bloomfields. Any hopes that the sale would go through quietly were unlikely to be realized. Judging by the gleeful look on Lucy's face, there was trouble brewing.

'That's what Mr Scraggs is here for,' Lucy continued.

'Who?'

'The gentleman in room 2. He's an artist.'

Her predecessor at breakfast. 'Really?' Polite interest. The word 'artist' covered a vast range of interpretation.

'He does houses, he says.'

Georgia suppressed the thought that Lucy might have mistaken the word 'painter' for 'artist', when she saw someone who could only be the said artist lingering in the open doorway. There was no doubt about it, at least from his looks: straggly brown hair, small equally straggling goatee beard and a pale anxious face above it.

'Good morning,' she said amicably, and the said artist turned briefly in her direction.

'Morning,' he managed.

'What can I do for you, Mr Scraggs?' Lucy cooed in her professional voice. Arrangements were made about evening meals, while Georgia returned to her grapefruit. It had been cut in a rush – naturally – but was none the worse for that. Ten days had passed since her first visit, but Georgia was beginning to feel at home both at Country Stop with the Todds and in Wickenham itself, even though she was aware that to them she was still very much an outsider. There were dangers in becoming too much part of the Wickenham 'family', however, for Ada Proctor's Wickenham was another country from the Wickenham of today. Somehow she had to forge a link between them. For her, the physical shape of Wickenham in the 1920s was now taking shape nicely, and this was a good base.

The online 1901 census had revealed that Major Stewart Randolph had a wife named Ethelind (where had that come from: a parentage devoted to Anglo-Saxon ancestry, a fanciful notion by a pregnant wife, a family name?) and two children, Guy and Gwendolen. Guy had been ten at the time of the census and Gwendolen six. A Dr John Proctor had been living at The Firs, together with Dr Edward Proctor, his wife Winifred and their daughter, Ada, then nine years old. The Hon Gerald Bloomfield had lived at Wickenham Manor with his wife Mary, their sons, Jack and Matthew, and a daughter, Anne. The only Sadler listed, however, was clearly not the family Marsh & Daughter was interested in. She was eighty-six, and her name was Queenie.

Nevertheless the census information in conjunction with Kelly's provided a useful picture of daily life, time though it took to compile it. There had been five grocery stores then (those were the days!), two bakers, a haberdasher, two butchers, a farrier, a dressmaker, three teashops, three pubs, two garages, a dairy, two greengrocers, the post office and a combined coal merchant and ironmonger. The carrier to Maidstone and to Gravesend ran twice weekly, buses and trains ran regular services and the fishman called on Thursdays. When can I move back? Georgia had thought ruefully.

Mary Elgin was quite impressed at her local knowledge when Georgia arrived.

'I remember old Stinky Tom – him and his stinking cod,' she remarked scathingly. 'Not good enough to give the cat, Mum would say. He had plenty of paws of his own, though, did Tom. I remember that too. So you're doing your home-work, are you?'

'That's right. An all-round picture comes first.'

'What use are pictures? What are you doing about my Davy?' Mary turned querulous.

'There's nothing I can do about Davy, unless we can find out how Ada really died, and who killed her.'

Mary grunted, but Georgia took this for encouragement or at least not disagreement. 'I need to find out if Ada really did have lovers or even admirers. She might not have

admired *them* but it would still give the men a possible role
in her death. I know you said you didn't know anything
about the other men in her life, but the name of Sadler has
been mentioned. Can you tell me anything about him?'

'Course I can. Why didn't you ask me? He were a scally-
wag, I can tell you. Good at his job at the Manor, but
fancied himself and expected everyone else to as well. He
was an old man to me, so I took no notice. Anyway, he
had a nice wife and kiddies. He was a foreigner though, so
were they all.'

'What nationality?'

'Oh, he were English. Wasn't Wickenham born and reared
though. Came here with the family when he started work
at the Manor.'

'When would that have been?'

'Can't say. I remember him coming, that's all, so must
have been after the war, probably in the twenties. Lot of
folk moving around then.'

'Do you know what happened to the family? They're no
longer in Wickenham.'

'He were there after the second war, I do remember that.
Must have gone sometime later, I suppose.'

'And you've no idea where?'

'Never had much to do with them. Went to live with one
of their kids perhaps. It's not like that today. No one wants
you, whether you got kids or not. Not even the government
wants you nowadays.'

Georgia took this as a cry against the outrage of growing
old. Mary Elgin was right. This home was good, compared
with many Georgia had visited, and the staff were good-
natured and helpful. But did they *want* her? 'What about
your own family?' she asked gently. 'I've met the Todds,
but no Elgins yet.'

'Not much lost there,' was Mary's immediate reply.

'You're still in touch with them?'

'Touch? They wouldn't touch me with a bargepole. Vi
and Emmie looked down on me for bringing shame on the

family by loving my Davy. Can't blame them, I suppose. That's what Mum and Dad told them, and they were younger than me, so they believed it.'

'What happened to you after your mother left and your father died?'

'The elder ones were married, so they took in Vi and Em. Didn't want me, thank you very much. I went to Grandma Higgins, my mum's mum. She'd more or less given up the travelling life by then, and lived in Meopham, so I went there and went into service. Then I met Bill Beaumont, and remembered him from Wickenham days, so that clinched it. I'd show them. So I married him and back I came to Wickenham bold as brass. Gran thought it a great joke. She never did like those Elgins. By the time Bill and me were married most of the talk had died down. We were in the Slump by that time, and folk had other things on their minds. The waters had closed over poor Davy. But I never forgot. I kept up Ada's grave while I could, since Davy didn't have one. I thought he'd like that. He was always a thoughtful one, was Davy. After the trial, the Todds wouldn't talk to me, they reckoned I was the cause of it all, though how that could be I don't know. Nor would the Elgins.

'It all blew over eventually – after the next war finished. My sisters were snooty but Bill was well liked, so they reckoned they could just about talk to me again. And their kids liked my cakes. The current lot just think of me as an old witch, nothing harmful, just bonkers. Daft, isn't it? Even if Davy had been guilty – which he wasn't – I was only a seventeen-year-old girl when it all happened. Life never gave you a second chance then. Now it's the other way round, seems to me. They give you all the chances you want, so it don't matter what you do. Why can't life be halfway down the middle?'

'You've had a tough time,' Georgia said sympathetically.

She was eyed sharply. 'I had Davy and Bill. Anyway, I reckons everyone has a tough time inside themselves. But we all march on somehow.'

Zac, Rick, her mother – was she marching on? Georgia wondered. She tried. Peter and she both did. That's what made them a good team. They had a common purpose, which they could not afford to let slip lest they too slid back into the mire of the past. That reminded her of the Randolphs, although her question as to whether anyone had gone missing about the same time as Ada drew a blank.

'Did you know the family?' she asked.

'I were only a kid when the Randolphs left the village. Went west, they did, and never came back. I remember the young lady, lovely she was. Gwendolen. Now there's a name.' Mary rolled it lovingly round her tongue several times. 'She was seven or eight years older than me. When I grow up I'm going to be like her, I told my mum. Don't be so daft, Mum said. Dad's sister Eileen did for the Randolphs, so I reckoned that was as good as knowing them. I think I remember the Major too. I do recall I was sick during the village hall party when the first war ended. I remember the men coming back from the army and talk of those that didn't. Didn't mean much to me. And before you ask, Auntie Eileen's long gone. Like the Randolphs. Like everyone.'

'But not you,' Georgia said quietly.

Mary roused herself again. 'Not blooming likely. Not before you find out about my Davy. So hurry up. God's knocking at my door and He's getting tired of waiting.'

As she drove away from Four Winds, Georgia began to realize she was suffering from indigestion. Not physical – thank heavens she'd avoided the full English breakfast – but mental. She stopped the car on the downs for a few minutes' reflection. That was the trouble at this stage of a case. There was a tendency to bolt one's 'food', rush at the information partly though enthusiasm and partly because of the pressure of limited time 'on site'. She knew what Peter meant by the need to lay it aside and listen to what the past was telling you. As in an archaeological site, the exposed skeleton lying in its resting place needed consideration far beyond what the date of the bones could produce. Consideration would bring some gleaned information to the fore, and let less important matters lie fallow.

Nevertheless, this was hard when someone like Mary Elgin poured his or her story into you. The swamp of emotion that it could justifiably arouse blotted out the distance you struggled so hard to retain. And yet, Georgia reflected, emotion was what led her to get involved in the first place. Thankfully, in her case, Luke stood as an upright pole in the middle of the swamp. If she made it as far as Luke, then she was out of the mud.

She suddenly had a great longing for home. Only three more ports of call, and then she could return to the safe distance of Haden Shaw. Safe? She picked up on this immediately. What was disturbing – threatening? – about Wickenham? The stirring up of the past or rumbles of the present?

Neither, she had told herself impatiently – nothing a good brisk walk wouldn't settle anyway.

Back in the open fields with the autumn wind blowing, this time clutching her detailed Ordnance Survey map, it was easier to visualize Mary's Wickenham of the late 1920s. Crown Lea had been a meadow then, though today it was cultivated, and the all but fruitless day in the PRO she had spent last week had revealed the coroner's inquest report, which concluded from the straw stubble on Ada's coat that she had actually been killed in the adjoining field, nearer to the wood in which she would have hoped to see the badgers and nightingales. Another point that might or might not have been referred to in the trial. Certainly it wasn't selected for the law reports.

Frustratingly, there had been no post-mortem report amongst the exhibits, which would have settled once and for all whether Ada had been a promiscuous trollop or virgo intacta. The inquest proceedings had concentrated on cause of death. Ada might well have been both flirtatious and a virgin, but it was yet another question mark still to be answered. On the plus side, the exhibits revealed that Ada had been wearing gloves. One to Davy Todd (and Marsh & Daughter).

'Ada,' Georgia said softly, as she stumbled over the rough footpath, '*what* on earth brought you here in the dark, if not the badgers?'

Map in hand, she continued on along the footpath to the wood, climbing over the stile. Even in the daylight she had a momentary qualm about entering it, public footpath or not. A large sign warned her to keep to the path. This was private property.

Whose? she wondered, orientating herself on the map. It could belong to Hole Farm who owned Crown Lea, or it could belong to the Manor. Wickenham Manor lay well to the east, but its estates were – or had been – large, so she should look into this. It was clear that few people used this footpath now. Overgrown brambles and nettles were dying off, but their trailing stems lay across the path, which according to the map led past the Manor and on to the hamlet of Wickenham Forstal.

There was no sign yet of a denehole, even though one was marked on the map. Then the footpath crossed a wide track – and she was in no doubt now that she had reached it. There were recent tyre marks leading to her left. No public footpath, according to the map, but even from here she could see where the denehole must be and she followed the track until she came to it, about ten yards along, boarded over, with danger signs and plenty of evidence of recent police activity.

'Okay, Peter, I've tried,' she told herself, but so far as she could see, to little purpose. Unless, of course, it occurred to her, Ada's rendezvous had been with John Sadler. Or, she was forced to admit, the skeleton in the denehole.

By the time she arrived at Alice White's home she was more than ready for late-morning coffee. Alice looked the part of pivot of Wickenham life, a bustling woman in her late fifties or early sixties, bright of eye and eager to communicate. Almost too eager. The words began to tumble out as though there were a pent-up nervousness there and Georgia noticed that as she talked Alice's eye contact remained with the cafetière, not with her visitor. Nevertheless, her cluttered dining-room table was a welcome antidote to Four Winds.

'Yes, my mother was in service at the Manor up to the time she married in the 1930s, and I think she went back there during the war. She was the only person who could work with the She-Wolf of Wickenham.'

'The *what*?'

Alice giggled, as she dispensed the coffee. 'Everyone called her that, not just Mum. I'm surprised you haven't run into Mrs Priscilla Bloomfield before now. Not in person, of course. Thankfully the old besom's no longer with us. She was the wife of Matthew, the old Squire, the present Trevor Bloomfield's grandmother. Matthew had just become Squire at the time of the Proctor case – that's what you're interested in, aren't you?' She looked up suddenly, caught Georgia's eye, and returned to her study of the coffee pot. 'He died during the war and her son Bertram took over the Manor. Until Bertram married, and long after it, his mother ruled the roost. She was a wicked old woman – didn't leave us till the 1980s – but my mum was a lovely soul, and could put up with anybody. Anyway it was so hard to get staff in those days that even the She-Wolf didn't dare go too far. She'd have had to do her own washing-up, and I can't see madam doing that. So what is it you want to know about the Proctor case?'

Georgia was hardly surprised that Alice White knew exactly what she was interested in. The whole village must have known by now. Even so Alice had seemed very eager to see her.

'The Sadlers primarily. He worked as a steward to the estate. Do you know them or what happened to them? Not that there's much chance they'd know anything about Ada Proctor's murder, but there seems to be this rumour that Ada was having an affair with John Sadler.'

'Oh yes, I knew Uncle John – that's what I called him as a child. And that went on till he and Auntie Rose left. She was a sweetie. Everyone loved her.'

'Even John Sadler?'

'I got the impression they were a devoted couple, but then I was a child, so I can't swear to it. Certainly Mum never said anything to the contrary, but then she wouldn't. He retired, probably in the late 1950s, and they went to live with or near their daughter. Out in the West Country somewhere.'

'As did the Randolphs,' Georgia commented, somewhat depressed at yet more vague statements that were getting her nowhere.

'The Randolphs?'

'Did your mother work for them too?' Georgia had caught the note of interest in Alice's voice.

'No, but it just reminded me of something. You know how some incidents in your childhood stand out but you can't tie them in with anything else. There was a day when I was about five or six when this wonderful man came to our house. He spoke in a funny way and Mum told me afterwards it was because he was French. He was in uniform, and even as a child I knew what that meant. He was fighting in the war. He was a charmer, and he paid special attention to me, asked me to show him round the village and Hazelwood House in particular. I fell head over heels in love and pestered Mum afterwards about him. She said his name was Randolph and he was looking for a family that used to live in Wickenham. I think I used to have fantasies that one day he'd come back and claim me for his own. I must have seen too many Hollywood films.'

'But he never did come back?'

'Never a whisper or whisker that I remember. But the name stuck in my mind, especially since not that long afterwards The Firs, which stood opposite Hazelwood House, was hit by a flying bomb, and Hazelwood was affected too. It stood derelict until long after the war and I used to imagine it was waiting to be *our* house, his and mine. Anyway,' she added quickly, 'Mum had no idea where the Randolphs were.'

'Or the Sadlers either?' Georgia asked without much hope.

'Oh yes, didn't I say? Mum stayed in touch with Rose, who's long dead now of course, and so probably is her daughter.'

'Would you have the address so that I can check that?' Georgia asked, as Alice suddenly stopped short, and her face reddened slightly.

'Yes, it's in my mother's old address book. I'll give it to you.' She went over to a desk, and scribbled it down on a piece of scrap paper. Then, in a rush, 'Look, do you mind not telling anyone if I do give it to you? I shouldn't have mentioned it really.'

'Of course not.' Georgia was surprised since Alice didn't seem the sort of woman to keep her mouth buttoned over trifles.

Alice looked relieved, and the words began to flow again. 'It's my husband. He's, well, funny over the past. That's why I never told him you were coming. He doesn't believe in raking up the old case. Says things are bad enough already, without giving the Todds more fuel.'

Georgia leapt on the salient point – the rest she could disentangle at her leisure.

'But *you're* interested in the case?'

'I'm sick of it all. I'm sick of being chair of the WI when all it makes me is a punchbag. It's time it was sorted, and if you can—'

The sound of the front door opening, followed by footsteps, silenced her. Her face went pale. 'Tell him you're here because Mary gave you a message about needing money.'

What on earth was this about? Georgia gulped, almost as nervous as Alice was, as the door opened and a tall, burly man in his sixties came in.

'Hello, George. You're early,' Alice managed brightly.

There was nothing bright about George White. He obviously recognized Georgia immediately, though she could not remember seeing him before.

'You're that journalist poking her nose in everywhere. What have you been telling her, Alice?'

'Mary Beaumont gave me a message for her, Mr White,' Georgia obediently lied.

'And what's Mary been yapping about this time?' But seeing Georgia about to speak, he continued viciously, 'Don't bother to tell me, and get out of my house. She's been bleating on about bloody Davy again. Right?'

'Wrong,' Georgia retorted, walking towards the door after thanking Alice. 'Mrs Beaumont doesn't *bleat.*'

She clutched the piece of paper on which the address was written like a lifebelt in the sea in which she felt she was gradually drowning. She shuddered at the thought of the marital row undoubtedly breaking over Alice's head behind her. Thank heavens for the single life. She could walk out, unlike Alice. What had all that been about? Surely not over the Sadler question. Even if she managed to get in touch with the family, a granddaughter was hardly going to know whether her grandfather had an affair with Ada Proctor over seventy years ago, let alone whether he had murdered her as a result of it.

'How are you getting on then?' Jim Hardbent asked, when she arrived at his home. He and his wife Janet lived in what used to be the village forge, though the house had obviously become grander and larger since it ceased trading. The old forge itself, where he ushered her, was now the room Jim devoted to village history but the fireplace still had the musty smell of smoke around it, and the heavy beams and brick walls still gave the impression that at any moment a few horses might amble in to be shod. On the bare red brick, old photographs were hung, and one wall was entirely covered with shelving, with neatly labelled box files.

Georgia made a face. 'Hardly brilliantly.' She decided to tell Jim about her latest conflict. It was time she got to the bottom of this antagonism. 'I don't understand,' she finished. 'Why should this George White be so sensitive about the case?'

'You know who he is, don't you?' Jim looked surprised. 'You were putting your head in the den and the lion bit it off. I'm amazed at Alice, I am. She was chancing it all right.'

A terrible suspicion came to her. 'He's not an Elgin, is he?'

'Head of the clan, m'dear. George Elgin White is Vi's son and so Mary's nephew, and Tom, the builder, is his brother. They're leading the opposition to the Todds over this appeal business.'

'But why should Ada Proctor affect that?' She found it unbelievable.

'Part of the feud.'

'Then why,' Georgia said, exasperated, 'was Alice so keen to talk about it? And she was, you know.'

'I do. She and I think the same – that this feud poisoned, and still is poisoning, Wickenham, and that there needs to be an end to it.'

'Then why –' it was time for plain speaking '– are you wary of me too?'

He grinned unoffended. 'Because an outsider's not the one to do it.'

'And do you still feel that?'

He thought about this. 'No. Now George has shot his mouth off, things have gone too far, and this appeal is going to bring the feud to a head anyway. Time for me to throw my weight in, I reckon.'

He threw it. In a trice he was pulling down a bound ledger, from the top of a pile of similar volumes. 'You can take a look at this, my love. It's the surgery accounts from 1927 to 1930, all written up in Ada's own hand, till she died, of course, and someone else took over.'

Georgia pounced on it. She was no handwriting expert but at least the contents must tell her something about Ada. 'How on earth did you get hold of this?'

'Ah well, medical records are one thing, but these are the private surgery records, cost of medicines, visits, etc. My dad got it, and more like it, after the bomb hit the house. There was a lot of stuff salvaged and no one in the Proctor family left.'

As she began to pore over the entries, Jim went on to explain: 'Dr Proctor was a panel doctor, meaning he was registered with the local National Insurance Committee under the 1911 Act. Some of his patients still had to pay, but those in work paid their dues and got everything free if they were sick. A few years after they retired, the benefits ran out though, and just as folks were really needing free treatment it was taken away from them. Daft, but it was a step in the right direction at the time.'

'"Mrs Hodges, 6d for ABC liniment, Mr Jacobs, nux vomica, Miss Gordon, sleeping draught,"' she read. But it was the handwriting that most interested her. It was neat but large, bold in black ink, not quite copperplate but a uniform style; this was the writing of a woman with a mind of her own.

The next volume Jim brought to her, containing household accounts, was equally well kept, including wages to 'Elsie'.

'Was Elsie their maid?' she asked.

'She was. She stayed on with the next owner after the doctor died, and never married, from what I can see. She died along with the new owners when the flying bomb dropped.'

Georgia spent several hours studying not only the ledgers and Jim's postcards but a collection of photographs. They were mostly fuzzy snapshots, but they included several of Ada with her father. One or two of them Georgia remembered seeing in the newspapers of the time, but others were new. If you gaze at old photographs long enough, she thought, you can live in the world in which they were created. Ada's photographs, as her handwriting, suggested a strong-willed lady, handsome rather than beautiful. That chin said it all. She looked tall, about Georgia's own height, five foot seven, with darker hair than her own honey-brown (as Luke insisted on calling it). Hard though it was to make judgements on such flimsy evidence, especially when one could not help being influenced by the long straight loose clothes and the button shoes, Ada didn't look to Georgia like a woman who would jeopardize her own and her father's reputations by carrying on with a married man – or with her gardener. If one was a doctor's daughter, known and respected with a position of one's own to maintain, one guarded one's reputation.

Just as she reluctantly felt she should tear herself away to return to Haden Shaw, she noticed the boxes labelled 'Oral History'. 'What are they?' she asked curiously. 'Written memoirs?'

'A few. Most are recordings.'

By the look on his face, Georgia realized Jim had been teasing her all this time, holding back a possible treasure trove. 'Recordings of people giving their impressions of life in their times?' She tried to contain her excitement, but failed.

'Not *their* times. Their *past* times. No one can describe their own today. What do you say about it? The refuse collectors call on Mondays? Yesterday is a different matter. Whether it's the truth or not is another question.'

Georgia hardly dared ask. 'How far do your records go back?'

Naturally he took his time about replying. 'You just might be lucky there. My grandfather, he was the first of us collectors. Had cat's whisker radio sets, and recorded on cylinders and the like. He always reckoned he would have been Edison only he were born too late. He spent a lot of time going round recording people, getting them to talk about the old times, mostly about the old Queen. Victoria that would be.'

'Was he recording in the 1920s?' Her mouth was dry with excitement.

'Well, now, I wouldn't be surprised if he were.'

'And can the recordings be listened to now?' she persevered.

'Wouldn't be much good as history if they couldn't be. A few years back I took the lot to one of these sound studios and remastered the recordings on to CDs.'

Steady. Her luck couldn't be this good. 'Is there,' she asked, 'by any chance one of Ada speaking?'

'Funny you should ask that, my dear. They're all indexed and so I had a look for you. There's a few more too you might be interested in, the old doctor, one of the Todds, the Squire—'

'This,' she said fervently, 'is my lucky day.'

'Don't get too excited, Georgia. They're only talking about a village and a past village at that. My grandfather wanted to set down how it changed after the first war. If you look at the war memorial there ain't a family in Wickenham didn't lose someone. Meant a big upheaval everywhere, as families from the Squire down to the butcher who expected sons to take over had to start grooming someone else; others were left without heirs at all, because war had touched everyone for the first time. Some men who survived wanted more than Wickenham could offer and left the village. There weren't the jobs for the heroes like they'd been led to believe.'

'I wish you'd told me about these recordings before.' She tried to keep accusation out of her voice.

'You had to get to know Wickenham before they'd make sense. I went to see Mary after you left the first time. "Is she a stayer?" I asked. "She'd better be," Mary said. "If she doesn't prove my Davy innocent no one will." So now we're all on the same course, I'll make you copies of these CDs.'

Still reeling from her good fortune, Georgia invited him to a drink at the pub before she left, and they walked over to the Green Man. The pub was crowded for early evening and, as she carried drinks over to the table she'd managed to bag in the window, she noticed the great Mr Scraggs. He didn't see her, for he was engaged in earnest discussion, presumably over the appeal, with Oliver Todd and one or two others whom she now recognized as being the Todd clan. The look on their faces read Do Not Disturb.

'The past looks easier than the present at the moment,' she commented to Jim as she set the drinks down.

He shot a look at the group. 'Past *is* the present, Georgia. No ignoring it. Growls away like a blessed volcano, it does. Then one day – whoosh. You mind you don't get in its way.'

'What have you brought me?' Peter's eyes were glued on the carrier bag that Georgia had borne in with such triumph, though his dinner was before him. It didn't seem the best of times to produce her trophies, but he refused to wait, so she continued.

'I've brought you the voice of Ada Proctor.'

He looked puzzled. 'You mean you've recreated her Wickenham. Describe it to me. And then I'll tell you what *I've* discovered.'

Blow him, she thought. He obviously had little faith in her research, so she'd do just as he commanded.

'In 1929 Wickenham is,' she began pompously, 'a quiet more or less self-sufficient village with good communications to London. The crime level seldom taxed the powers of Policeman Plod. Football and cricket were played on the fields of Wickenham Manor, and no one thought leases were necessary for everyone knew that Squire Gerald Bloomfield would never turn them out. He died that year, and the new Squire was the second son Matthew, since Jack had been killed in the war. No one knew much about Matthew, but they didn't expect anything to change – even though he had a fierce wife, known as the She-Wolf of Wickenham.'

'*What?*'

'Her name was Priscilla. Fortunately her ferociousness didn't include wanting to build on the cricket and football pitches. Matthew was to die during the Second World War of natural causes, and his son Bertram – then away fighting in Sicily – inherited. In time money became a problem. However, back to 1929, when the Slump, as it was known in Wickenham, hadn't yet hit Britain. Wickenham was prosperous because of its hops, not yet a noticeably declining industry.'

'You can cut the economics.'

'Do you want this picture painted or not?'

'Dearest Georgia, go ahead.'

'There was a National Health Insurance scheme of a sort, which benefited those in work, but Dr Proctor had to temper the wind to the shorn lambs of the parish. Consequently he was highly respected, as was his daughter.'

'What about the rumours of her being a scarlet woman?'

'I've decided provisionally to discount them. You know how easily they can start. Goodness knows what Haden Shaw thinks of me and Luke.'

Peter ignored this, and she suspected it was because he dreaded the thought of a day when Luke and she might get together permanently so that it would become Marsh, Daughter & Son in Law. Three is rarely a working partnership.

'Why didn't she marry someone else after Guy went missing?' Peter interrupted.

'Not enough men,' Georgia answered succinctly. 'An elderly vicar would be all the likes of Ada could hope for.'

'And did Wickenham possess that invaluable social asset?'

'No. The Reverend Percy Standing was middle aged – and at least by the time he was bumped off (according only to malicious rumour; more factually he died of food poisoning) he was married with a family. He died during the second war, and his widow and kids went to live on the south coast somewhere. Address available, but may be well out of date.' She had gleaned this from the present vicar.

'Worth following up?'

'If I read the gleam in your eye correctly to mean that Ada might have confessed her sins to him, I can only say that according to the photos I've seen not only would she not have sinned but, even if she had, she wouldn't see any need to confess anything to anyone. Very self-contained. We can consider it further if you like.'

'On what grounds might I ask?'

'The grounds of Ada's voice.'

'But –' he caught sight of her face – 'you're not telling me something. What is it?' His voice ended in a howl of rage.

'You wouldn't stop to let me. You insisted on the picture of the village. So now let's listen to Ada.'

Peter was silenced, as she drew out the CD on which Ada featured. Then: 'Have you listened to this?' he asked her accusingly.

'No. Jim suggested we should hear it together if we're writing the book together.'

'Decent of him,' Peter grunted. It was equally decent of Jim to have put Ada's contribution first on the CD, Georgia thought. The remastering of the original had still left the crackling and background noise intact presumably for the sake of not risking any change to the voices, but Georgia found it increased her excitement, like listening to an old wireless broadcast.

And then came Ada's deep voice, beginning with a laugh, a voice she instantly liked:

'I really don't know what you would like me to say, Fred. [A few words lost]. The turn of the century? Well, there were the hoppers of course, some of them still come. There was old Maud – remember her? Enormous size, brought her own bed with her, and all ten children. Some of them still come but Maud has gone. My grandfather was alive then. How old-fashioned it seems now, the old doctor in his frock coat and his pony trap. I would go on his rounds with him sometimes. He took me up to the Manor from time to time, and I'd have something nice in the kitchen while he talked to the Squire. He let me collect the money too, that's how I learned about keeping records, so that I could help my father. And I remember the celebrations for Edward VII's coronation, and how they had to be postponed because he was ill. Guy –' an all but imperceptible pause – 'and I were so cross that the children's party at the Manor had to be postponed too. We didn't believe it would ever happen, but it did. In August, I think, and we had the party on the Manor lawns. It wasn't the same though.'

Georgia stopped the player. Enough for the moment. The rest could wait. 'What do you think, Peter?'

'A confident voice, and a certain humanity, would you say? Certain of herself and her place in life.' Peter brooded. 'Poor woman. She wasn't so safe as she thought. Someone killed her.'

'It's over seventy years ago,' she said gently.

'Only yesterday, once one begins delving.'

'What were you going to tell me?' she asked quickly, to divert him, seeing where this might lead.

Fortunately Peter obliged. 'I had a call from Mike. At his prompting, Darenth Area gave him some more info on the forensic work done on the rubbish in the denehole. There were a few coins that might not have been the deceased's, but there's a chance they were.'

'What about them?'

'Two of them were French franc pieces dated 1919. That's way before the change in their currency. You wouldn't remember, but some time around the late 1950s, their 100 francs became one franc. Before that a franc piece had only been worth tuppence or so, the sort that might be lingering in his pocket if our skeleton had come from France. Which might explain why the list of missing persons in the Wickenham area doesn't tie in with it.'

Georgia couldn't resist the temptation. 'And why a French officer by name of Randolph could not be connected.'

'Just what, Georgia, is this all about?' Peter glared at her.

'He only came to Wickenham in the Second World War,' she finished aggravatingly. 'Sorry.'

Chapter Six

Georgia parked behind the Green Man, uncertain as to why Jim had summoned her so quickly. She ought to come was all he'd said on the telephone, and since she wanted more time to study his records she'd agreed. The village protest meeting on 16th October was not the time she would have chosen, but at least it had the merit that the village would be concentrating so hard on its present crisis that her doings would not be the focus of attention.

Marsh & Daughter had been living in the Wickenham of 1929 for the past week, and the village of today was beginning to feel a mere overlay to the one she knew. Today she would be looking not at the dull plaster-rendering on the façade of Todds the butcher's, but a smart white-painted, black-beamed frontage. The Green Man would no longer be under the management of Thomsons Ales, and a chara-banc stop for excursions from London. The village hall was no longer the Victorian building on the Green, about to be converted, so she'd gathered, into a trendy restaurant, but the brand-new Lottery-built edifice on the new development. The Manor was no longer a private home, there were no longer tennis parties at Hazelwood House, and Dr Proctor no longer descended each morning to breakfast cooked by Elsie or Ada, before walking into his morning surgery. The Firs' gardens were now those of the council houses that had replaced them, and were lovingly or unlovingly tended by hands other than those of Davy Todd. In 1929 the Old Forge, now Jim's home, had been run by John Wilson, whose blacksmith business must then have been on the verge of extinction.

And on 31 October 1929 seventeen-year-old Mary Elgin, in the throes of young love, would have been looking forward to an illicit evening with her Davy while her parents were out at the Hallowe'en dance.

The protest meeting was not until the morrow, but the moment Georgia had driven into Wickenham past the Manor, she had seen evidence of the escalation of feeling. There had been a small but dogged band of protesters standing at the gateway to the Bloomfields' home, and a similar sized group on the opposite side of the road just inside the Manor gates. They looked peaceable enough at present, just holding up placards reading 'Stop globalization now, Say no to conglomerates, Village land for village people,' but making no attempt to lobby passers-by or traffic. To her, it had the depressing air of a well-orchestrated event, even though the protesters were laughing and joking amongst themselves, and it did not bode well for the meeting.

It would be a mistake to imagine there were no such conflicts in 1929. There was no point seeing Ada's Wickenham through rose-tinted spectacles. The early twenties had been a time of slump after the rosy expectations of peace-time following the First World War had been disappointed; 1926 had seen the General Strike; in the month Ada had died, the Wall Street Crash was causing the first ripples of the Great Depression of the 1930s in Europe. Compared with the Jarrow March of 1936, a local protest over football and cricket pitches seemed small beer. It wasn't that small, however, if there were indeed an orchestrated attempt to tie the sale of the sports fields in with global issues, as if the World Trade Organization were moving its HQ to Wickenham. When she had left Wickenham just over a week ago, it had been a local issue of discontent. How had it changed so quickly and why?

As she walked into the Green Man for a lunchtime sandwich, she saw the Bloomfields' Jaguar driving along the

High Street, and caught a glimpse of Trevor's face: set, hardened, that of a troubled man, aware of the reception he would get at his gates. This was unlikely to be the first day such protests had been mounted, and the pressure was – by the look of him – getting through. She wondered if he would have second thoughts about the fields, but knew it was unlikely. The Trevor Bloomfields of this world didn't get where they were today by having second thoughts, even where their own or their family's safety was concerned.

When she returned to the pub, the answer to her question of how the dispute had escalated became clear. The public bar was packed with some kind of meeting. She could see Bert and Oliver Todd in the thick of it, pints were flowing and angry voices were raised. There were perhaps thirty people gathered, both men and women and of all age groups. She could see Lucy, and other people looked familiar, but it was her glimpse of the pale face of Terence Scraggs, now transformed with the look of the fanatic, that convinced Georgia she was right. Terence wasn't just an outsider who'd been roped in for general support. He had either come – or been asked to come – as a prime mover in this protest.

Georgia decided to sit in solitary state, and perched on a bar stool in the saloon bar. She wouldn't be welcome at the meeting, and was determined to steer clear of any active involvement in the dispute. That didn't prevent her from talking about it, however. It would look odd if she didn't.

'Tomorrow's the night, then,' she began conversationally to Steve Faraday, the pub landlord, who seemed to bear her no ill will for deserting his accommodation.

'Firework night's early this year.'

'You think there'll be trouble?'

'That's what it's for. Trouble's what they're after.'

'Verbal fireworks only, I hope.'

'We'll have to wait to see. I've got no time for the

Bloomfields myself, but I don't hold with punch-ups. Especially not outside my pub.'

'Why don't you like the Bloomfields?'

'I don't like or dislike them. It's what they're doing. Sneaky they are. We've only just cottoned on to the fact that there are two sales going on. The two sports fields are a separate deal to the hotel and rest of the estate. They've been keeping quiet about that.'

'Does it make any difference?'

'That Mr Scraggs says it does. Don't see how myself. Either way, I don't want no supermarkets here. We have enough problems in Kent with people stocking up with booze from France instead of drinking in our pubs. Besides –' Steve busily polished a glass and squinted at the results – 'I'm half Todd myself.'

'I thought you were a foreigner from London?'

'So I am, but my mum was a landgirl here in the war. Lodged with Bert's parents, said they were a great family. The farm she worked on was Elgin-run, but she didn't take to the farmer. A slave-driver was Joseph White. He was George and Tom's dad. The Todds and the Elgins pulled together during the war, so no one thought amiss of it when she lodged with Todds. When this pub came up for sale, down I came. Found things had changed though, and this is a Todd pub.'

'Don't tell me. The Red Dragon is where the Elgins drink. No wonder I got funny looks when I went in.' She'd popped in there one lunchtime to see if they served food and promptly retreated again. 'They'd know I was staying at Country Stop. How could I guess about its being an Elgin hang-out though? They don't call themselves Elgins any more. The landlord's name at the Red Dragon is Billy Parsons, isn't it?'

'They're all called Elgin, Georgia,' Steve informed her gloomily. 'You take a look at the parish register some day. Billy's name is William Elgin Parsons. Just like builder Tom Elgin White and his son Daniel Elgin White. One generation of Elgins was mostly girls, so they all agreed to give their kids the name Elgin as a second forename. Still do it. Amazing, isn't it?'

Georgia groaned. 'And now I've fallen foul of George.'

Steve was highly amused. 'Go and stand your ground at the Red Dragon again, the Elgins ain't *that* bad. Only –' he paused – 'I wouldn't go today if I were you.'

'Or tomorrow?' Georgia asked resignedly.

'Right. You're lodging with Todds, and that might be misunderstood. Things are sensitive just now. See?'

Georgia saw. The Elgins could hardly lynch her even if she did go into the Red Dragon, but she didn't want to risk stirring up more ill feeling. What on earth had Jim been thinking of by telling her to come now?

When she arrived at the Old Forge, Jim was out, and Janet welcomed her in. She was a small, rather tight-lipped woman, more reserved than her ebullient husband, but Georgia was coming to like her a lot. She spent a pleasant afternoon, poring over Proctor household books and photos, although she wasn't sure she had learnt anything material from them. They were helpful in rounding out the picture yet further but it was time for the central players to move out of their black and white snapshots and into life. Janet also filled her in on more family background for the Todds and Elgins – too much so, perhaps, for Georgia's head began to spin. This case, she tried to remind herself, centred on Ada and Davy, not village feuds.

Jim returned just as she was about to leave, and she promptly tackled him as to why he'd suggested she come back to Wickenham today. 'There's Steve Faraday suggesting I keep out of trouble, and you're inviting me into it,' she joked.

'Keep out of it, I agree,' Jim replied gravely. 'You need to observe though. Didn't I say Wickenham was like a volcano waiting to blow its lid? You never know what muck will be chucked out of it, but it'll get you, you can count on that. I reckoned you should be here to see it in action.'

Georgia made her way back to Country Stop with a vague feeling of irritation. Jim seemed to be implying that there were links between what was happening now, and what happened in 1929. She couldn't see how. Had the Elgins been covering up the true murderer for the sake of seeing a Todd hung? It was a gripping theory, but that's all it was. A theory. The fingerprints on Time could hardly turn themselves into whopping fists so long after the murder, unless of course it had been the feud, rather than Mary Elgin herself, that had been responsible for the sense of unfinished business in the Wickenham air. If so, it followed that she and Peter might be barking up the wrong tree so far as the Proctor case was concerned. Well, they were too far into Ada's story to retract now, and a village feud, however ugly, was outside their power to resolve.

Into the frying pan, she thought as she entered Country Stop and Lucy Todd's flushed excited face greeted her.

'Hello, Georgia. Sorry I couldn't stop to chat at lunchtime.' She had an air of great self-importance.

'I understand. It's a big day for you all tomorrow.'

'Yes, we Todds have got to stick together. Half the village will be out of a job otherwise.'

Especially the butcher, the baker and the small grocery-cum-stationery store all run by Todds, Georgia thought. Lucy ignored the fact that the other half of the village might gain by it.

'You'll be eating with Mr Scraggs tonight. I hope you don't mind,' Lucy added. 'With both of you in for dinner, it's best to serve you together. Seven o'clock all right? Earlier than you like, I know, but—'

'You've got another meeting.' Georgia grinned.

'And there's tomorrow,' Lucy muttered awkwardly.

'I understand. I'll go to the pub tomorrow evening. Even if Steve's at the meeting, I'm sure someone can stick something in a microwave for me.'

Lucy looked relieved. 'I could do you a poached egg at six,' she offered half-heartedly, but Georgia politely turned down this offer.

In fact the pub would suit her splendidly. She'd probably be there alone since everyone who was anybody would be at the meeting. Georgia Marsh, however, would remain a non-contender in the Wickenham battle.

Once back in her own – albeit temporary – space, her feeling of irritation continued. Here she was in the heartland of the Todd empire and yet instead of drawing closer to the truth of the past, she felt more like a heavy stone stuck in the middle of the fast-flowing river of the present. If she leant out of her window she could see the place where The Firs had once stood, but that would only increase her frustration. There was still nearly an hour before supper, and a shower, even with a hair wash, wouldn't take that long.

Perhaps – yes, she'd fall back on the remedy that had often worked in the past. It was time for a 'Somebody's Son' – her private phrase for it, never shared with Peter for obvious reasons, for setting someone in a family context and thereby giving the name a reality it might otherwise lack. No man is an island; even the darkest villain or the purest saint had parents and ancestors, and probably siblings and descendants. Seeing the names set down on paper could often clarify her thoughts. She grabbed a notepad and pencil to make a start, and half an hour later – after much scrabbling through her notes – she looked at the results of her work with great satisfaction, blanks and question marks notwithstanding. The Todds and the Elgins shared the same page in her pad, and this gave her a odd sense of power over them, which she had been far from feeling earlier.

'That,' she declared, gazing with satisfaction at the name of George Elgin White, 'fixes you. Even a blundering bully like you was a proud mum's offspring once, bawling your head off and dirtying your nappy.'

The Todds

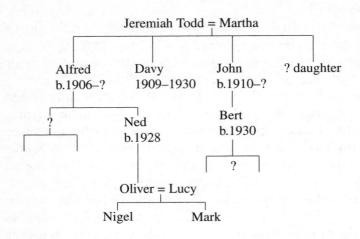

The Elgins

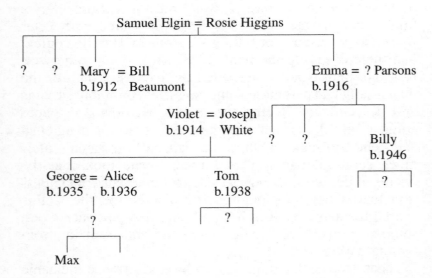

When she came down for dinner promptly at 7 p.m., Terence Scraggs was already at the table.

'Still painting?' she asked brightly as she sat down opposite him. She tried to sum him up anew, as an outside 'professional' protestor, but here in Country Stop he presented just the same somewhat forlorn image she'd first seen.

'Right.' He seemed to be regarding her as a problem he had to endure, and she pitied him. In a way, this enforced companionship was worse for him than for her, since she might at least pick up interesting snippets about the protest.

'Where have you been today?' she persevered.

'The Bloomfields' place.'

'But they'll probably be selling up, so why do they want a picture of their house?' Georgia could play the innocent well when required.

'Not to paint. I was marching.' The last word came out with pride: clearly he wasn't shy about his involvement.

'So you must feel strongly about the sale of the Manor and the grounds?' As if she didn't know.

His face flushed, and not from the mulligatawny soup Lucy had plonked down before them. Georgia had seen that look before. It meant a zealot's speech was on the way.

'Someone has to stand up to those conglomerates,' Terence said fiercely. 'The rights of the common man have to be respected. Look what they're doing to the farmers of the Third World.'

'But a supermarket opening in Wickenham doesn't seem related to that.'

'It's part of it, you see,' he explained eagerly. 'You have to make a stand somewhere. Like El Alamein. Far enough, we said. This is where we stand and fight. These supermarkets are buying up these EU surpluses cheaply and driving everyone else out of business. All the developing countries' farmers and our food stores here don't get a look in. Nor the fish. Nor the butchers. Bakers will go soon. It's time to say no.' He banged a fist on the table, which Lucy took as a signal that their soup was finished, and shot in to remove the plates. 'I tell you –' Terence disregarded the interruption – 'the Third World is here in Wickenham. We have to help.'

Georgia agreed with his cause in principle, but to use the sale of two sports fields for attacking global issues smacked of hijacking to her.

'So that's primarily what brought you to Wickenham,' she said admiringly, 'not the painting.'

He glanced at her warily, perhaps surprised that she had twigged this. 'I saw the publicity in the newspapers. There's something I can do there, I thought.'

'But doesn't making a living have to take precedence?'

'Justice does,' he announced.

'Do you live in a village yourself?'

'My parents do.'

Locally, she presumed, since otherwise how could he have seen the local publicity about the sale? She decided she had gone far enough with her questions, however. Fortunately Terence was the sort of man to whom it would never occur to enquire what she was herself doing here. Unless he already knew of course. This was answered for her when he said: 'Lucy says you're looking into the Ada Proctor case.'

'That's right. Have you heard of it?'

'Not before I came here. It was a Todd versus Elgin thing, wasn't it? Did it start this feud?'

'No, but I'm sure it didn't help.'

'And you think Davy Todd was innocent?'

'He might have been.'

'Who did kill her then?'

'As yet I've no idea.'

'There was a body found recently, in the woods or something.' His turn to persevere.

'Yes, a skeleton in a denehole. Did you read about that too?' Perfectly natural that he should have done, but he seemed more interested than she would have expected. Usually zealots were one-subject people.

'No.' Terence didn't seem disposed to go any further, then perhaps realizing that her eyes were still on him, as Lucy brought in their braised beef, he added: 'Someone in the pub mentioned it. Wouldn't have anything to do with this Ada Proctor, would it?'

'I can't see why it should.' Georgia was taken aback at the coincidence of his querying this, though she supposed it was a natural enough connection in a village where murders were comparatively rare.

'A tramp, probably. Nothing to do with Todds or Elgins anyway.' A pause. 'Families can be odd,' he added inconsequentially.

'There'll certainly be two very odd ones meeting tomorrow night, or do you think the Elgins will boycott the meeting?'

He grinned, but no warmth from it reached his eyes. A cold fish, Georgia decided. 'They'll be there. Either inside or outside.'

'The meeting's in Todd hands though. You, or rather they, are the ones opposing the sale.'

'But the Elgins will kick up a rumpus somehow or other. Hypocrites,' he added darkly. 'They want to keep in with the Manor, so they get the building contracts when the sale's complete.'

'Some things never change, do they? ' Georgia decided to move on to safer territory. It was a Wednesday. How about discussing *The Bill*? At least she'd be watching it, even if Terence had mightier matters in mind. She had no desire to be sitting in the pub while yet another Todd meeting took place. *The Bill* would be escapist in comparison.

The next morning was grey and even when the sun came out briefly, it was quickly overtaken again by dark clouds.

Not a good omen, Georgia thought. Then: nonsense, this was just an ordinary day in Wickenham with an important meeting at the end of it. The weather symbolized *nothing*. The post office was busy with pensions that morning, judging by the queue, and mothers with pushchairs were shopping in the general store and the bakers. This, she reminded herself, was not Tonypandy. No major eruptions of civil unrest here.

Nevertheless, once at the Forge, she tried in vain to concentrate on Dr Proctor's appointment book. Despite her best intentions, the Wickenham of today kept taking precedence over 1929, and she had to force herself to study the book. After Ada's murder there were two weeks with nothing but the word 'locum' scribbled on the otherwise empty pages. Then a different handwriting began recording the doctor's appointments. She learned little new. The old Squire had died earlier that year and the doctor had been visiting him regularly, with all appointments recorded in Ada's hand. After the murder the doctor was still visiting the Manor, this time to see the new Squire, or his wife of course, the famous She-Wolf of Wickenham.

The She-Wolf had been one of the other voices on Jim's tape. Not so deep a voice as Ada's, not unpleasant, but very assured. She was talking of the Wickenham she had come to as a young bride in 1920, and of the role she played in the village, a subservient one to that of her husband, and one which, even to their ears, it was obvious she was eager to change. She saw her job not as bearing comforts for the sick, but of sharing in her husband's managerial responsibilities for the welfare of Wickenham. Unless the Manor thrived, the village would fail to do so, and the Manor's duty was to ensure the village became increasingly prosperous and independent – as she was sure it would. The Manor might be the guardian of the village's soul, but that included making sure the village could fuel its own body. Fine words, Peter had commented, but they had apparently won few friends. Why had she been dubbed the She-Wolf of Wickenham? he asked. A good question, and one to which Georgia had as yet no answer.

There was one phrase from her contribution that had stuck in Georgia's mind, however: that the Manor was the guardian of Wickenham's soul. Merely fine flourish, or was there something in it? Now that the said soul was being so rudely rejected by the Manor, perhaps there was. The sports fields were only symbols of a bond far more ancient. If the core was rotten, the rot would spread outwards.

Psychological claptrap, she told herself. This meeting was beginning to get to her, yet the protest was only a dispute between two warring parties, nothing to do with ancient relationships. And to prove it, she decided she would take her lunch at the Red Dragon today, just as she had gone to the Green Man yesterday. Blow Steve's warning. She had nothing to feel guilty about – quite the contrary since she was supporting Mary Elgin.

The first face she saw as she walked inside was a man who always seemed to be in the bank queue with big boots, and have a continuous snuffle, not to mention his present belligerent way of planting his two fat elbows possessively on the counter. She also recognized the woman who served in the ironmongers, and the man she'd seen retiling the roof on a cottage under renovation on the Green. Now she knew it was odds-on they were from the Elgin clan.

No George here today though. At least she was grateful for that. Nevertheless, she was immediately conscious that she was still not wanted here. Although she nodded pleasantly as she walked to the bar, there was no reaction. Eyes stared at her, backs were turned, although there didn't seem to be a formal meeting going on here. The first back that turned, he of the big boots – Tom Elgin White? – sent a ripple through the bar, with groups edging away, leaving her isolated. From behind the bar Billy Parsons gave her a shamefaced nod, obviously remembering her from her earlier visit, but he was the only one, while the low rumble of voices made it clear she was the object of discussion and that her presence was resented. Every so often she caught a word – and was probably meant to: Todd, bitch, cow . . .

She realized that she was shivering, although the day wasn't cold. It had been a mistake to come. By doing so, she had not only rubber-stamped the idea that she was a Todd supporter, but thrown her hat into the ring of active participants. She left as quickly as she could, aware that the groups behind her were uniting as she moved towards the door. Battlelines had been drawn. 'By the pricking of my thumbs/Something evil this way comes.' The play you never quoted from on stage. Nor perhaps in Wickenham.

'Are you going to the protest meeting this evening, Jim?' Back at the Forge, she sensed that Jim was waiting for her to mention it, and he answered promptly.

'Got to, my love. It's about Wickenham, isn't it? Historic, you might say.'

'It's a football field and a cricket field,' she objected, trying to convince herself as much as Jim. 'Important to those who play there but not fundamental to the village.'

'You're wrong there. It's about the Manor. About who's boss here. We reckon we are, because we live here. That's democracy. But it wasn't always so. Commoners and King, villages and lords of the manor. That isn't democracy. We stopped the first by chopping his head off, now we have to deal with the other.'

Jim was an intelligent man, and obviously saw this as more than a squabble over two sports fields between two feuding groups. That finally convinced her. Georgia's blood was up, furious with herself firstly for going to the Red Dragon and secondly for retreating so quickly. She was going to the meeting, whether it branded her as a Todd or not. If the Elgins believed she was an active player, then she might as well behave like one.

'Do the Bloomfields have children? And if so, do they mind about their "inheritance" here being sold?'

'Three. Jacob, he'd be about twenty-five, don't mind about nothing but making money in the City. Sarah, she's a looker and a sensible lass. Twenty or so, at university. And Crispin, he must be eighteen now. He's spoiled rotten. Fast cars and drugs is what he cares about. There's always a bad streak in every family comes out every so often, and I reckon he's the streaker in the Bloomfields at the moment.'

'Aren't you—' Georgia broke off, fearing to sound rude.

'Overdramatizing? No, Georgia,' Jim replied gravely. 'I'm not. You ought to come this evening. You won't understand Wickenham till you see the clash of the Titans. And I reckon that will happen tonight. You come to sit with Janet and me. You'll be safe enough if you do that.'

'I don't care about the Elgins, but won't the Todds resent me too? Everyone knows I'm here to investigate Ada Proctor, and tonight's meeting is nothing to do with that.'

'The Elgins and the Todds are though. After all, if Davy Todd was innocent, it was the Elgins let him die. Mary's father lied, if she's to be believed.'

'No one seems interested in the case though.'

'They weren't, my love. All long forgotten – till you came here, talking about Davy maybe being innocent. Then those Todds got to thinking what that meant.'

Georgia went white. 'You mean I'm responsible for stirring up—'

'No, you might have caused it, but you can't be held responsible for tribal warfare.' Jim was looking serious. 'Let's hope they take it out on the Manor folk by yelling and shouting, that's all, not fighting it out over Ada Proctor.'

She took her dinner soberly in the Green Man – soberly since as she walked up to the door, a passer-by had spat at her. When she swung round indignantly she saw two men, one of whom she recognized, laughing and walking away. He'd been in the Red Dragon earlier. She was about to have it out with them, then realized she had only herself to blame. She'd nailed her colours to the mast, and all she could hope was that this rancour towards her would die down after the meeting.

The pub was almost deserted, with only a few commuters having a drink after their return from London. Jim's words had shaken her as much as the Elgin spittle, despite his assurance that no blame could be attached to her. She realized she should take care that her view of Davy Todd's guilt shouldn't be swayed by the fact that she could only justify Marsh & Daughter's investigation into the case if he was innocent. If he was guilty, she might have unleashed this tornado for nothing. And then, to her relief, she remembered Terence Scraggs. No, she wasn't responsible for this eruption of the feud. For whatever reason, he had come independently to rabble-rouse.

The new village hall could easily seat, at a guess, five hundred or so in its main hall. Even so it was full to overflowing. She was wedged in between George and Janet near the back of the hall – and near the aisle. 'Just in case,' Jim said, whether comfortingly or not.

'I don't see any Elgins,' she whispered. There were still twenty minutes to go, but some should surely be here?

'This is a protest meeting,' Jim answered,' and since they aren't protesting that's probably why they're not here. Bet they've got a spy or two here though. Still, I'd feel a darn sight more comfortable if we could see some. Better to have the verbals in here than . . .'

'Than in the dark of the night?' she finished for him.

He nodded. 'Take a look behind you,' he said. 'You'll see Mr Blasted Bloomfield's two male offspring standing right at the back by the door. No sign of the great man himself. Sensible of him.'

Georgia glanced back over her shoulder. Jacob looked a younger version of her father, confident, assured – and rich. How did a twenty-five-year-old manage to look like that? Crispin was in jeans, a T-shirt, a shock of curly dark hair and a gleam in his arrogant eye that suggested that he could easily add women to fast cars and drugs. She thought of

Trevor Bloomfield as she had glimpsed him earlier that day, and wondered if fear or prudence made him stay away tonight. The local volunteer policeman was guarding the doorway (or the Bloomfield sons?) as if in answer to her question.

Terence Scraggs was already on the platform, together with one of the older Todds whom Georgia recognized from the pub and Oliver, who was chairing the meeting. He was going to keep the ball in his court judging by the size of the butcher's mallet lying before him on the desk.

She had expected an evening in which both the rights and wrongs of the sale would be at least represented even if both weren't examined in the same detail. From the outset, however, it was clear that the wrongs were taken for granted; not even the action to be taken was under discussion. That had already been decided. A formal appeal to the Secretary of State for the Department of the Environment, Transport and the Regions had been drawn up, Oliver announced, on the grounds that the circumstances under which the original planning permission had been granted and regularly updated were now radically altered. Planning permission for Class A1 retail use had been given when the land was still part of the Wickenham estate and went with the hotel. Now it was being sold separately, which was an entirely different kettle of fish, since it transformed ancillary use into dominant use, which was a material change to the original permission.

It also, Georgia thought, had brought a material change to Oliver Todd. Seen in a new role, he had a gravitas alien to the homeloving butcher she was used to. What was required of the audience this evening was a willingness to show its support of the appeal, Oliver concluded, as he yielded the floor to Terence. Mr Scraggs would explain.

As Terence stood up and began to speak, Georgia watched another unexpected and even more powerful transformation. This wasn't the pale nervous co-lodger of Country Stop. Having an audience obviously brought out latent powers in him. Like Hitler, once before an audience, the hesitant man turned into the impassioned leader of men. Perhaps it was unfair to compare poor Terence to Hitler but, as she witnessed his control of the audience, there seemed to be something in it. He'd certainly done his homework, quoting specific cases on revocation of planning permissions. One High Court case in particular, brought by a district council against the Secretary of State, against the latter's decision to in effect scrap a planning permission that allowed the building of a supermarket, seemed very relevant to Wickenham. The council had lost, and the supermarket's enormous costs became a major issue. If she were Jacob Bloomfield, Georgia thought, she'd be listening very intently indeed to carry the message home to Father.

It became apparent that the solicitor who had drawn up the appeal was a contact of Terence's, confirming Georgia's suspicion that this wasn't the first time that he had taken up such a cause. He was moving on to the common law on immemorial custom, and their need now to establish a substantial period of usage of the fields for recreation. Once again he impressively cited chapter and verse.

By the time he sat down, most of the audience was on its feet, cheering, and punching the air in approval. Georgia almost joined them. Terence had inspired a sense that there was a legal path forward and that even if the Elgins were waiting outside to duff up the Todds, they couldn't stop this roller-coaster.

'Good, eh?' Jim commented.

She agreed, but was uneasily aware that this didn't bode well for peace in Wickenham, especially since Oliver then announced that all those who could swear that sports had been played unchallenged on those grounds for over twenty years should sign two copies of an attachment to the appeal. One was for the formal appeal, and one for a protest to be delivered to the Manor, which would be passed through the audience. The tension palpably increased while this long procedure took place. The noise level grew as some of the audience left and the rest united.

It took Jacob Bloomfield to blow the top of the volcano. As the last depositions were handed in to Oliver Todd, and the noise abated, his voice was suddenly heard from the back of the hall.

'You'll achieve nothing by giving a copy of your appeal to my father.'

Georgia turned quickly round, to see him standing right by the door and no sign of Brother Crispin. The roar that greeted him, caused either by the obvious sneer in his voice or by disagreement, silenced him only for a moment. As soon as it died down, he began to speak again. 'It should be presented to the new owners, when the contract is signed tomorrow.' The roar that greeted this final word was more than angry. It was ugly. It was a shock to Georgia – and perhaps to all the audience – that it was being rushed through so quickly.

'I don't like this,' Jim muttered. 'Bloomfield must have known what he'd be doing, the fool, so why's he doing it?'

Oliver banged the mallet for order, as Jacob continued. 'If you'll kindly let me speak, the new owners are offering an alternative site.' The hush that followed this announcement held a strange quality as though the volcano merely paused to gather its energy, and Georgia's stomach muscles tensed.

'Where would that be?' Oliver shouted stonily.

'Dickens Field.'

The volcano blew. No longer a concerted roar but shouts of abuse, the scraping of chairs, as the audience began to move.

'What's this about?' Georgia had to yell at Jim to make herself heard.

'Bloody insult, that's what. Dickens Field is a waste dump by the motorway on the edge of the parish several miles out. They know it's useless. It's to kill the appeal, that's all. If they offer an alternative site, what's a chap in

105

Whitehall going to know about Dickens Field? It sounds good, and that's all they care about.'

The whole audience was now moving towards the exits. 'This is where we get out, Georgia. Janet, come on love. Move quickly.' Jim grabbed her arm and then, keeping Janet between them, with Jim ahead they were swept along in the crush to the exit, squeezed through and at last they were out. Georgia breathed in the cold fresh air thankfully, as Jim pulled them to one side, apart from the mass of people swelling out into the narrow road leading to the Green.

'Keep to the side, and then make for home,' Jim ordered. Once at the Old Forge, they stopped to look behind them, but Georgia could see nothing.

'Where are the Elgins?' she asked. She'd assumed they would be gathering en masse by the Green, or in front of the pub, but there was nothing but the dark grass and the amber light from the street lamps.

'They'll be waiting somewhere, you can be sure of that.'

'And the police?'

'If the village bobby's wise he'll have sent for them. They'll likely be too late though.'

She watched as the Todds swept down by the side of the Green to the main road, their placards sprouting like magic. And somewhere, probably at the entrance to the Manor and the Bloomfields' house, the Elgins must be waiting.

Georgia turned down the offer of a nightcap, preferring to make her way home safely while the village was venting its wrath at this end. This clash was nothing to do with her, and yet she felt a sense of guilt at leaving. Involvement? If so, that was bad. She half walked, half ran along the top of the Green and down the far side to the main road, then along past the silent Red Dragon to Country Stop.

The house was dark and cheerless and she was half sorry she had turned down the offer of a nightcap. Tomorrow she would leave Wickenham, at least for a while. She tried to get the thoughts of what might be happening at the

Bloomfields' house out of her mind, but it was impossible. There was a noise from far away like the hum of a motorway. She had just reached her room when the sound of police sirens swept by, and she instantly went to the window. She could see nothing. The distant hum resumed, but as she climbed into bed fifteen minutes later the sound of the sirens blared out again. Once more she ran to the window to look out, only to see that the flashing lights of the police were followed by those of an ambulance.

Chapter Seven

Georgia slept badly. Distant noise advanced, retreated, fell silent, and then advanced again in a different guise. If she woke, all seemed quiet and she fell back asleep, only to find herself once more on the battlefield. She longed for the reassurance of another human body beside her. Not anyone's. Luke's. When she finally awoke, it was due not to light, but to a banging on her door. It took her a moment to realize where she was, and why this had to be an unusual summons.

'Who is it?' she shouted.

'Your father's here, Georgia.' She just about registered that it was Lucy calling out, and that she sounded agitated. The words didn't make sense, though. She shook the remainder of sleep from her eyes and head, the latter still spinning from the dreams of the night, and glanced at her watch: 7.30.

Peter? Here? What could be urgent enough to justify that? Rick? There was news of her brother, was her first thought, as she swung her legs out of bed. Luke? Her mother? No, please God, to any of these.

'I'll be with you,' she called, in a voice she hardly recognized as her own. She carried out the speediest toilet possible; though the shower woke her up, it didn't stop her mind racing round as she pulled on trousers and sweater, brushed her hair, hoicked out some shoes from under the bed and ran downstairs.

There was her father, his wheelchair wedged in between the three tables, his eyes fixed impatiently on the doorway for her arrival. The entrance to Country Stop was hardly

108

wheelchair friendly, so to see him here represented some considerable manoeuvring on somebody's part, more than Lucy could have managed. Lucy appeared from the kitchen door, still in her dressing gown, and looking drawn and pale. 'I'll get you both some tea.'

'Coffee today, please.' Georgia knew she needed it, and Peter seldom looked at tea. 'Now, what's happened?' She looked fearfully at her father.

'Not any of those,' he answered simply. It couldn't have been difficult to read her mind, she supposed.

'Poor Mr Scraggs is dead,' Lucy burst out. 'And him staying here. I couldn't sleep a wink after Olly told me. And the police are coming *here*.'

Georgia's head spun with shock and instant scenarios and questions. She needed breathing space to assimilate this shocking news and to talk to Peter. Somehow his arrival had to be connected with this event, though she couldn't see how Terence Scraggs' death would affect Peter.

'Lucy, you need coffee yourself,' she hinted, and to her relief Lucy obediently returned to the kitchen.

'How,' she asked her father, 'did he die, and what are you doing here? Did he –' she remembered her sickening dreams – 'die here?' She remembered her conversation at dinner with him, and the different personality he'd shown last night at the meeting. She hadn't taken to Terence Scraggs, but even her brief acquaintance made her mourn him and the devastating uncertainties of life.

'No, Georgia. He was stabbed in a fight last night, I gather. Mike Gilroy telephoned me this morning when the SIO requested his presence via Darenth Area HQ. He's here too, but he's gone to the incident van at the scene of crime.'

Georgia couldn't make sense of this. Why on earth should the senior investigating officer send for Mike, who was in a different police area?

'Mike remembered you were here, and he immediately rang me, so of course I came too,' Peter continued. 'I had to get myself up,' he announced offhandedly.

'You were worried about me? Trust me, I always avoid a fight.' Mechanical banter while her brain grappled with Terence Scraggs.

'I did. But if Mike was going to be here I didn't want to miss out.'

'On what?' She began to see where he might be heading now, and she resisted it more in the hope of convincing herself than to deter Peter.

'Don't you think it's odd there's another murder in Wickenham?'

'No, not if this fight was connected to the Elgin–Todd feud that had just erupted when I came home last night. Terence Scraggs was here because he was probably a semi-professional protestor, and because he was a freelance artist, not because of the Ada Proctor murder.' Even if he had questioned her about the case, his interest had only been a polite one, hadn't it? 'So why was Mike involved?' she continued firmly.

'The SIO was short-handed, and remembered he'd been showing an undue interest in Wickenham. So he was called in.'

'I bet Mike was thrilled to bits to be asked,' Georgia rejoined, and Peter looked guilty. He was saved by the – now welcome – reappearance of Lucy bringing coffee, orange juice and toast.

'Were you there, Lucy, when Terence died?' Georgia asked sympathetically, her mind still racing over connections between a murder during a fight and Marsh & Daughter's sphere of interest.

'No. Yes. I mean, at first I was.'

'Last night was the protest meeting I told you about,' Georgia explained to Peter. 'After it, I came home, but much of the audience joined a march to the Bloomfields' house. Is that when the fight happened, Lucy?'

'Mr Mighty Trevor Bloomfield didn't even bother to come to the meeting, ' Lucy sniffed. 'He just sent his two posh sons, who did a quick disappearing act once they'd

110

said their dirty piece. So we *had* to march to the house, perfectly peacefully, and look what happened.'

'The Elgins appeared,' Georgia answered. It hardly took a PhD to work that out. 'Perfectly peacefully' was unlikely to have been a correct description either. She had seen plenty of booze flowing at the meeting.

'I don't know where the Elgins had been waiting.' The words began to spill out of Lucy now. 'Probably in the pubs. They were drunk, broken bottles, everything, and we hadn't had a drop. We went into the drive, and we no sooner got there than Mr Blooming Bloomfield threw open the front door and him and his two precious sons came storming out to meet us, demanding to know what the hell we were playing at disturbing the peace. Terence told them good and proper how they were breaking the law doing away with ancient rights . . .'

Lucy began to choke, but continued: 'They wouldn't stop to listen. I was with Olly and Mr Scraggs at the front, the Bloomfields charged up to talk to us, and then the Elgins suddenly appeared in front of us. Hundreds of them, pouring through the far entrance, coming straight for us. You get home, Luce, Olly said. This is no place for women, and he pushed me back and me and the other women got out of it. What with us peace-marchers pushing forward and the Elgins charging us we were lucky to get out of it. We heard the police sirens coming and we hung around for a while on the Green, until most of the men joined us. Not Olly, though. The police wanted to talk to him, being one of the organizers. So I went home, and Olly didn't come for another hour. I couldn't sleep a wink till he was back safe. But when I heard what had happened! Oh, it was awful, Olly said. It took ages to break up the fight even with the police and Olly doing all they could to stop it and when there were only Olly and a couple of others and that George Elgin White and his cronies they found poor Mr Scraggs half hidden by the bushes. It was dark and no one noticed till the crowd went. All Olly said was the knife was still in him. Oh poor Olly. And poor Mr Scraggs. All he wanted to do was fight for right and justice for the village and look what happens. He's murdered for it. Those Elgins have got a lot to answer for.'

Peter leapt on this. 'Do the police think they know who killed him then?'

'Olly didn't know. He had to leave, didn't he? But it stands to reason it was one of them Elgins. Can't see the Bloomfields bloodying their hands, though they're the cause of all this. Oh *poor* Mr Scraggs. He died for us.'

Peter shot a glance at Georgia, who interpreted it correctly. 'Lucy, you need rest. Why don't you have a lie down?'

'I can't. Olly's had to go to the shop, and the police said they'd be coming to look at his room. They told Olly to lock it, so I'll have to be here.'

Georgia grimaced at Peter. Too much to hope for! 'Look, we'll rouse you if they come within the next hour or so. Then we'll be going out –' She made it deliberately vague – 'so we'll rouse you then.'

'But your breakfast,' Lucy wailed. 'Won't you want your full English, Georgia? And Mr Marsh?'

'Thank you, no,' Peter said in lordly manner. 'The use of your loo would oblige however.' Between the two of them, this was accomplished fairly easily, since the Country Stop toilet was a reasonable-sized room on the ground floor, and once they were on their own Georgia replenished the coffee and produced some cereal.

'Now,' Peter said, 'that sanity reigns, kindly tell me more about this Terence Scraggs. *Everything.*'

Georgia obeyed. 'It seems to have been a stab in a general fight,' she reminded him, as she finished, 'so I still don't see why Mike was summoned here.'

'Even in drunken brawls, one would be fairly careful whom you fought and Scraggs was an outsider. Odd, isn't it?'

'Yes, but he was an outsider who was the power behind the appeal.'

'An appeal over a contract that you say is being signed today. A trifle belated.'

'No one knew till the meeting that the contract was to be signed so quickly. And it wouldn't invalidate their claim anyway, it would merely change the point of attack from the Bloomfields to the new owners.'

'Ah, yes, the Bloomfields. That, I deduce, is why the SIO thought Mike would be interested in joining the Darenth team, though it's fair to say it could simply be revenge for his hassling them on our behalf over the Wickenham denehole. This particular SIO has, so Mike informs me, a warped sense of humour.'

'Unlike Mike, who has none at all,' Georgia observed.

'Chief Inspector Lockhart,' Peter continued oblivious, 'pointed out that the crimes both happened on Bloomfield land.'

'What crimes?' Georgia asked blankly.

'Last night's and the denehole man. The coroner has decided to hold an inquest on him, since it's possible he died a violent death in the absence of evidence either way. Lockhart picked up that the denehole is on the Bloomfield estate.'

Was it indeed? Remiss of her not to have followed through on that after the possibility occurred to her. And then she thought further. 'Does the SIO know that the denehole is close to the public footpath right through the estate? Or,' she added sweetly, 'that these crimes – if indeed the first one was – would be over seventy years apart?'

'You told me Ada Proctor was found on the same footpath, heading towards the woods.'

'True, and it's also true the coroner's report suggested she was moved from a point nearer to the wood.'

Peter gloated in silence. Only for a moment, however. 'Don't you think it odd that this fellow announced he was an artist—'

'He had a portfolio. I saw him carrying it once,' she

interrupted. Be blowed if she would let Peter's theories get ahead of evidence *again*.

'But he obviously wanted to fight on the Todd front, thus stirring up the feud. Why have two reasons for coming to Wickenham?'

'People don't have to conform to reason.'

'Not even you, Georgia.'

She ceded victory.

'Wickenham – ah, I remember it well.' Peter looked round complacently as Georgia pushed him along The Street towards the Green. He was self-mobile in his chair, but relished the occasional lordliness of her pushing him, so she stifled her complaints. He had chosen this method of going to the scene of crime rather than by car in order to 'sniff'. One can't sniff through car windows, he pointed out. He had already sniffed once this morning. As they emerged from Country Stop he had spotted Terence's car parked there, a Citroën Deux Chevaux.

'That his?' he asked, and, when she nodded, added, 'Thought so. Wanted to be different, to make a point. That would figure. Anorak man aiming at power.'

His second sniff was at Georgia's suggestion, as she stopped outside what had once been Mary Beaumont's tearoom.

He was silent for a moment, as he regarded the house. 'Nothing here, is there?' He didn't seem perturbed. 'But of course *she*'s no longer here.'

'Do you want to meet her?'

'Naturally. This afternoon?'

'What about Margaret?' Peter had a habit of going off and giving Margaret the fright of her life when she arrived to silence in the house.

'I left her a note. Don't fuss. I'll be back tomorrow.'

'Lucy only has two rooms so—'

He twisted round indignantly in his chair. 'My dear girl, if you think I'm going to stay with that maniac of a woman, you are vastly mistaken. I'll book into the Manor of course.'

'Of course.'

'I take it it's well thought of as a hotel?'

'Jim Hardbent says so.'

'You seem to place reliance on his word. I see no such need. Remember there is power in being the only historian in a village, and all power corrupts. Is he a Todd or an Elgin?'

'Neither. He's for Wickenham.'

'I'll reserve judgement until I meet him.'

Wickenham today, Georgia realized, would have no time for fingerprints from the past. The suppressed excitement and tension over the present were almost tangible, as even on this chilly autumn day groups outside pubs and shops buzzed with discussion. Georgia recognized Todd groups and now the lesser-known Elgins. She had wondered whether the murder would unite them, but from the look of things there was little chance of that. The Todds would be all too anxious to distance themselves from the more obvious culprits, the drunken Elgins, and they would be all for blaming the Todds or maybe even the Bloomfields.

Autumn leaves were scampering over the grass, still damp from overnight rain. The crime scene examiners must have had their work cut out recording and logging the scene of crime before rain overtook it, she thought, perhaps obliterating some forensic evidence for good. Mud could be a good companion before a crime but a hindrance after it, and not the whole crime scene could be protected from rain, especially when there were questions of access concerned, as here. Doubtless the Bloomfields were making the most of that.

As they drew near the Bloomfields' home she could see the incident van established a little way up the main road that ran past the house. With Elgins and Todds present in large numbers last night, the scene of crime to be taped could be enormous, but she could see that as they reached the house that reason had had to prevail and only the immediate pavement outside and the forecourt to the house were taped off.

'Typical,' Peter grunted as they reached the van. 'No access for us poor sods in wheelchairs.'

As he rapped with his stick on the van door, Mike came grumpily to meet him.

'No need for that. We've got a ramp. I'll come down though. Morning, Georgia.'

Mike's lugubriousness hid his quick mind and eye. He might not possess humour, but Georgia felt if she were a villain and saw his lanky figure descending upon her, she'd give herself up on the spot. At one time she and Peter had used a private nickname for him, 'Squash', which had nothing to do with his physical appearance but sprang from Peter's observation that you could bounce balls off Mike with impunity, but if you ran up against him yourself, you'd land up floored. Then Mike had overheard this one day, instantly diagnosed its rationale – and they never used it again.

'So what's the story, Mike?' Peter asked as he came down the steps.

'Presumed story. Death by sharp instrument in the chest either deliberate or accidental. More like the former, since the sharp instrument was a kitchen knife left in the wound. No pulling it out in panic and covering yourself in blood for this villain. It's with the lab now.'

'Suspects?'

'Very funny. A couple of hundred or so at a guess. That –' he cast a mournful look at Peter – 'is why I'm here. They need legwork to get round these blasted Elgins and Todds.'

'And the Bloomfields?' Georgia asked.

'Them too. The SIO's taking them on.'

'Other forensic evidence?'

'Nicely packaged up and on its way to the lab. A few circular splashes of blood lifted from the brick paving and several others spattered around, which could be Scraggs's, could be others', and plenty of broken glass around. There are signs the body was pushed further into the bushes where it was darker and no one could fall over it too soon. One damaged placard found in the bushes, obviously used as a weapon at some point to bash someone good and proper.'

'When can I see the scene video?' Peter demanded. 'You must have it in there.' He glanced enviously at the van. Not 'can I' but 'when' with Peter, Georgia knew all too well.

'You don't. Not unless you have a valid reason.'

'I'll find one,' Peter assured him confidently.

'Don't you mean you'll give me evidence of one?' Mike suggested.

'Easy with Georgia's help. She knew him.'

'You'll have your work cut out with Lockhart as SIO. Wait till I can bring you in as some kind of expert witness. See?'

'Yes, Mike,' Peter said meekly. 'By the way, I presume Darenth Area will be paying for DNA samples?'

Mike eyed him suspiciously. '*One* sample at the moment, Peter. Of Terence Scraggs. Not the several hundred possible suspects yet. *Or*,' he added scathingly, 'getting excited about the man in the denehole. The lab got a profile for him and there it stays.'

Georgia groaned to herself. Mike had given Peter the perfect opening. 'What's happened to him, by the way? All seems to have gone quiet. You said you'd let me know when the inquest report came in.' Peter sounded aggrieved.

'It hasn't. You'll be pleased to know it's been adjourned, thanks to you getting me to badger Darenth with questions about that skeleton. It's pending enquiries. Satisfied?'

'Yes.' Peter glowed.

'And, before you ask,' Mike added dourly, 'no doubt you'll be asking to see the artefacts collected with Denehole Man. They're back with Darenth.'

'That's very good of you, Mike. If you'll just arrange it . . .'

*   *   *

Peter transferred from his Alfa Romeo to wheelchair outside the Manor, leaving Georgia to drive it to the official car park.

'Proper ramp, I see. Nice wide door,' he remarked of the hotel before them, when she returned.

'That's as well. You'd complain about Traitor's Gate not being wide enough.'

'Nonsense. I'm eminently reasonable in such matters.' Unfortunately the nice wide door was closed, and the stick was raised to be brought into play again just as a uniformed doorman swept it open.

The park had looked magnificent, and in the October sunlight Wickenham Manor itself looked a brighter place than Georgia remembered from her earlier visit. Part of the park had been turned into a golf course, but there were also formal gardens, woodland and lawns. She wondered whether the contract had gone through yet, and whether the murder would have any effect on that. Even more important: was the sports fields' sale still going through today? Certainly if the appeal went ahead, that must affect the supermarket deal; she hoped it would scupper it completely, if only for Terence Scraggs's sake.

The calm of the Manor seemed a world away from what was happening in the village today. It appeared unassailable, and she supposed that was and always had been its strength. Whatever happened in the village, the Manor went on for ever. Or perhaps that was a mere illusion. The fingerprints on Time might be covered by silken gloves here, but that wouldn't eradicate them.

Ada would have known this place so well. Quite apart from delivering medicines here, either by pony cart or by footpath to cut off the corner, she must have attended countless social occasions too. The doctor, the schoolmaster, the vicar, all had status in a village, and Ada must have known the Bloomfields, just as she knew the Randolphs. Matthew, who became Squire the year she died, would have been, she calculated, four years younger than her. There would, to Georgia's knowledge alone, have been quite a youthful circle here in the years before the First World War, with Matthew and Jack, their sister Anne, who was Ada's age, and Guy and Gwendolen Randolph. By the 1920s, only Matthew and the women were left; what had happened to Anne and Gwendolen? she wondered.

When Peter emerged from his room, on the whole approvingly, they made their way to the bar for a drink and bar snack. Since the hotel had a conference centre, the bar was crowded and – not altogether to her surprise – she saw Trevor and Julia Bloomfield. The contract was presumably being signed here, and they would undoubtedly wish to escape the presence of the police van at their home as much as possible. They looked strained, whether through lack of sleep, or because the business meeting had not yet taken place. Nevertheless Georgia seized the opportunity to push their company upon them. She had as little liking for the couple as they seemed to have for her, and saw no reason to be tactful. Introducing Peter, she promptly took advantage of their lacklustre invitation to join them. There wasn't any choice, in fact, since the bar was so crowded.

Georgia made all the right noises: she was so very sorry to hear about the tragedy last evening, how upset they must be, particularly with such an important day today, and how violent today's society was. Peter remained silent, only because, she knew full well, he was busy summing them up. Outwardly he was doing his impression of an old man only interested in digging up the past.

'It makes your 1929 murder seem positively attractive,' Julia remarked bitterly. 'One on one's own doorstep doesn't carry the same interest.' She must have seen Georgia blink for she scowled and then added, 'Of course we're deeply involved because we live so close to it. A 1929 murder doesn't seem so *real*.'

It did to Georgia, and it surely did to anyone with imagination. It only required concentration. Take away Nefertiti's Egyptian headdress – and there you had a fashion-conscious

119

teenager of today. Take away Ada's cloche hat and there stood today's smart professional. Take away Sir Philip Sydney's ruff and doublet, give him a sweater, jeans and anorak and there might stand Terence Scraggs.

Nevertheless Georgia did her best to murmur something that could be taken for sympathy.

'It was all quite ridiculous and scaring,' Trevor took over angrily and with a speed that made Georgia suspect he was eager to put their side of the story. His grievance must be real from his viewpoint, she supposed, trying to be charitable. 'My sons came back from the meeting to warn us that a march was on its way with this ridiculous appeal, so I went out with them to collect it, thank them and ask them to disperse. But as soon as we were outside, all hell descended as that other scrum pitched in and we were caught in the middle. Fortunately Julia saw what was happening and rang the police – though it turned out they were already on their way. Our village policeman had summoned them too. They took their time, I must say, and look what happened.'

'Typical of today,' Peter said earnestly. 'Did you see this Terence Scraggs in the scrimmage?' he continued with bland innocence.

'It was chiefly Oliver Todd I went out to see. Scraggs isn't local. He came to see me some ten days ago, wanting to paint my house. I'd have told him where to put his blessed paints if I'd known he was behind this appeal.'

'Did he get the commission?' Georgia asked.

'I told him there was no point, we were selling up. As a goodwill gesture though I said he could paint Wickenham Manor and I'd pay for that. The stuff he showed me looked quite good. Look what he did to me. Talk about a stab in the back.'

There was an awkward silence as he realized the inappropriateness of the comment, and Georgia turned quickly to Julia, nauseated by this farce, and the need for it. Here they were, sitting in an upmarket hotel, with drinks in their hands, discussing a murder that had taken place only last night a few hundred yards away. How useful it would be if forensic science could strip away the layers of speech to reveal the thoughts underneath. Instead, they were doomed to seek truth the hard way, sifting the dross of everyday words in the hope of infinitesimal nuggets. 'A terrible shock for you when the body was found,' Georgia said earnestly, though she doubted whether anything other than a blow to her purse could shock Julia from her detachment.

Julia obviously thought it was time for a shudder. 'I was watching from the window when the policeman found him, and everyone started shouting and rushing around. I didn't know what was happening, till Trevor came to tell me. After that it went on for hours, police and doctors and ambulances, men and women in white suits, and lights being put up. And those ghastly powerful torches they have. Quite dreadful.'

'For Scraggs too,' Peter remarked, shaking his head sadly.

Trevor looked at him sharply, but didn't comment.

'And then the police must have wanted to talk to you,' Georgia persevered.

'Endlessly,' Julia replied. 'We didn't get to bed until four, and then it started again at seven.'

Peter took up the conversation seamlessly – one of the benefits of their working together. 'Dreadful to have the police sniffing around just when you don't need it.'

'Sniffing?' Trevor stiffened.

'They must see you as a suspect after Scraggs's campaign against you.'

Georgia waited with interest for his reply to this, but Trevor actually laughed. 'What on earth would I want to kill him for?'

'It could be argued you did it to ease the sale of the land for the supermarket.'

He shrugged, still apparently amused. 'You've been reading too many Agatha Christies. Stick to Ada Proctor, that's more your forte. I live in today's world. What good would it do me to kill Scraggs? The appeal won't stop just because Scraggs is dead, even if the sale for the two sports fields did go through. In fact, it won't. I know that already. We're meeting this afternoon, but it's a lost cause. They had an alternative bid they were urgently considering, and they were already concerned at talk of this appeal. They need to build quickly and the last thing they want is to begin pouring money into something with a possible sword of Damocles hanging over it. The alternative site was a last-minute hope. With that given the thumbs down, we knew it was all over well before Scraggs died. The cash from the sale of two piffling fields would be jolly nice, but it won't make or break us fortunately and the main deal won't be affected. So there'd hardly be any point in any of the Bloomfields sticking a knife in the chap. It would simply make one more reason for the sale not to go through.'

'Someone killed him,' Georgia pointed out quietly. 'Don't you care who?'

Trevor shrugged. 'In a fight like that, who can say? One of the Elgins, probably. Get a few beers inside them and they don't know who or what they're attacking.'

His lack of concern sickened her. Just one more knifing in a fight didn't count apparently. Involuntarily she turned her head away – and instantly froze.

It was Zac. She was sure of it. He'd just passed through the swing doors from reception leading to the residential part of the hotel. She'd only had a sideways view, but she knew that profile, and that curly black hair, that careless disregard of his surroundings, animate or inanimate. Oh *damn*! How could fate spin round and hit her in the face again? Why now? Why here?

Some people have a greater hold over you in absence than they do when they are with you. Georgia could never quite decide whether Zac was one of them or not. In absence he acquired a sinister attraction that chilled her, but in his presence, despite his exasperating charm, she found herself wondering what all the fuss was about – and that was his most chilling weapon of all, damn him.

She had first met him when she was a twenty-year-old student and overwhelmed by his casual seven-year seniority and sophistication. Wine was his stock-in-trade as a conman then – though Zac would have been horrified even now to think of himself as such; he buzzed in all the wine connoisseur groups in London and even more fruitfully around the rest of the British Isles. If there were a celeb party, Zac would be there – or pretend he had been. Not, she discovered later, under his own name of course. His was the usual scam. He travelled the world and dealt, he claimed, with only the best vineyards, and those directly in order to obtain the grandest of the *grand cru* at a fraction of the price it would be through the usual channels. He shared a bottle with the chosen victims to confirm his judgement, which they inevitably did, and then departed with their money. The wine never materialized and nor did Zac reappear.

When she had married him immediately after her graduation he was already – again discovered later – the proud victor in a Ponzi-type sting for investment in a struggling co-operative vineyard concern in Italy, paying dividends to the first round of investors out of the investments of the next round. The crazy thing was that Zac never bothered to do his homework properly, and he knew very little about wine. He eventually fell foul of a rich and canny lady, who smelt a rat when, presenting her with a bottle of sweet Monbazillac dessert wine, he casually assured her it would go admirably with oysters, and the lady proceeded to make some enquiries of the vineyard before placing her order. Since Zac had been incompetent enough to operate occasionally in his own back yard, Kent, the case had landed by coincidence on Peter's desk, and as Peter had been privately pursuing a few enquiries of his own about his son-in-law, it had led to Zac receiving a five-year sentence of which he served just over half.

When they were first married, Georgia, in love with Zac,

with life and with the romance of country living, had found work in a bookshop. Zac laughed at her for such steady ways, compared with his own easy-come easy-go approach to money. True, his way was fun, and up to a point she enjoyed the excitement, but it was only after her father had broken the devastating news to her about her husband's 'profession' – she'd thought him a genuine wine dealer – that she discovered the bills he had left strewn in his wake.

Georgia never forgot the way Zac looked at her after the sentence had been announced. It was simply his familiar bewildered expression of 'how can they do this to me?' Was there a real Zac behind it? If so, she had realized at that moment that she had never known him – and this still terrified her. Behind the public mask of anyone and everyone, what might there lie?

Even Luke's.

'Are you sure it was Zac, Georgia?' Peter gloomily regarded the cajun chicken and rice, courtesy of the Green Man, instead of the more gourmet-conscious food of Wickenham Manor. No way was she staying around there.

'Of course, I am,' she said wearily. 'What on earth's he doing here?'

'Knowing Zac,' his ex-father-in-law observed mildly, 'I would assume he was conning someone.'

'It's not going to be me.'

'You can't play hide and seek in a village this size. Face him.'

'I can't. Maybe he's only passing through.' She didn't believe it. Once in a good hotel, Zac would settle in and wait for custom. If he saw either of them, he would assume his bill was as good as paid for him.

'I'll find out. You stay at the Todds this evening and I'll zap Zac.'

That made her giggle – for a moment. 'What did you make of the Bloomfields?'

'I bet he drives a new S-type Jag,' Peter threw back

instantly, 'and she's used to sitting in it. I wouldn't like to be the one that suggested she downsize to a Mini.'

'My feeling too,' Georgia agreed. 'The lady's not for swerving. Nor's he either.'

'Now before *I* go to see Mary Elgin,' Peter announced, 'I've had an okay from Mike on my mobile in my room for you to look round Scraggs's room provided Mike's present. The police have done all they need.'

'Which was?'

'Mike will tell you. Precious little. They've found the parents' address – they're coming to identify the body at the mortuary, and the personal possessions will be sent on to them. They don't want to come to Wickenham themselves. Too traumatic. So go quickly – and don't tell the world. Mike will meet you there.'

'You're glad about this, aren't you? You want to see Mary alone.'

'I must admit that is the case.'

Peter versus Mary. Formidable force meets formidable force. Which of them would win, or would it be a draw?

She went straight back to Country Stop, where, with Mike at her side, she entered Terence Scraggs's room. It was creepily like her own, the same floral pattern on duvet cover and curtains, merely in a different colour. Hers was the pink room, Terence's had been yellow. Yellow for sunshine, but there was little joy left here. If he had ever poured any of his personality into this room during his stay it had vanished now. She concentrated hard on summoning up Terence in her mind – if only to banish Zac's sick-making image. Lucy hadn't yet packed his belongings, so his toothbrush, soap and razor were still on the washbasin, a testament to how carefully he tended that wispy beard. His sparse belongings still hung in the wardrobe, or lay in one of the drawers. His spare shoes poked from under the bed. Soulless or not, it seemed like prying and she let Mike take the running in going through his few papers.

Mike had come to the force via the profession of

window-cleaning, which he'd taken up as soon as he could get shot of school. He'd told Peter that this was what turned him into a policeman. He'd learnt so much about the way human beings lived, and their quirks and idiosyncrasies, through window-cleaning that he thought he'd put it to good use. To look at him quickly, one would see nothing other than a Policeman Plod; a second look at his watchful eyes would explain exactly why he was now a DI and climbing. He had a knack for absorbing every detail and was going through Scraggs's scribbling pads, his draft speech about the protest, and a note from his parents about a forthcoming family weekend with equal zeal.

Georgia noted down the parents' address, although this wasn't her main reason for coming here. While Mike was still occupied elsewhere, she picked up Terence's portfolio, which was propped up by the wardrobe together with his paints, crayons, pencils and a portable easel. Donning the gloves Mike handed to her, she hauled the portfolio on to the bed and looked through it. Halfway through she found an unfinished watercolour of Country Stop, and a rough pencil sketch of Wickenham Manor. Presumably the latter had been a botched attempt and the finished painting had been handed over, which bore out Trevor's story. One or two other sketches showed Terence had had a boldness of approach that she would not have expected, although his sterling performance at the meeting should have suggested it. There was nothing on Jim's Forge, so that too must have been handed over.

Then came two sketches that were not of houses, but of what she identified after some thought as the Wickenham Manor estate, perhaps because Terence had considered a double hit by offering landscape paintings of the park as well as the house. The next one was a finished watercolour of a Victorian house in its own grounds which seemed familiar though she could not quite place it. Why had this one remained? Did the prospective purchaser not like it?

Was it perhaps not even in Wickenham? It wasn't so good as the other work. It had a static quality without the life suggested by the others.

And then she realized why it seemed familiar. 'Mike, look at this. It must have been done from a postcard, one of Jim's probably. It's Hazelwood House.'

'Where's that?'

'We're probably standing on it. It was pulled down in the 1960s.'

'So?'

'Why did Scraggs go to this trouble when there'd be no buyer for it? Don't you think he must have had more interest in Wickenham than just protests?'

'What sort of interest?' Mike was not to be moved.

'Hazelwood House is where the Randolphs lived. Peter's got a bee in his bonnet that the man in the denehole was one of them.'

Chapter Eight

'Rested?' Peter looked at her keenly as she arrived at the Manor next morning. Georgia was hardly surprised he asked. She must have looked a fright. She had slept badly again, probably because she spent much of the night walking in through the front door of Hazelwood House, just as it had appeared in Terence Scragg's drawing. She had felt like Gretel, entering the unknown to meet the wicked witch, and yet once inside there had seemed nothing to fear. There had been merely a jolly family Edwardian Christmas, à la Hollywood, in progress, with a large Christmas tree and benevolent father handing out gifts. There had even been one for her, a painting of Wickenham Manor, for which she was ecstatically grateful – in her dream. However, when she left the Hazelwood House, much relieved, it always called her back again, but the next time she entered there was no sign of benevolent father or presents. Instead Zac leapt out at her from behind a door. 'Didn't you expect me?' he would say with his hurt look. 'I'm always here.' Then he'd smirk . . .

'I can see you're not,' Peter continued. 'We'll go home tonight. Staying at Country Stop is a bad idea for you. You need to keep away from this current mess or you'll lose track of the past.'

'Suppose they're related,' she said reluctantly. The nightmare about Hazelwood House still loomed in her mind, and she tried in vain to convince herself she was making too much of one simple painting in Scraggs's portfolio. She told Peter what she had found in Terence's room, surprised he hadn't badgered her immediately for this information. 'Interesting, don't you think?' she managed to conclude, hoping against hope that he'd pooh-pooh her fear. If there were more to it than coincidence, that brought Terence Scraggs's murder closer to her.

'Very. As you say, why bother to paint from a postcard a house long gone?'

'Is that a rhetorical question, or do you want an answer?'

'Answer please,' Peter requested.

'He had some interest in the house, either architectural, or more probably because it had some significance for him.'

'Hmm.' Peter mused on this. 'Remember the car he drove?'

'You can't make a thesis out of that. Suppose he borrowed it. Suppose it belonged to his mum.'

'Get real. It's not a mum's car.'

'You don't know his mum.' Georgia was irritated. Peter was always doing this, playing with his own pet theories, and then goading her to the point where she'd have to cry: 'Where's your evidence?'

This time Peter didn't carry the clash any further, which was again unusual. Instead, he helped himself to some more coffee, and remarked, 'Georgia, would you be interested to know I had a pleasant drink in the bar last night with a marketing rep for a shampoo and hair products distributor?' She looked at him warily, but he was serious. 'He had black curly hair, and a sharp profile,' Peter continued, 'as did your former husband, but—'

'It wasn't.' Georgia slumped back in her chair in relief, as her tension slipped away.

'At a second look this gentleman was nothing like Zac. It worried me, Georgia. I thought he was safely behind you, whether he turned up occasionally or not, but what this episode suggests is that he's still lurking inside you.'

'I don't love him any more,' she replied immediately. It sounded inadequate even to her. Love was no longer the point. There were other forces even less controllable than love, including a sexual one that both attracted and repelled.

'That wasn't what I meant, and you know it. Think about it.'

She would. She had to, she was aware of that. Peter too was involved in this sphere of her life, as by one of those ghastly coincidences of which life is capable he had been the one who finally put Zac behind bars to receive his come-uppance. But this was not the time or place to put this under the microscope yet again. Instead: 'How did you get on with Mary Elgin?'

'Interesting. I had to see her downstairs of course in the communal room, which was buzzing with the news of the murder and the fight. It's not often they get so animated, so one of the staff told me, but Mary ignored all chat of her tribe's involvement with the murder. Nor was she in the least concerned about the sale of the sports fields, but she did want to know, very much, about our progress over Davy Todd.'

'Did you show her printouts of the trial reports?' Georgia was not surprised at Mary's one-track mind. Davy was the driving force keeping her alive.

'No. Too heavy going. Instead I reminded her of the evidence. And she listened very carefully, making some pertinent comments. She didn't get upset either, which is a good sign. It suggests it's been in her mind all along. She remembers the grilling on the stand she received from the crown prosecutor. It can't have been easy with her father having sworn blind he'd never seen Davy that night. Assuming we're believing Mary's story, I wonder whether her father thought about the consequences of what he was doing in virtually condemning the boy to death, or whether he had convinced himself that somehow Davy was guilty.'

'I don't see how he could have done, do you? If Mary's right, he was with them from about ten until eleven thirty or so. Even if Ada's time of death was somewhat later than the post-mortem stated, surely no one could rush straight out after a thrashing like that to make a sexual assault on their employer's daughter. Nor would there have been much time since those witnesses said they saw him in the street about a quarter to twelve.'

'She remembered everything, Georgia.' Peter had clearly been impressed. 'She described the entire courtroom to me, and Davy "dawthering and doddering", as she called it, when he gave his evidence, knowing no one believed him. Poor Davy, she said, with his pocketful of dead hopes.'

Kentish dialect was more graphic then than now. Georgia had a sudden thought. 'Had Davy and Ada ever been out at night before looking for birds and animals?'

'Yes. Once at least. But again he'd been advised not to talk about that in case the Crown claimed he'd got a taste for it.'

'But that's surely a point in his favour too. If he had made any sign of a pass at Ada she would never have arranged to meet him again.'

'Unless she enjoyed it, and next time he went further,' Peter pointed out, which silenced her. 'And if he'd laid on a hand on her before, and she *didn't* like it, she wouldn't just have avoided his company, she'd have had him sacked.'

'So the jury's still out on that. Damn,' Georgia said crossly.

'And remember the maid testified that Ada was excited about going out later, so a solitary walk on the spur of the moment seems ruled out. So,' Peter suggested craftily, 'how about considering Guy Randolph now? You seem to be coming round to my way of thinking.'

'Certainly not. Not without more proof at least,' she shot back at him. 'One painting from a postcard does not add up to a skeleton in the denehole – even,' she added guiltily, 'if Terence did ask me about it.'

'Aha. Now you tell me!' Peter roared. 'So our Terence knew about that before he came to Wickenham.'

'Not necessarily.'

'Nonsense. You've been holding back on me. That could

have been the reason he came here in the first place. The sale of the sports fields was a cover.'

'If you care to add two and two and make fifteen and a half, certainly,' Georgia whipped back.

'You must agree Terence Scraggs needs more investigation.'

'And the police will be doing it.'

'Perhaps, Georgia dear, you could offer to take his belongings back to his parents. They might even be glad of a visit. You talked to him here and there'll be no funeral yet for them to concentrate on.' Their eyes met. No funeral. Many religions believed the spirits of the unburied wandered between heaven and earth. Like Rick's. The pit of the unknown heaved inside her, but she managed to suppress it, and for Peter's sake to make her voice sound normal.

'I'll try.'

'And I'll get stuck into the Internet, to see if I can find out more about our friend Terence. Not that –' he suddenly raised his voice – 'our magnificent police force aren't pulling out all the stops to solve this crime.' Georgia turned round to see Mike Gilroy marching across the lounge area to join them.

'No need to shout,' he remarked stolidly. 'I can hear you loud and clear. And we *are* pulling out stops. That,' he said, pulling up a chair, 'is why I'm here. I'm halfway through interviewing the Elgin family.'

'Good of you to keep us informed, Mike. I appreciate that,' Peter said genially.

'I'm not here for PR. I'm here to say there's feeling about, especially amongst the Elgins.'

'No doubt. About the murder or the sports fields?'

'Both and neither. To be blunt –' he looked apologetic – 'against you two, especially you, Georgia, since you've had the highest profile here.'

'In what way?' Georgia put her cappuccino carefully down on the table.

'The way you seem to be heading for position of chief

scapegoat for arousing trouble between Elgins and Todds.'

'But that's ridiculous,' she exploded. 'The sports fields are the problem. Surely you've got it wrong, Mike? I clashed with George White, but I've hardly met any of the others.'

'The Elgins know that they're in the hot seat over the murder, Georgia. Their line is that your bringing up the Ada Proctor case sparked off the old trouble again. Whether it's the Todds or Elgins responsible, there's been vandalism in the churchyard. Ada Proctor's grave has been daubed with red paint.'

Georgia went cold. This trouble went much deeper than she thought. Desecration of a grave in a village like Wickenham was as bad as it could get – short of murder. 'What did it read?' she asked levelly. 'Or was it just splodges of paint?' Please, the latter. *Please.*

'It read: Get out, bitch,' Mike replied. 'And that's you, Georgia, not Ada. See what I mean by linking the two of you?'

She was appalled. 'They can't say I killed Terence. I wasn't there.'

'They're not wanting to pin the murder on you, just shifting blame for the uproar. Get you silenced, so the thinking is going, and Wickenham might start pulling together. I may be wrong,' Mike added hastily, 'but that's how they're talking to me, a copper, so there must be a lot more going on that I don't know about.'

'Who is the ringleader?' asked Peter grimly.

'George Elgin White. Behaves like the village chieftain, and a nasty piece of work if you ask me. You said you'd met him, Georgia?'

'You could say that. He ordered me out of his house.' Next time, Georgia vowed to herself, she'd research the village more deeply before even thinking about the crime.

'The other side of the family, descended from Mary's sister Emmie, aren't so bad. Those are the Parsons. There's a lot of grandchildren around though from both families making a nuisance of themselves. The older ones don't tend to go sticking knives into people, but the kids – there were a lot of them there Thursday night – could easily have done. The young 'uns are dividing into their clans now, and it's coming to the fore. There's Patrick Todd, he's descended from Davy's older brother, Alfred. He's a real tearaway, and George's grandson Max is a chip off the old block on the Elgin side.'

'You've been doing your homework, Mike.' Peter didn't often offer compliments, and Georgia too was impressed at how quickly Mike had enveloped himself in Wickenham matters. 'What about the fight itself? Anyone admit to seeing what Scraggs was doing?' Peter continued.

'Yes, a few of them are anxious to help, chiefly the oldies. The consensus seems to be that Olly Todd and wife, and his sons Nigel and Mark, were in front when Trevor Bloomfield and his sons came out, and Terence was on the far left of the line. They all seem to have closed around the Bloomfields, until someone shouted, "Here come the Elgins", or something less polite. They pushed the women out of the way, and immediately were rushed, fell back and lost touch with what was going on.'

This more or less confirmed what Lucy had said, Georgia thought – though being a mother hen she hadn't mentioned Nigel or Mark.

'Even in fights there's usually a bit of verbal before they get down to the physical. Are you telling me the Elgins just came straight in and went for the Todd jugulars?' Peter asked.

'Not quite. According to the Todds, George and his sons came straight at them, so did the rest of the Elgin kids. The older more sensible ones tried to get their brood out of harm's way by pushing them away from the Todds. Young Max White got hold of Scraggs, and starting shouting at him to get lost. He helped one of the Bloomfields tear the placard out of his hands, and when he saw a Todd tackling his younger brother, used the board to separate them. He swears he didn't see Scraggs again.

'Oliver Todd says at some time he caught sight of Terence pushed towards the bushes,' Mike continued, 'but the physical had started in earnest and no one seems to know what happened next. The Bloomfields say they made themselves scarce as soon as they were separated from Oliver – who was the person they wanted to deal with. First two of them, then the other, retreated into the house. Trevor Bloomfield claims he didn't mind discussing the situation with the villagers but Scraggs was an outsider.'

'And no one heard yells for help?' Peter queried. 'I'd like to see that scene video,' he added hopefully.

'Too much racket, I gather. And don't push your luck. Anyway, the result is that we're asking for DNA buccal swabs to be taken from the Elgins, Todds and blooming Bloomfields thought to have been near the centre of the fight. It seems we have got a fair proportion of the village represented in the lab.'

'But,' Georgia objected, 'you'd think that if the Elgins were going to stab anyone it would be a Todd and not an outsider.'

'Maybe he was another scapegoat,' Mike pointed out. 'We don't know what enemies he might have made in his time here. I meant what I said, Georgia, word's got round that you're raking up Ada Proctor, and in the mood they're in now, they don't like it, the Elgins in particular. The way they see it is that the Todds seduced an Elgin, then murdered another woman and now here you are trying to clear his name by saying an Elgin lied under oath. That's what it amounts to, isn't it?'

'And suppose he did lie?'

'Then the Elgins don't want to know. Not now. Let everything quieten down a bit.' Mike hesitated.

'We're leaving today,' Peter told him. 'That should satisfy the bloodhounds.'

'We're not abandoning the case though,' Georgia said vehemently. 'If they're so het up over me, it must mean there's something to discover.'

'Don't tell me,' Mike groaned. 'You can sniff it. I'd like to see DCI Lockhart's face if I told him I could sniff evidence.'

More shaken that she had realized, Georgia went out to the car park to drive back to Country Stop for her luggage. As she turned into the entrance though, she immediately saw something was wrong. Heart in her boots, she walked up to her Alfa Romeo to find all four tyres were flat and on the windscreen was another painted suggestion that she get out of town.

'Contradictory,' she pointed out ruefully to Peter when she returned to the Manor to ring the garage. Half of her wanted to have it out with – with who? Oliver Todd? George White? The other half wanted to go to the church-yard right away with bucket and scrubbing brush. She at least owed that to Ada.

Her father looked grave. 'It's only lowgrade at present, but Mike's right. Georgia, my love, it seems that our finger-prints on Time have talons in this instance.'

Oh, the luxury of reaching home, of garaging her car, dumping her bags inside, taking off her shoes and padding through the blissful quiet of 4 The Street, Haden Shaw. Although she had reluctantly agreed with her father that they should leave as soon as her car was ready, there had been no sign of hostility at Country Stop. On the contrary, Lucy had been quite wistful when she left. 'You will be back?' she asked anxiously. 'Don't take any notice of those dreadful Elgins. They're all mouth, they are.'

Maybe, but someone had vandalized Ada's grave, as well as Georgia's car, and someone had killed Terence Scraggs. Until the police found out who, it would clearly not be wise to have too high a profile. With police permission, there-fore, she had packed Terence's belongings into Peter's car while her own was being attended to.

Distance, she told herself, would lend objectivity. Haden Shaw, with its unassuming streets, its post office-cum-general store, surviving by the skin of its teeth, and its friendly pub, small green and part-time church, seemed a haven. The White Horse would shortly be open, and there she would find amiable neighbours. No Elgins, no Todds, no ancient feuds, no murders. She wondered if this were really the case, or whether if the dust were disturbed here, as it had been in Wickenham, nasty things would crawl out of the woodwork, turning friend into stranger. Such tragedies, as had happened here, seem to have been absorbed into the village psyche; there were no mysteries left in Haden Shaw. Or was it that she could not see them, because she was part of the village?

How blissful to change, make some tea, and then to wander next door for a quiet Saturday evening with her father, sharing a takeaway from the pub (a special courtesy for Peter).

Did she say 'quiet'? The moment she let herself into his house, she knew she was wrong.

'Is that you, Georgia? In here, quickly.'

She dumped their dinner on the kitchen table and ran back to the study. It sounded like a three-line whip, and so it was for Peter was crouched over his computer.

'Look what's happened,' he invited her. 'I thought I'd glance at my emails and then for fun flicked to the Internet. What do you know! Gwendolen Norgood's daughter has materialized.'

'Who, *father* dear, 'she emphasized since this was out of office hours, 'is Gwendolen Norgood, let alone her daughter?'

'You disappoint me, Georgia. Gwendolen Randolph to you. She married.'

Randolph? She should have guessed it. The blessed name was everywhere, unlike Proctor. She cast her mind back, and became more interested. 'You don't mean Guy's sister?'

'Yes, but this is Gwendolen's daughter, Mrs Jean Atwater. She must be a fair age herself, but here she is large as life. I asked for anyone knowing where the Major, his wife and Gwendolen moved to in the 1920s, and of any descendants.

Apparently they moved to Hassocks in Sussex.'

'Is the daughter still there?'

'This is a family search request for information over the Internet. She hasn't mentioned her address obviously, so I've put a message on asking her to ring me, and giving my credentials as a bone fide researcher. Great!'

Georgia agreed. 'A step forward, I grant you.'

'You see,' Peter crowed, 'perseverance is all one needs.'

'Perhaps if we go on persevering, a Proctor will appear.'

'Nothing yet. I did try. There was also a message from Darenth about fixing a time to view the artefacts of Denehole Man. I've fixed it for Hallowe'en, which seemed appropriate. You don't have to come.'

'Try and stop me.' Perhaps she'd call in to see Luke on her way back. No. The fright over Zac was too close. If she saw too much of Luke now, she might be flying to safety to escape the night for the wrong reasons. Her father might have been right; something lodged within her might need to be exorcised before, not after, she stepped into the future.

There was nothing like a motorway (or two in this case) to dull one's mind. Perhaps this was a good thing, for she needed to be calm to face Terence Scraggs's family. Georgia wasn't looking forward to handling this. Terence had only been dead a week, and his parents, William and Celia, could hardly have taken in his death, let alone adjusted, even though they had sounded calm when she telephoned them. It remained open as to whether she should ask them anything about him. She'd have to keep her antennae going at full tilt.

They lived at Beaconsfield, and Terence had had a flat in High Wycombe. Mike had told them it had been searched as a matter of form, but no priority had been given to it since the crime was being taken as a result of the fight. She turned off the M40, and had some lunch in a small restaurant in the main street of Beaconsfield. It tasted amazingly good and fortified her for what was to come. She found the house easily enough afterwards, and braced herself for what seemed certain to be an ordeal. As the door opened, she saw what she had expected and feared. His parents were on the point of, if not actually, retired, and their expression was the puzzled vacancy of those who have been faced with a tragic reality that they couldn't yet grasp. What they saw in Georgia must have reassured them for they invited her in almost eagerly, even helping bring in their son's belongings.

'It's good of you to come.' Eager or not, Georgia felt the vibes of sadness even as she entered the living room, where there were photographs of what was obviously the Scraggses' wedding and of Terence himself. Celia saw Georgia looking at a much younger Terence.

'We hoped Terry would marry soon, but he told us he hadn't met the right person.'

The usual story and Georgia wasn't surprised. She didn't think Terence had been gay; more likely he was one of those people for whom absorption in a cause occupied their entire life. If they chanced upon a like-minded soul, fine; if not, they would not set out to seek one. What really hit home to her was this photograph of a ten-year-old boy with an eager look and engaging smile. Déjà vu. Seventy years earlier it could almost have been Davy Todd. Judging by the era of the photo, it had to be Terence, but there wasn't a lot recognizable as the man she had breakfasted with.

William Scraggs looked away, as if knowing exactly what she was thinking, and cleared his throat. 'You would like some tea?'

'That would be lovely.'

She didn't really want it, but she guessed it would be helpful for them to be able to replace thoughts even with this small action.

'Who did you say you were? I didn't take it in when you rang, I'm afraid,' Celia asked diffidently, as she brought in an already prepared tray.

'I was staying in the same guesthouse as Terence. I know one of the policemen involved in the case, so rather than having his belongings delivered by courier it seemed more personal for me to bring them back to you. I had met him, you see.'

'You knew Terry?' Their eyes immediately lit up, as if by Georgia's presence their son had somehow come close to them again, and they could connect with him through her.

'I talked to him, and I saw him in the village quite often. I'm so sorry. He was doing a great job for the village. You must have been very proud of him.'

'Oh, we were. Such a talented artist. His lovely pictures. And now it's all gone,' he mother said dully. 'We don't even know when we can bury him.'

'No, I'm sorry. That must be terrible.' It was. She knew that so well.

'What did you talk about to him? How was he? Happy?' asked Celia fiercely, as though this might compensate in some small way for what happened to him.

Georgia thought carefully about this, instead of giving an instant answer. 'I think he was. You know he was involved in a protest to stop the sale of the sports fields?'

'He was always doing that sort of thing. He had a social conscience, did Terence. And look where it got him,' William Scraggs put in bitterly.

'A valuable job though. It sets an example.'

William looked doubtful at this platitude, but Georgia meant it. And seeing the conversation going the right way, she pushed it a little further.

'Do you think that was why Terence chose Wickenham to visit? He did some nice paintings there as well. I looked at the portfolio that I brought back to you. I hope you don't mind.' Everything had been placed out of sight in an understairs cupboard, obviously to wait for a day when they had the courage to look at it all. It was one thing helping her with it in her presence, quite another for them to see it there when they were alone.

'He was very talented,' Celia murmured.

'His paints and easel and so on are there too,' Georgia added desperately, wondering what to say next.

'I suppose we should keep them. Perhaps Judith would like them for the children. That's his sister.'

Georgia sensed she had taken a wrong turn. She'd brought reality too close, and made haste to swing it back. 'One of the paintings was interesting. May I show you or would it upset you?'

They looked at each other. 'Fire away,' William said – too hastily. Hating herself, Georgia fetched the portfolio and showed them the painting of Hazelwood House. It was clear it meant nothing to them, though. 'I was in Wickenham to look up some of its history,' Georgia told them diplomatically, 'so this house interested me, since it's no longer standing.'

'Yes, I remember now. Terence told us on the telephone about you. Ada something. Is that right?'

'Yes.' So Terence found Ada Proctor interesting enough to mention to his parents. Was that significant? 'Hazelwood House once belonged to a family called Randolph and Ada—' She broke off because both William and Celia reacted instantly, and were looking at her in amazement.

'That's funny. My father was a Randolph,' Celia told her.

It was the last thing Georgia had expected, especially since the Randolph connection with Wickenham had obviously been a surprise to them. Anyway, it couldn't be the same Randolphs, she realized. 'I don't think your father could have lived in Hazelwood House because the Randolphs moved away in the early 1920s. Their only son was killed in the First World War, so it must be a different family.'

'My father didn't live in Kent. He couldn't have done. He was French and brought up in France.'

Georgia remembered Alice and the French officer, and

struggled to think logically. Was this coincidence or a jigsaw at last beginning to take shape? 'Was he in the Free French air forces during the second war?' she heard herself asking, already imagining Peter's jubilation.

'Yes, he was.' Celia looked even more surprised. 'He met my mother and settled down here. Look, I'll show you a picture of him.' Eagerly she hurried to a bookshelf, the bottom shelf of which was stacked with photograph albums. She extracted one to show Georgia, and turned to a black and white photograph of a posed handsome uniformed young man. No wonder Alice remembered him. He was stunning. There followed a series of family photographs in which the young man gradually aged.

'Did he ever mention Wickenham?' she asked.

'Not that I can recall. He might have done to Terence, because Terry got interested in the war and all that. Dad gave him all his medals and stuff just before he died. That was nearly five years ago.'

'Do you have them here?' Georgia feared she was going too far now, but Celia seemed to see nothing odd about the question.

'They'd be in Terence's flat.'

Memo, ask Mike about that. 'Where was your father brought up in France?' She tried to sound casual.

'On a farm up near Lille somewhere. I've got the address somewhere. I think the family still own it, but he had nothing to do with them. I never went there. Of course things were difficult when I was small, because of the aftermath of the war and he'd had a row with his mother anyway. There was a lot of bitterness over the farm, he told me. His father walked out when he was six, that would have been in the 1920s sometime, and his mother carried on alone. During the war my dad came to fly over here with the Free French forces, and France was occupied of course. His brothers took over the farm and that was that. Froze him out, didn't want him back after the war, so Dad said, so he had to start again. He never spoke to his family again.'

Peter was totally focused now on the skeleton. Any mention Georgia made of Ada was ignored. They had visited the mortuary to see the collection of bones, but had learnt nothing new, save that it brought a reality to what they were doing. The bag of artefacts found near the body had been more fruitful. Besides scraps of cloth, the old francs and something they had identified as a British threepenny piece, they had found the remains of an old watch, whose metal had survived the interment well, though its leather strap had long vanished. Peter was fairly certain it was a Bréguet, since he discovered the tiny blue-jewelled crown from the winder, which had become separated from the watch remains.

'Well, well,' Peter had said softly. 'French, eh? Those coins were no coincidence then.' After begging for permission from a doubtful DCI Lockhart, he had taken the watch to an expert in Canterbury for cleaning, 'Just in case,' Peter explained. 'He might have had his initials on it.'

It cleared up one point: Denehole Man was probably no vagrant. Vagrants and casual hop-pickers couldn't afford Bréguet watches, and the chances of one picking up such a treasure by chance or gift were slim.

'We're going to find the man's name,' Peter declared. 'Blowed if I'll let him be immortalized as Unknown Man. When he's released by the coroner, he'll be given a church-yard burial with headstone, complete with name, even if we have to pay for the whole bang-shoot.'

After Georgia's visit to William and Celia Scraggs, Peter was even more convinced there was a case to answer for the skeleton being Guy Randolph. Part of Georgia still fought it, however, despite the fact that the lover returned from the war was an attractive idea, and Luke was all for it. A terrific story for the book, he pointed out on the telephone.

'What story?' she had countered. 'He murdered his fiancée, then fell in a hole. Answers are needed, Luke.'

'I'll help you look for them in France,' he told her placidly. 'I'm sure you've already made plans to go there. I need a break.'

'The Elgins are not going to follow me to France.' She was half pleased, half irritated that Luke was determined to be present, but the pleasure won.

'I'll bring my trusty sword in case. Only it won't be between us in bed. Okay?'

Chapter Nine

L uke had his own ways of doing things, and this was one of which Georgia approved: taking the Eurostar to Lille rather than driving. The short journey to northern France by rail made the switch in countries pass imperceptibly, and – for her – removed the need for the conscious effort of driving on to French soil from the shuttle or ferry. In the ten years since Rick's disappearance she had only visited France once, and then it had been to Paris. Not the vast expanses of flat fields of the north, the mountains and valleys of the Midi, the scorched hills and plains of the far south, or the Celtic mysteries of Brittany, where he had vanished. The countryside held question marks, whereas a city offered a cocoon to those safe within its walls. Georgia had never visited her mother in the Dordogne, and nor had her mother – with rare tact – ever suggested it. They met in London or Kent instead. Georgia often marvelled that Elena was able to close her mind so completely to Rick's loss, but then that was Elena. If it was too much to cope with, she turned her back and walked away. Or at least, Georgia conceded, appeared to do so.

Georgia had (feebly she admitted) protested to Luke about the expense of train travel compared with driving one of their own cars, but Luke had merely retorted, 'This may be work for you, but it's my holiday.'

She had taken to Lille immediately. She had passed through it years ago when she was a student, and had had no desire to linger in its grey industrial gloom. Now it seemed a different city: on the one hand, geared for tourism;

145

on the other, sporting a life of its own, from its bustling brasseries to the winding cobbled streets of the old quarter, and from magnificent museums and parks to the bedlam of the flea markets. For all its flaunted Euro-culture it remained, thank heavens, stubbornly French.

'What precisely are you hoping to discover at this farm?' Luke asked her at breakfast in their small, comfortable hotel. Dinner last night had been too precious a time to discuss work. They had laughed, they had drunk, they had eaten well, strolled back to the hotel and made love.

'After all,' he continued, 'Terence Scraggs's parents didn't seem to know much about the Randolphs, although it was her father who came visiting Wickenham in the war. What worries me is that you seem to be dodging between Randolphs and Proctors. I thought the book was to be centred on the Proctor case, yet apart from the fact that Ada was once engaged to a Randolph there's no evidence that the two are connected.'

'Not *yet*,' she remarked. 'This coffee is exceptionally good, isn't it?'

'If that's to put me in my place as a mere publisher, tough.' He reached across to seize another croissant. 'You and Peter work in your own way and you usually produce results, but every so often we poor publishers have to be reassured that we're still on the same tramline so far as our precious books are concerned.'

'A week or two ago I'd have been right with you,' she assured him. 'I thought Peter had a bee in his bonnet about Guy Randolph.'

'Carried away with the old Victorian melodrama scenario?'

'Yes. Now I'm not so sure and, since there are no leads to follow up on the Proctor side, I might as well look into the Randolph theory, if only to dismiss it. And after all it was Wickenham we were interested in at the beginning of this case; I plumped for Ada, Peter for Denehole Man as the chief line to follow.'

'You said you'd got an address for some chum of Ada's, though the jury was out as to whether it was the husband or the wife.'

'The Sadlers. I've written to them. No reply.'

'Ring them.'

'Unfair. They might at this very moment be crawling around their attic turning out old boxes of correspondence and photographs that will give us the vital clue to what happened to Ada. Meanwhile, on to the Randolphs. At least now we know about that watch, we have a somewhat more credible thesis to work on that Denehole Man came from France.'

The watch: Peter had been over the moon when he got the report that it was indeed a Bréguet, and in good condition considering its incarceration. It was still sealed, which meant that, once cleaned, the hands were visible. It had stopped at six thirty.

'Which,' Georgia had immediately pointed out to Peter, 'tells us nothing at all.'

The watch could have gone on merrily ticking away until the mechanism ran down, irrespective of when it landed in the denehole. She suspected her father had been hoping that like the clock in the old song, it had 'stopped short, never to go again, when the old man died'. Evidence was seldom as positive as that. All the watch told them was that its owner had liked quality possessions (who doesn't, given the choice?), that he could afford to buy such a watch and that, coupled with the French coins, which might or might not have belonged to the same person, he probably came from France.

'Let me get this straight, though,' Luke persisted, 'all we really *know* about Guy Randolph is that he went missing, believed killed, in the war, and nothing has been heard of him since.'

'Peter's heard from his niece,' Georgia offered defensively.

Luke heaved a sigh. 'These Randolphs could well be

complete red herrings unless you change the approach of the book.'

'They could,' she agreed, 'but since this is a holiday for you, you don't have to worry about that.'

'Authors are supposed to keep quiet and not answer back.'

'Even when they're sleeping with the producer?'

Luke reached for her hand. 'Tonight, Josephine. Right now, there's work to do.'

The worst part of any city was finding one's way out in a car, particularly a hired car, and Lille was no exception. By the time Luke had been honked at several times in traditional French style, Georgia was beginning to wish she had forced herself to go one stage further in her resolution to face France again, and stayed in the countryside, rather than a city. But then she wouldn't have had that night-time walk round floodlit Lille or the meal at Brasserie André. Next time, perhaps – if there was one. Luke was no poodle, and wouldn't wait for ever, and whereas she would travel the rest of the world quite happily on her own, France was another matter.

Once out of Lille and on to the Dunkirk road, she relaxed. The farm, she calculated, was about twenty miles away, and when they turned south at Armentières on to a minor road they found themselves in a familiar northern landscape of flat fields, with the occasional village or farm tucked away, often approached only by single-track lanes. A village meant a few houses, the church, the estaminet. Georgia realized she was slipping into First World War terminology, but it was difficult not to do so here, especially since it would be Remembrance Sunday shortly. The land around them had all been fought over at some time during the two wars, especially in the first, and the surrounding towns, St-Omer, Béthune, Armentières and Hazebrouck had been transport, rest or training areas. Lille itself had been in German hands not only in the second war, in common with the rest of France, but for most of the first war too; areas such as this so close to the front line even during the long stalemate periods had been under constant bombardment.

Only twenty miles or so across the Franco-Belgian border lay Ypres, an epicentre of bitter fighting for four years with its salient bulging into the front line, which led from Switzerland to the North Sea. Ypres itself never fell but the men defending it did, in their hundreds of thousands, and their remains were still being dug up. One of those missing was Guy Randolph, and it was a valid thesis at least that he was not an unidentifiable or unfound corpse, but that the Randolphs of Berthès Farm, where they were heading, were descended from Guy. Randolph was a reasonably common name, but the coincidence was a strong one.

If Guy had been made a POW, news would have got back to Britain. He could have left the battlefield in a fit of genuine amnesia or shell-shock, as it was termed then. Many men did genuinely lose all memory of who they were in these circumstances and would wander off, finding work where they could, especially on farms. The other alternative was that he was a conscious deserter, and in 1917 deserters were shot. That would be reason enough for a man who could not take any more of the horrors of trench life to hide away until after the war. Even afterwards they would face trial, so was it all beginning to add up?

Berthès Farm was near Estville, a tiny village on the River Lys. The farmhouse was a neat twentieth-century bungalow and neither it nor the farm itself hinted of the terrible past history of the area. The house looked well maintained, and the farm prosperous. The farmer's wife, Jeanne Randolph, had been highly suspicious when Georgia spoke to her on the telephone, and it was only after Georgia explained about Denehole Man that she grudgingly agreed to seeing them. She was still grudging when she opened the door. She was a small tidy woman with dark hair and beady eyes, perhaps in her late forties, and there was nothing of the friendliness of the Lillois to be seen here.

'But then there wouldn't be,' Luke pointed out cynically when Georgia mentioned this later. She knew he was right.

This was a different culture to that of Lille itself. Out here there was no need to be friendly with anyone if one did not wish to be. The Randolphs would run their lives on the price paid for their produce and the subsidy they would receive for producing it.

The outside of the house might have been standard twentieth-century, but the interior did not match it. Any antique dealers would give their eye teeth for a look at this, Georgia thought. There was a magnificent eighteenth-century longcase moon clock in the living room, ancient rustic table, chairs and settle, a glorious array of old china on the dresser, and a hearth of old Flemish tiles. To crown this, in a typically French gesture, three flying china ducks and a pink fluffy teddy bear gazed down at them from walls and settle respectively. The bear looked much friendlier than Madame.

Madame Randolph wasted no time over the courtesies, but immediately summoned her husband, who lumbered in from the rear of the house. Roland Randolph was a huge man in height and girth though not so formidable as Madame. '*Ah. Les Anglais*,' he roared. '*Une petite absinthe, peut-être?*'

This was declined, if regretfully by Luke, but a small apéritif of some home-made wine or liqueur made its appearance nevertheless, and a plate of Madame's biscuits joined it.

A certain amount of ceremony followed, while Georgia explained with Luke's help (his French was better than hers) why they were here. This was none too easy, since she wasn't sure whether to centre the reason on the murder of Terence Scraggs or Denehole Man.

Madame watched eagle-eyed, obviously still suspicious that they might run off with the spoons, but Roland concentrated on what Georgia was telling them.

'You are the police?' Madame enquired, after Georgia elected to begin with the Scraggs connection.

'No, madame. We're investigating privately.'

'Ah, from the newspapers.'

'No, madame. I am a publisher,' Luke weighed in. He could be impressive when he chose, and this was one such occasion, as he spoke offhandedly of the reputable books he published.

'And you write a book of this murder?'

'No. The book's about a murder in the past,' Georgia took up the story, 'but the one of Terence Scraggs, which took place only two, three weeks ago, does have a connection with you. I met his parents, and his mother's father was born on this farm. His name was Randolph.'

'*Ah!*' Roland cried. '*Mon oncle. François.*'

'I gathered there had been a disagreement, and he left the farm after the war.'

This caused an excited spate of rapid French between Monsieur and Madame, followed by a wry: 'Disagreement, yes. My father Bernard and his brother Joseph worked on this farm throughout the second war. François then came home, and say as eldest brother he want all of it. He does not want to help us, he want to rule us. My father and uncle say no, and my mother agree with them.'

This was a different version from the Scraggs's story, and this François bore little relation to the gallant airman of Alice White's dreams. Georgia listened intently.

'He think that because he fly with the Royal Air Force he do more for France than we do here,' Roland continued. 'My father tell him he, François, is the deserter. The true fight was here, with the Germans who occupied our country and took all our family had.'

'Was it just the two brothers on the farm? What about your grandfather?' Georgia held her breath. Roland must be in his late forties, and his father must therefore be over seventy. François, Bernard and Joseph could have been Denehole Man's sons.

'Grandfather? He was not here. It was my grandmother ran the farm in the war. My uncles were young men, and she feared they would be taken by the Germans to work for them as slave labour, but she managed to get help to stop that. So they stayed here. She was truly *formidable*, my grandmother.'

'And her husband died when? He was the first Randolph in the family?'

'*Oui*, but the farm was hers, left her by her father. My grandfather helped her run it, but then he left.'

'Was his name Guy?'

'I am sorry?'

Luke intervened, pronouncing it in the French way, and light dawned.

'Yes, that is so,' Roland agreed.

Another rung on the ladder climbed. A cautious hope sprang up that she was getting somewhere at last. 'When did he leave here?' she asked eagerly. 'Was it to go to England?'

Luke shot a look that read 'leading question'.

'That I do not know. My father died last year, but my uncle still lives. He likes to keep to his room, he is old, you understand, but perhaps he will talk to you.'

'Pah!' snorted Madame, which made her views on her uncle-in-law quite clear. 'I will call him. That one, if there is something in it for him, he will run here fast.' She could be heard screaming upstairs and shortly she returned in triumph. 'See, he comes.'

When Uncle Joseph appeared, wearing the blue blouson and trousers of the French worker, he looked far from decrepit, though he must be over eighty, Georgia thought. His eyes were sharp though. He talked rapidly with Roland in French for a while until Georgia decided to intervene. She began carefully in French. 'I am interested in the bones of a dead man found in Kent. It is possible they are your father's.'

'*Angleterre?*' Joseph looked interested and took a healthy (or unhealthy) swig of absinthe, contemplated his glass, then banged it down on the table. A decision had obviously been arrived at.

Luke translated the stream of patois that followed as best

he could. 'I think he's saying that he was a child when his father left home, only about five. And a good thing that he left, because he was a lazy layabout. They were better off without him.'

'Yet his wife kept the name,' she pointed out.

'*Mais oui*,' Joseph sounded indignant. 'They were married. My father told her he came from a good English family and one day he would inherit a big house, much land and much money. We waited but it never came, but my grandmother said if it did she wanted them to know she was married to him, even though he had left her.'

Georgia smiled. 'I'm afraid I've brought no fortune with me.'

The old man rattled something else off, in dialect, which was strongly Flemish-influenced, Georgia guessed. 'Also,' Luke interpreted, 'she wished her neighbours to know she is married because she has three children. She did not want the new *curé* to think she was a sinful woman. Everyone knew that old Berthès left her the farm, so she kept that name going.'

'Your mother was very wise,' Georgia told Joseph gravely. Hang on to your marriage lines, she thought. Some things never change.

'You are married, madame?' he asked.

'Not now.'

'You should be,' he told her. 'Too much time is wasted while one thinks about such things, and then, *pouf*, one wakes up and one is too old to . . .'

He used a word that Georgia didn't recognize but Luke laughed and Joseph's gesture accompanying had been clear enough.

'Never too old,' she declared roundly.

That caused a laugh all round, and even Madame raised a smile.

'So your father left to go to England to hunt his fortune?' she prompted Joseph again.

'*Non*,' he immediately replied and her heart sank. Surely

this wasn't going to be yet another dead end. 'He left to live with Madame Rosanne of the Chat d'Or in Lille. My grandfather not a good man. He think there more money in a restaurant. My grandmother not give him much money, because he not like to work on the farm. So he go to Chez Rosanne. She had been a brothel keeper in Paris, and when she have much money and wishes to be respectable she come to Lille to open a restaurant. Restaurants are indeed respectable, but also hard work. One day Madame Rosanne come here to my mother and ask: "Where is Guy? He steal some money and go." "He not here," said Maman. Rosanne did not believe her but she went to the village and the whole village say, "Monsieur Guy not come here."'

'A sad story,' Georgia commented politely.

'*Pas du tout*,' was Joseph's shrugged reaction. 'Life is practical, madame. Rosanne and my mother become very good friends, so she come to run the café in Estville. When the next war comes, she very against the Germans, but she pretend to be great friends. This way she get information and can protect us all. Through Rosanne my brother and I allowed to stay here through the war. So, Guy good father to me, all because of his whore.' He wheezed and cackled to Madame's obvious disgust.

'And who runs the café now?'

'Rosanne died many years ago, my mother very sad. No one left of her family.'

Georgia judged it was time for the big question. 'Do you know where your mother met her husband?'

There followed an earnest discussion in French but Georgia couldn't understand anything but the odd word.

'She met him after the first war ended,' Roland finally said. 'They marry in 1919.'

'Not earlier?' she asked puzzled. He must have been in the army near here and the war was over in 1918.

Another discussion and finally Joseph admitted: 'It is a long time ago now, so I tell you the truth. The farm was my mother's anyway, and Brussels cannot take that away from us, even if they find out about my father. They met when he came here for help in 1917. He had run away from the war, he told Maman, and he pretended to be shell-shocked but she did not believe that. He had found himself in Wytschaete, he said. That is a small village south of Ypres on the road to Armentières, where there was a British army rest centre. He had been a week or two earlier with his battalion before the battle. If he were recognized after he run away that would be bad, so he go south to cross the river into France and get as far away as possible. But he was hungry and tired and saw our farm. My mother opened the door and he said he was English and if he were sent back he would be shot. My mother who was a practical woman needed help on the farm, because her father, old Berthès, was ill, and her brothers were dead in the war at Verdun. She cannot run it alone, so she takes him in, though being so close to the fighting front it is a big risk. If the Germans come and find him, she will be shot. But they did not, and after the war they marry. But he no good. He run away from British army, she say to me, I should have known he would run away from me. And from Rosanne too! How could he do that? The English, they do not know how to work like we French.'

Georgia let this pass, in the interests of co-operation.

'Maman said he come here,' Joseph continued, 'to work on farm, but it is too hard for him. He is a gentleman of England, he tells her, and gentlemen do not work. So he give her three children and disappears after they were married seven years.'

'Would you have any proof of his identity as Guy Randolph?' Luke asked.

Three pairs of eyes fixed on him. 'There is money to be had?' asked Madame eagerly.

'I would not think so,' Georgia answered for him. Even if this was indeed the Guy Randolph of the denehole, the legal position over the estate would surely be affected if he had been declared officially dead at the end of the war.

Madame lost interest, but Joseph was more co-operative. 'He had a few things from the war, but our brother François took them from Rosanne after the war, she told us. Perhaps he thought it might help him find the fortune or even our father himself. Who knows? Perhaps he did, but I do not think so. We heard no more of our papa and little from François.'

And years later, Georgia reflected, his grandson went on the same mission to seek his heritage, got caught up in a protest about something entirely different and was murdered.

'Good, wasn't it?' she asked Luke as they drove away. 'Peter should be happy. There were some interesting questions here. For example, if this were indeed the Guy Randolph who went to England in 1929, why did he leave his war medals behind? Did he still fear being arrested as a deserter? What do you think?'

'I think it's time for lunch, Luke said practically. 'I have a French meal-shaped space in *mon estomac.*'

'We could try the village café.'

'My thoughts exactly.' It proved to be full of smoke and lunchtime eaters, but the food coming out in steaming bowls looked promising. They were no sooner through the door than they were buttonholed as prime prospects by madame, who had a definite gleam in her eye, especially as it weighed up Luke.

'*Vous voulez manger?*'

'*Oui, madame.*'

Madame could have been a dead ringer for Rosanne, Georgia thought, as they sat down at the table, quickly covered for them in a red-check cloth, and sturdy glasses, plates, cutlery and paper napkins plonked upon it. There was no menu here – one would not dare ask for one, Georgia whispered to Luke. On the walls were old newspaper cuttings of the armistice, the liberation, and of

General de Gaulle, one of the famous sons of Lille. It only needed Edith Piaf to growl out 'Chanson d'Amour' to complete the illusion that fifty years had just vanished. They accepted the platefuls as they emerged one after the other: crudités, saucisses, salade, vegetables and carbonade of beef.

'It begins to make sense, doesn't it?' Luke eventually returned to the purpose of their visit. 'We could try to prove Guy Randolph of Wickenham was the Guy Randolph of Berthès Farm by checking army records. With a father as a major he'd have been at least a junior officer, so he should be quite easily traceable. Or,' he paused, 'you ask Uncle Joseph for a DNA sample. You said there was one taken from the bones, didn't you?'

'Yes.' She hesitated. 'But I'd rather put my money on Gwendolen's daughter. At first, anyway.'

'Explain, if you please.'

'Two reasons. Firstly, since the skeleton is fairly ancient, there's a better chance of a match through the female line, Guy's and Gwendolen's mother. Mitochondrial DNA – inherited only from the mother – is more likely to be intact in poor tissue samples, as the skeleton's probably are. Secondly' – she paused – 'if we woo Uncle Joseph we're approaching the puzzle backwards. There's nothing but circumstantial evidence to suggest their Guy Randolph is the one we're after, yet with Gwendolen's daughter we're on sure ground.'

'Hum. No harm in our checking army records though.'

'*Our* trying?'

Luke grinned. 'Sorry. You could. I was merely being a concerned publisher.'

'Apology accepted, especially as you're my partner at the moment, not publisher. Sharing work is permitted.'

'Another halfway house. Just like you. Do you ever think you're going to cross the Rubicon, Georgia?'

'Probably,' she answered honestly.

'Then why not now?'

'There's too many loose cannons floating around inside me,' she tried to explain.

'Which there always will be.'

'Wait a little longer, Luke?'

'Of course. If only for dessert,' he added practically. 'That tart looks rather good.'

'As no doubt Guy said when he set eyes on Rosanne.'

'Shall I stay on for lunch?' Luke asked, as he drove Georgia back the next day to Haden Shaw from the Ashford International station.

'Yes, Peter would love it. Besides, I can print him out the Randolph family tree according to the testimony of the French connection, so that you can help answer his usual barrage of suspicious questions.' She'd forced herself to compose this on her laptop the previous evening, feeling a martyr for working even this short period with so many temptations in the form of Lille and Luke to divert her.

'Good. It seems a pity to spoil the day by going back too early. They don't expect me back in the office till about four.'

She was even more glad of Luke's presence as they let themselves into her father's house. She always feared coming back to find there had been some problem with Peter, and to have Luke there was a boost. If he were grumpy, Luke would get him out of it more quickly than she could; if he were ill, there would be someone to share the anxiety for an hour or two. Today all was well, however, and when she opened the door and saw her father at his computer a rush of affection swept over her.

'Good news,' she called. 'Luke and I are taking you out for lunch.'

'Good,' came the instant reply. 'Margaret's prepared that dreadful cauliflower cheese for me. Have a word with her, will you?'

Georgia obediently went to find Margaret, who was

engaged in dusting the upstairs rooms. 'Tell him, I'm not wasting the cauliflower,' Margaret said cheerfully. 'He needn't worry. He can have it for his supper. It's good for him.'

There was wheelchair access at the back of the White Horse, and Peter had his favourite table quite close to the rear entrance. If he found others sitting there, he could stare them out until they picked up their plates and walked. 'I'm very grateful,' he would then quaver. 'It's the only table I can manoeuvre this thing up to.' A complete fib but he had come to believe it himself by now.

The White Horse hovered successfully between the trendy and the traditional village pub. The trendy element was not formed of casual passers-by but by word of mouth. The cook here was good, and though the lunchtime trade was largely local the evenings drew their clientele from far and wide. Even with the best of landlords it wasn't easy to make a living running a pub in this part of Kent, and Ken Davies, the publican, was perpetually muttering dark threats about his not being appreciated in this place, judging by the lack of profits. One of his regulars had become so sick of this ritual he presented the pub with a huge pink plastic piggy bank labelled 'Ken's Pauper's Fund', in which pennies were solemnly deposited. Then someone ran off with it, and that was that.

'How did you get on?' Peter asked at last, once he had made his decision between baked gammon and fish and chips.

Georgia produced her Randolph family tree and laid it before him.

'Not proven,' she pointed out, 'but it looks good.'

'Tell me more,' Peter commanded, and listened remarkably patiently for him. 'A deserter,' he murmured when they had finished. 'Why didn't I think of that, or perhaps I did. I expect you pooh-poohed me at the time, Georgia. But you see it's all glueing itself together at last.'

159

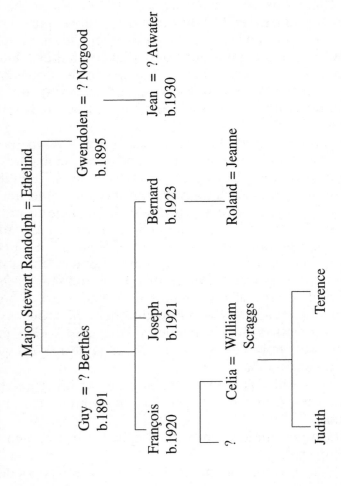

The Randolphs

Major Stewart Randolph = Ethelind

Guy = ? Berthès
b.1891

Gwendolen = ? Norgood
b.1895

François
b.1920

Joseph
b.1921

Bernard
b.1923

Jean = ? Atwater
b.1930

? Celia = William
Scraggs

Roland = Jeanne

Judith

Terence

'It's collecting itself, but it's not tying up with Ada Proctor, and it's still not certain Guy is Denehole Man.'

'Ah, well, we're a step forward on that,' Peter announced complacently. 'Gwendolen Randolph's granddaughter Jean wants to visit Wickenham. What do you think of that?'

'Terrific,' Georgia answered. Then: 'What for?'

'She wants to see the ground her ancestors trod. I had a long talk with her on the phone, but the only information that I gained was negative. Her mother and grandparents heard nothing of Guy after the war and he was officially presumed dead. There weren't even any rumours that he might still be alive. Nothing. She was definite about it. She also mentioned that Guy didn't sound the sort of person to stay away if he were in need either. He was a charming scrounger, according to what she was told by her mother. Anyway, I said if she visited Wickenham, you would show her round, provided the hoo-ha has died down. I'll come, too, of course.'

'There's no need,' Georgia said.

'You're not thinking straight. Of course there is.'

Luke chipped in. 'You want to use your charm to persuade her to have a DNA test, don't you?'

'Of course,' Peter replied with dignity. 'She wouldn't want her uncle lying in an unidentified grave, would she?'

Chapter Ten

Georgia drove cautiously through Wickenham. Jim Hardbent had assured her on the telephone that the village was relatively quiet, at least superficially. He couldn't see it getting back to 'normal', however, until there was someone under arrest, and that hadn't happened yet, but as for her meeting Jean Atwater, he thought, Georgia could risk returning here.

The signs of Christmas were making their appearance in earnest now that December had arrived. Lights were strung over the shops and around the Green. She could see the baker's sporting holly and frosted windows, and those of the general store displaying Father Christmas and jolly sleigh stickers. The season of goodwill was providing at least a veneer over the village's troubles; Christmas was an armistice in the war of real life. She sensed an unnatural calm everywhere, but perhaps she was influenced by the grey of a December morning. Nevertheless, she was glad she had chosen not to stay here tonight, but to return to Haden Shaw.

She had gathered from Jim that the sale of the Manor and estate had duly gone through, but that the fate of the sports fields was as yet unknown. The supermarket deal had collapsed just as Trevor Bloomfield had expected, but what that implied for the future – including that of the appeal – was still to be revealed.

The investigation had obviously been scaled down. No sign of the incident van now, but its absence didn't mean there wasn't still a police presence in the village. They were still interviewing, Mike had told them, working their way through the protestors. The good news was that at last some alien DNA had been found on a scrap of hair caught under Scraggs's fingernail, but the bad news was that so far none of those admitting to be close enough to Terence to have killed him had provided a match, and nor had the National DNA Database. The DNA bill was mounting, Mike told them, but the SIO was considering paying for an intelligence-led screen by the FSS, if they decided to broaden the scope and request samples from virtually the whole village. Mike was no longer officially on the case, but was being kept informed of what was happening, chiefly, he suspected, because Lockhart wanted to keep tabs on the Marshes, especially now the name of Randolph was providing a theoretical link between Darenth's unidentified skeleton and unsolved murder.

Georgia's first call here this morning had been to Lucy Todd to explain she was only here for the day, in case she was spotted in the village. Lucy had been distinctly sniffy at first, but then relaxed.

'Are things quieter now?' Georgia had asked her. It was a trite question, but since the murder was still in everybody's minds, it wouldn't seem so to Lucy.

Lucy heaved a sigh. 'Still rumbling on. Oliver's hopping mad the way they've taken his DNA swab as a suspect, just because the Elgins are saying the murder's our fault for starting the protest. I ask you, what's democracy coming to if you can't protest peacefully? And you're a witness that it was peaceful, till those Neanderthals came charging up.'

'Surely the police have the Elgins in their sights too?'

'Oh yes, and the Bloomfields. It's all very democratic in that sense. But the Elgins are wriggling out, saying they were infiltrated by outsiders in balaclavas over their faces, who were thugs hired by the Todds to stir up trouble. Crazy, they are. Of course it was an Elgin or one of those Bloomfields done it. Why should we want to kill the man

163

who was leading our protest? Poor Mr Scraggs. He didn't deserve to be killed.'

There Georgia was all with her. 'It seems unlikely certainly, but it wasn't in the Bloomfields' interest to kill him because it would ensure their deal was off right away.'

'Perhaps,' agreed Lucy darkly. 'But after all it could have been an accident,' she added hopefully.

'With a killer deliberately carrying a knife, that seems unlikely for anyone on a peaceful protest.'

'Not where the Elgins are concerned.' Lucy cheered up, now back on familiar ground. 'You tell your policeman friend that. Dab hands at darts are the Elgins.'

Georgia wasn't sure of the logic of this, and furthermore, she thought wearily as she drove away from Country Stop, she would be glad if she never heard the words Todd or Elgin again. If there had to be feuds, why did they have to be inflicted on everyone else? The Todds and Elgins had succeeded in affecting the entire community – albeit, Georgia conceded, in unusual circumstances. Whatever the reason, back in Wickenham she was finding it harder to fight her way through the thorn bushes to Ada Proctor's day and the Randolphs'. In France it had all seemed so straightforward, but now she felt herself sinking into the bog of Wickenham politics once more.

When she walked into the hotel after parking the car, she stiffened as she saw Peter chatting amiably with Trevor Bloomfield. Try as she might, she couldn't reconcile her image of this man with the role of local lord of the manor. It was he, over the sale of the sports fields, who had set Wickenham by its ears, not Georgia with her enquiries into Ada Proctor. Now he was proposing to walk calmly out of the mess, clutching his millions, to set up wherever he chose in the world. True, the days of paternal feudalism had gone for good, and good riddance, but she resented Trevor Bloomfield on Wickenham's behalf. His family owed something to its past, which should provide a bond with the village.

When had it been broken? she wondered. It seemed to be there in Ada's day, judging by the doctor's record books; and so had it during the war, according to Jim. She remembered his telling her about the way the village and Manor had drawn together over the blackout, rationing, call-up, and through the dark summer days of the Battle of Britain when the skies of Kent were full of Messerschmitts, Heinkels and RAF defenders. Had the break in the bond come when the Bloomfields first turned the Manor into a hotel, or had it happened earlier? Matthew Bloomfield died in 1943, and perhaps that had been the beginning of the decline. Perhaps the She-Wolf influenced her son Bertram, the new owner of Wickenham Manor, into her way of thinking, that the estate was just another business, with no commitment to the village save of employer to employee. An interesting thought, that the She-Wolf's prophecy in the recording about the role of the Manor had been fulfilled. Wickenham was economically independent of its Manor, but its soul still had expectations of it.

'I was glad to hear the sale of the Manor had gone smoothly,' she managed to say to the She-Wolf's grandson, noting that he hadn't bothered to get up to greet her.

'Amazing the way news gets around. Yes, that at least went through.'

'But not the supermarket,' she pressed. Be damned if she'd go easy on him.

'No problem there. The deal fell through, as I'd expected. There's no point throwing the fields in with the sale of the Manor – the new owners would hardly thank me for handing them that smoking gun – so I haven't decided what to do yet.' He grinned. 'I have to admit, I haven't tried very hard. I'm enjoying seeing Oliver Todd and George Elgin White both going around with long faces, wondering what's going to happen.'

'When will you put them out of their misery?'

'They'll have to wait a while longer. I might sell to the first bidder. I might keep the fields and be an absentee landlord. I might make them a charitable trust for this village, which is so fond of my family. Who knows? I assure you, I don't.'

And you don't care either, Georgia thought. No paternal interest here. 'And meanwhile,' she observed, 'the Todds won't do anything about the appeal because there's no current direct threat and they wouldn't want to spend good money on legal bills until there's something to appeal against.'

'You seem very involved, Georgia,' he sniped back. 'All those Todds getting to you, are they? They've put my family through the mill for long enough, now they can stew in their own juice. I wouldn't get too mixed up with them, if I were you. Remember you are an outsider.'

'And so was Terence Scraggs. Is that a threat, Trevor?' Her simmering rage at this unexpected attack was only just kept at bay.

'Good heavens no,' he laughed. But the sneer was still present. 'Nevertheless if you were my daughter, I wouldn't want you here at the moment.'

Peter stirred. 'Fortunately,' he rumbled, 'she's not your daughter. Georgia's DNA has better stuff in her molecules than sterling, euros and dollars.'

Trevor stood up. The smile had vanished. 'I do advise you not to meddle too far into Wickenham affairs. You are intending to write a book for your own profit, after all. It hasn't gone unnoticed in the village.'

'It seems to me,' Georgia remarked, somewhat shaken, after Trevor had stalked off, 'that the fingerprints on Time have suddenly become knuckle-dusters rather eager to get rid of us.'

'Keep your path straight ahead,' Peter replied. 'We didn't bring this about. The protest over the fields has nothing to do with Ada Proctor or Denehole Man. Remember that, and ask yourself why Wickenham – or parts of it – is getting so riled up about us. Although,' he added honestly, 'I can't answer that myself.'

'Scraggs's death at least links with the protest, if Denehole Man turns out to be the missing Randolph.'

'I don't agree. It would only link if that were the reason he was killed.'

Georgia stared at him. 'How on earth could it be that? It's neat, but there's not a shred of evidence or even a theory to back it up. Nice one, Peter, but let's plod on along the slow but sure route. What time's your Mrs Atwater arriving?' She was driving over from East Sussex where she was staying with friends.

'Elevenish.'

Georgia had formed a mental picture of Jean Atwater as a fluffy-haired rose-cheeked lady, and was not prepared for the determined lady who strode into the hotel bar lounge. She might be seventy-odd, but she was very definitely living in the present, not her mother's past. She was trouser-suited, styled white hair, and very professional looking. As indeed she proved to be. She ran a local charity and owned and ran a chain of florist shops into the bargain.

'It's good of you to offer to show me round the land of my father, Peter.' Jean firmly shook their hands, and first names were arrived at easily and quickly.

'Didn't your mother ever return here?' Georgia asked.

'I don't believe so. It was associated with bad times for her and for my grandparents. Charmer or not, she told me, Guy was always causing ructions at home. My grandfather was of the old school and there were constant rows and clashes. When Guy died, I suspect my grandmother remained full of silent, and probably unjustified, guilt.'

'Your mother too?'

'She told me family life was a lot more peaceful without Guy but a light had gone out of it. That's why she didn't want to return here. She used to talk about the Manor and the parties they had there, especially when she was in her teens before the outbreak of war in 1914. There were Guy and herself, the three at the Manor, Matthew, Jack and Anne, and Ada Proctor. Ada's the one you're interested in, aren't you? She was the sixth of our core group, though of course there were lots of others who came and went. Jack was a madcap like Guy so they got on well; Matthew fancied Ada, so Mum reckoned, and they were more disciplined, and Anne, who was most academically inclined, married young and went to live in the States after the war.'

'And Guy was officially engaged to Ada?'

'I don't know about official. Mum always spoke of them as a couple, but Guy apparently chased everything in skirts. We were all young, of course. Guy was twenty-three when war broke out. I've brought some photos, if you'd like to see them.'

'That's very good of you.' Peter dived forward eagerly, swinging his chair round to peer over the table, leaving Georgia to peer over him.

'Not at all. It's good to show them to someone who's interested, for whatever reason. My children aren't. They're just names to them. I shall be dead and long gone by the time they get to the age to be interested in their family's past.'

Jean produced sepia studio photos of a good-looking young man, one of a toddler in skirts on his mother's knee, and a delightful one of a posed family group on the steps of what Georgia recognized as Hazelwood House, obviously taken in late Edwardian times judging by the clothes and the children's ages. Guy must have been about eighteen or nineteen in this photo. A strong face? No, determined, but not strong. She could see this young man taking ill to farmwork. Don't assume too much, Georgia, she warned herself. We don't know this is Denehole Man, and we don't know this is the Guy Randolph of Berthès farm. This case was a greyhound straining at the leash, waiting for the magic word. Perhaps Peter was feeling the same for he was taking inordinate pains with the photographs, giving them very careful attention. There was another family group on the steps of Hazelwood House, in early 1920s dress, and this time Gwendolen looked to be in her mid-twenties, very glamorous, and aware of it. No Guy, of course.

'Do you want to see the denehole?' Peter asked Jean.

'No, thanks very much,' she replied briskly. 'I never knew Guy, so the old house and village will mean more to me than where Guy might or might not have met his death. It's sad to think he might have come back here after the war – if you're right, that is – only to find us all gone. I suppose finding strangers in Hazelwood House he would have come to the Manor to find out where we'd gone, and fallen into the denehole, somehow.'

'It's a possibility,' Georgia agreed. A pretty unlikely one though, in her view.

'Or was he pushed?' Jean asked outright. 'That's what you're after, aren't you, otherwise you wouldn't be interested?'

'That too is a possibility.'

'If I understand you both correctly, the landscape is swarming with Randolphs who might or might not be related to me. There's this French family – who might be direct descendants of Guy, there's this poor lad who's recently been murdered, and a Randolph living in Beaconsfield who is related to the French family. Yet you can't prove any of this for certain. How can you ever hope to?'

'There is a way,' Peter began, avoiding Georgia's eye. Too soon, too soon, she was silently telegraphing through to him. He didn't get the message, or didn't want to. 'And that's for you to have a DNA test. A sample has been extracted from the skeleton.'

Jean frowned and took her time about replying. 'I'm not sure about that. I'll think about it. Suppose . . .'

'There are always supposes,' Georgia said gently to fill in the gap, as Jean broke off. She was taken aback at this reluctance, since she appeared such a down-to-earth woman.

'It makes it too real,' Jean explained. 'It brings it into the here and now. And what for? So you can write your book. Sorry, if that sounds rude, but it is a factor.'

'It is,' Peter agreed. 'Nevertheless, it's also a step towards identifying a nameless skeleton for the coroner and giving a name to an eventual gravestone.'

'There must be other ways to find out for sure whether it's Guy.' Jean stuck doggedly to her decision. 'But I promise I'll think about it.'

Peter wisely dropped the subject, and after lunch, Georgia offered to drive Jean round the village. She elected to walk, however, to Georgia's approval. 'If I'm going to see Wickenham, I need to see it properly,' she pointed out.

Georgia did her best to describe the village as it would have been in Gwendolen's day, as they strolled through, and became so wrapped up in recreating it that she had completely forgotten DNA when Jean later returned to it.

'I feel a wimp for not agreeing to your father's suggestion,' she admitted. 'I know it seems a small step to you, but your evidence about the skeleton is only circumstantial. You see, my mother had a tough time with Brother Guy, for all that they got on well. He was always coming *back*, she told me. Just when you had sorted out the disastrous effects of his last prank, he'd produce a new humdinger. Just as they thought he was all set to marry Ada, he'd up and away and fall for some other woman. Then back he'd come. I feel that's what he's doing to me now. I want to squash him, to say he can't *do* that. Go away.'

It was a point of view. The dead could reach out from beyond the grave with a power that was denied the living. 'An unfair fight for you,' was all Georgia could reply.

'Tell me about this Ada Proctor,' Jean asked.

Georgia obliged so far as she was able, pointing out the Elgin house, which was later the teashop, and the grass lane to Crown Lea. 'This was where The Firs stood, where Ada and her father lived, and over there –' Georgia indicated the other side of the road – 'was Hazelwood House.'

Jean stared at the 1960s housing estate for so long that Georgia began to share her disappointment. 'It's hard to imagine how it was eighty years ago.'

'Perhaps not, if one looks and then *sees*.' Jean frowned in concentration. 'Some of those trees could have been here then. Not the ones in front of us, they're too young, but over there.'

There was a large oak tree that Jean managed to identify as being the young sapling in the photographs. She gazed at it for some time, while Georgia stood silently at her side. 'You said Hazelwood was pulled down in the 1950s?' Jean asked at last.

'It was damaged during the war when the flying bomb hit The Firs and it more or less fell down by itself after that.'

'I think the house must have been here,' Jean decided. 'That porch, where the photo was taken, was at this angle to the road.'

More or less in the Todds' driveway, Georgia realized.

'This Randolph you mentioned, who came looking for us in the second war, and went to see the former maid at the Manor,' Jean changed tack. 'I've been wondering, why didn't he go to the Manor, instead of to her?'

'Perhaps he did.' Georgia hadn't thought about this, and Jean had a valid point. 'Matthew, the then Squire, died in 1943 though, so perhaps Randolph came after that and no one else could give him any information.'

'But you told me his wife survived him and she would have been at the Manor in 1929 too. Why send him off to the maid?'

'I've no idea,' Georgia admitted. 'The wife seems to have been a woman of strong mind, and not too agreeable, so perhaps she just couldn't be bothered, or maybe she was out and someone else directed him to the maid. That's the problem with these cases, there are always irritating details that one can never quite grasp. Are they significant or are they the hiccups of daily life that don't fall neatly into place? If I don't leave my milk bottles out for collection, does it mean that I'm lying injured inside or simply that I've forgotten? Easy enough to solve in cases set in the present day, but another matter when it comes to mysteries in the past.'

'I understand that. Now, it seems to me that the French airman's visit is good evidence of a link between us and this French family, so tell me, Georgia, when do you get to the point that you can be certain that you are right?'

Georgia considered this. 'When the evidence satisfies us. It's like a trial by judge, if not by jury.'

'Do you think I was wrong not to agree to the DNA sample?'

'There's no right or wrong about this,' Georgia declared firmly, as they walked back to the village. 'My father is very keen to put a name to the skeleton that we buried but, as you say, there are other means, so you mustn't be too influenced by our wishes.'

'He could get DNA through the French family. Why me?'

'Because you are the *sure* point in the evidence. You are without doubt descended from Guy Randolph's family. The others *probably* are.' She went on to explain the intricacies of mitochondrial DNA from the maternal line.

'But why, Georgia, are you both so keen to name this skeleton? I can understand you're being eager, and that there's the book to write, but there seems something more personal than that.'

Georgia hesitated. She was beginning to feel hedged in. Did she remain the objective investigator, or should she delve deep into herself in the effort to answer her question? 'Let's go here for some tea.' The Green Man was not Wickenham Manor, but it did serve tea (with some persuasion).

'It's the living with uncertainty,' Georgia began, to ease herself in to the subject, reluctant to go further than necessary. 'If we don't get the French family to agree, or if they are not related to Guy, then like us, you will never know for sure whether the skeleton is your missing uncle. We want you to realize that, and what it might mean.'

'But that's not important to me,' Jean objected.

'It might become so. You might begin to wonder whether it was or wasn't his skeleton, now that the idea has been planted in your mind. The image of a gravestone without a name is a powerful one.'

'I can live with that. Why did you say, like us?' Her eyes were studying Georgia keenly.

Georgia made a valiant effort, since she had no choice. 'We,' she began painfully, 'had a similar tragedy. My brother Rick disappeared like Guy, not in war, just on holiday. We never heard any more but we have to believe he is dead. Your mother had to live through that, just as we did. Your grandparents couldn't seriously have hoped that Guy would return from the slaughter of the trenches just as my parents can't hope that Rick is alive somewhere, yet in dreams the not knowing, where and what and how is agonizing and for my father unbearable. Even if your family believed Guy died in battle they would never have known how, whether his death was instantaneous, whether he lay in agony, whether he died trying to save someone, or the opposite. His death leaves a question mark, and this skeleton provides at least a chance that you could complete the story for your family.'

'You said it was Ada Proctor who was your main interest in Wickenham. What does this skeleton have to do with her?'

'Because if the man in the denehole was Guy, and he appears to have died about the same time as her, there's a chance that Ada was going to meet him and not the lad who was hung for her murder.'

'Who was?'

'A young man, a gardener called Davy Todd. His sweetheart, who swore in vain she was with him all that evening, is still alive.'

'In the village?'

'No, in a retirement home on the Downs.'

'Could I meet her?'

'We could go there and ask the staff if she's well enough.' Georgia was taken aback by Jean's unexpected request, not immediately seeing the reason for it. She couldn't deny Mary visitors, however, especially Gwendolen Randolph's daughter. 'Let's go now. The light's already fading.'

'My mother loved Kent,' Jean remarked as they drove up on to the downs. 'A pity she never came back here. It's lovely even in wintertime. The light has an interesting quality, and the trees are themselves, not covered with their greenery. Their skeletons are much more – Ah,' she said wrily, 'there we have it, don't we?'

Georgia laughed. 'We do.'

'You want me to clothe yours for you.'

'We do.'

'I'm still thinking.'

The duty nurse at Four Winds looked doubtful at their request to see Mary, however. 'She's not good today, not good at all.'

'Tell her Miss Gwendolen's daughter is here to see her,' Georgia pleaded.

The answer came back promptly, though the nurse still looked dubious. When they reached the room, Georgia saw why. Mary was in bed, eyes sunken and looking fully her age. Her eyes were closed but she opened them as Georgia leant over. 'A visitor to see you, Mary,' she said gently.

'Sit down,' Mary ordered hoarsely, a gleam in her eye that suggested she was preparing to rally fast. 'Let me look at you.' She examined Jean very carefully. 'Nice lady, your mother, very smart,' she said at last. 'She wouldn't remember me. I was a child.'

'I've brought you a photograph,' Jean said matter of factly, rummaging in her handbag and producing the 1920s photograph of the Randolph family on the steps of Hazelwood House.

Mary's eyes lit up, and after a delay while glasses and

magnifying glass were tracked down, she studied a it intently. At last she handed it back.

'I remember her. Lovely she was. You come here about my Davy too?' She looked hopeful.

'No, about my uncle Guy. You wouldn't remember him. You must only have been a toddler when he went off to the war.'

'She's trying to prove my Davy innocent.' Mary jabbed a dismissive thumb towards Georgia. 'She's taking her time about it. I shan't last much longer. Tell her to hurry up.'

'If you know he's innocent,' Jean shot back at her, 'why do you need to know what really happened?' Georgia sensed a weird communion between the two of them. Two strong characters meeting on some kind of common ground.

'It's unfinished business, ain't it?'

Georgia tiptoed out, to leave them alone as Mary's eyes closed, and after a few minutes Jean followed her. 'Georgia,' she began, as they walked back to the car, 'even if that skeleton is Guy's, that still wouldn't give Mary closure over Ada Proctor and Davy Todd, would it? It would only raise more questions. How and why did Guy get there and what happened then?'

'That becomes Marsh & Daughter's job, to find out how the two strands link. We think they do, but we need stepping stones, and that's awkward in this village at present. Ada's grave was vandalized recently.'

Jean looked aghast. 'A *grave*? Coincidence?'

'Far from it. Some people in Wickenham don't want the case examined. Mary's wishes count for nothing with them.'

Jean gave a nod. 'I don't like graves being desecrated. I'll tell your father he can fix up for me to give that blessed sample.'

'All in all, a good day's work.' Peter was mentally patting his back with both hands as Georgia and he reviewed the day in his beloved study after returning home. 'Well done,' he added belatedly, noting Georgia's steely eye. 'I

175

acknowledge that you were successful where I was not in persuading the lady to our point of view.'

'Did we do right though?'

'Of course we did. We always do.'

Georgia kicked off her shoes. 'I can't help feeling we're barking up a wrong tree, though. How is the Scraggs investigation going?'

'Nowhere fast, according to Mike. All the combatants were too busy with what they themselves were doing to notice what was happening elsewhere. The police must still be crawling over their budget for a mass DNA screen, so nothing's moving forward much. Oliver Todd blames the front-line Elgins, the Elgins first blamed the Todds, then had a go at the Bloomfields, now it's aliens from outer space who popped in with knives in their hands. Even your name's been mentioned,' he added casually.

'I was at home in bed!' Georgia was astounded.

'Any proof of that? Luke with you, was he?'

'I work alone, you know that. Except in Lille,' she conceded.

Peter grinned. 'The police aren't taking the accusation seriously.'

'Good.' She changed this uncomfortable subject. 'Mary's fading fast, and yet we're not an inch further forward in finding out the truth about Davy. It's as if Ada Proctor lived in another country, marching around in her Wickenham, while we footle around in ours.'

'Something,' Peter declared Micawber-style, 'will turn up.'

'Maybe it's supper if you play your cards right,' Georgia said sourly, going out to fix it. Yesterday's beef stew filled the bill nicely. She wondered if she could get away with pasta or frozen veg and decided she could. Or at least would try to. Next time she wouldn't so rashly tell Margaret not to bother about supper.

'How long will Jean's DNA sample take to process? I assume it won't be fast-tracked,' she asked, when she had served this sumptuous meal. The latter was eyed askance, when he saw the pasta, but Peter obviously realized discretion was the better part of valour this evening.

'Mike says the SIO has arranged for it to be taken next week, with a strong suggestion my blood will be next if it leads nowhere.'

When Georgia returned to her own home, she realized she still felt disgruntled, which was irrational in view of the step forward over Denehole Man. She'd banked on having something at least by year's end, and that was unlikely now. The living room, usually so inviting, tonight looked empty and cheerless. Damn, she said softly, could it be I'm missing Luke? This was an ominous sign. She tried to convince herself in vain that her depression was only over the Ada Proctor investigation going so slowly, and picked up a pile of Christmas cards still waiting to be written. Everywhere lights were going up, turkeys were being ordered, presents chosen and children getting excited. She was thirty-four, the biological clock was running faster now, and if ever she wanted kids of her own enjoying Christmas, steps would have to be taken. This was an even more ominous thought, so she turned her mind to wondering what sort of Christmas Ada would have had if she hadn't met her murderer that Hallowe'en night. It failed to produce anything.

Irritably she flung aside her list ten minutes later. She needed communication with the outside world, but Christmas cards were a longwinded path to it. Any messages on the answerphone? There were not. E-mails? She ploughed her way through, deleting spam, Christmas offers from supermarkets, bookshops and gift shops, but found not one single one that could be called a message from a real person. Would Ada have taken to e-mails? she wondered idly. She hadn't the slightest idea, and wasn't that some kind of admission of failure? They were off chasing wild geese about deneholes while Mary Elgin's life ebbed slowly away, tired at last of waiting. And yet, for the life of her, Georgia couldn't see her next step ahead. She needed a light to guide her through the field, just as Ada must have had her torch.

Since some sort of communication with the outside world suddenly seemed essential. She tried to ring Luke. He was out. Very well, she would spend the rest of the evening, such as it was, with Peter. As she padded back through the hallway to put her outdoor shoes on, her eye fell on the one method of communication she hadn't yet checked. She was so used to seeing flyers and bills she tended to forget nowadays that there could still be such things as real letters.

'Peter!' It was her turn to yell out as she closed his front door behind her, making him jump. He was deep in a book about facial reconstruction of skeletons. Guy Randolph in this house, living next door to Ada Proctor.

'I hear excitement in your voice,' he observed. 'A Lottery win?'

'In a way. So far as Ada's concerned anyway. And probably Denehole Man too. Maybe he'll get his gravestone yet.'

'Tell me. Waste not a single second.'

'I've had a letter from Rose Sadler's granddaughter, Meg Watson. Hardly surprisingly, Rose is dead, but her daughter Angela, Meg's mother, is still alive, although she remembers little about the Ada Proctor case. She had the impression, however, that Ada was Rose's friend, rather than her father's, but that might not be so of course.'

Peter made a face. 'And this passes for a breakthrough?'

'Patience, patience, Peter dear. Here it comes. Meg, the granddaughter, is a solicitor specializing in criminal cases, so always had her ears pricked up when her grandmother talked of having been ready to give evidence in the Ada Proctor case and not being called. What was the evidence? she asked. Her grandmother was vague at first, explaining said it wasn't very important, which was why she wasn't called. Ada had been in London that day and Rose Sadler met her as she walked home from the station at about six o'clock. Ada chattered on about her trip and asked Rose if she were going to the Hallowe'en dance that evening. Rose said no, she and John had offered to look after the Bloomfield children as well as their own, so that the Squire and his wife, and the maid, could all go to the dance. But when Rose went to the Manor to collect the children, the maid had told her it wasn't necessary, for Mr and Mrs Bloomfield had had an unexpected visitor, a Mr Guy Randolph.'

Chapter Eleven

'Three cheers for Ada,' Peter shouted.

'For who?' Georgia took up the well-worn response.

'For *Ada*,' Peter roared. 'I think this calls for a drink,' he suggested tentatively, and looked surprised as Georgia wholeheartedly agreed, and put the deed to the idea.

Three cheers for Ada, three cheers for Pooh. Very nearly Christmas and how often had her parents sat by the fire on December night with them when she and Rick were children, reading the Winnie-the-Pooh stories. She and Rick were allowed to burst in with the Pooh 'hum' songs at appropriate – and often inappropriate – places. Rick's specialty was 'Here's a mystery'. Nostalgia of course. How about all those evenings when Peter was working, or those when Elena was out organizing something or other? Yet there must have been some Pooh evenings for them to catch so painfully at her memory.

She lifted her glass to Peter and perhaps to Ada as well. 'It looks as if you were right about Denehole Man.'

'Why did you ever doubt me? And it brings Bête Noir Bloomfield back into the frame.'

'Hold on,' Georgia laughed. 'I know it's late at night, but isn't there a tiny flaw in that reasoning? Bête Noir Bloomfield was nowhere near born in 1929.'

'His ancestors then. All tarred with the same brush no doubt.'

'That's a fairly wide-sweeping statement,' she pointed out.

'Evening talk. I wouldn't put that to Mike.'

'Not a good idea.' An image of stolid Mike cheerily sitting here between them, knocking back even a small whisky while they indulged in fantasy, was a happy one.

'Of course,' Peter reminded her, 'we need to go steady on this. It's still only a theory.'

'Tonight we rejoice, tomorrow we slog on. Here's to Denehole Man.'

'Seriously, Georgia,' Peter began, holding his empty glass out expectantly, 'this disproves all that stuff about her series of lovers, and Luke is going to love it. Shall we indulge ourselves and consider it?'

He was right. It was time for one of their periodic ritual reconstructions during a case.

'Yes,' Georgia said decidedly. 'It was a dark and stormy night,' she began theatrically, then caught her father's eye. Although the deaths they were dealing with were seventy-odd years earlier, they should be no less real to them than that of Terence Scraggs. It was all too easy to fall into the trap of treating their cases as 'stories', something for the mind to puzzle out, rather than for imagination to picture, and humanity to grieve for. 'Ada had returned in a good mood from London that day,' she began again. 'She was well respected in Wickenham – except by scandalmongers—'

'The source for whose scandals we haven't yet marked down.'

' – and was looking forward to going out badger-hunting and nightingale listening with Davy the following night. As she left the train, she was glad she had put off their trip until the morrow, for she was tired after the day in London, and ought to spend the evening doing the household accounts and cooking her father supper, since their maid might have wanted to go to the dance. Once, with Guy and their usual crowd, she remembered, she had liked dancing herself, but that had been in the old days before the war that changed everything. She was quite happy with her present life, however. Her father needed her and she did a useful job in the surgery, etc.'

'Where had she been in London?' Peter interrupted.

'She'd been in London to go to a matinée,' Georgia conjectured. 'She went with a friend of hers from the war days when she was—'

'Hey,' Peter interrupted again, 'what did she do in the war?'

'Let's assume she had trained as a VAD, yes? She did some hospital work, maybe she even went to France, and all that training helped when she returned home at war's end—'

'So when the news came that Guy had died, why didn't she make use of that training and go away and nurse some-where other than Wickenham?'

Georgia frowned. 'Is a guess in order?'

'For tonight, yes.'

'She would have been twenty-six when the war ended. Perhaps she thought she had been away from Wickenham long enough, and liked living at home. Perhaps there was someone else there she was attracted to. Or perhaps she decided to work in a local hospital, to put her skills to work, Gravesend perhaps, somewhere she could get to easily by bus or train. Country doctors aren't rich, and cars were expensive luxuries then. Ada enjoyed her job, or at least she felt she was performing her duty. She probably met other men and had a social life, which is how the stories of other men crept in. She brought them home to meet her parents, like any respectable girl at that time.'

'Yes,' Peter said. 'I'm with you there. That's a real possi-bility.'

Encouraged, Georgia continued. 'But for poor Ada every-thing changed yet again. Before she could settle down in a new relationship, tragedy struck. After her mother died, her father needed someone to run the house and even more importantly to do the jobs in the surgery that Winifred Proctor had formerly performed. Back comes Ada, the dutiful daughter.'

'Unwillingly?'

Georgia considered this. 'Probably not. Daughters on the whole tended to do what was expected of them, and there would be perks in coming back.'

'Even if love passed her by?'

'Perhaps it already had. Perhaps she was only too glad to return to the cocoon of The Firs, if there had been another disappointing relationship.'

'All conjecture, of course,' Peter said. 'Ada could have lived at The Firs all the time, nursing her woes in losing Guy.'

'I don't see Ada as a "nursing her woes" type of woman. With so many men of her generation wiped out in the war, that happened to a lot of women. She was more likely to have assumed that life was over for her in the field of love. That's why there was all the excitement when Rose told her Guy was back. Rose only came to the village in the early twenties so she wouldn't have known what a bomb-shell she was tossing Ada.'

'Wouldn't she?' Peter queried. 'Girls in those days were just the same as now. They'd talk over their past boyfriends.'

'Perhaps not Ada. Ada was a practical sort of woman. She might have mentioned a fiancé killed in the war, but she wouldn't necessarily have gone into details; the Randolphs had left by 1921 so Rose wouldn't have known the Randolphs either, except perhaps as past history.'

'Humph,' remarked Peter. 'I'm more or less with you. So what happened after Ada left Rose that night?'

'She was even more glad that she hadn't arranged to go out with Davy Todd, though it would have been easy to call off the meeting since he was still here. She dashed into the garden still in her best London-going coat, gave Davy a few instructions for the morrow—'

'Why? She'd expect to be there.'

'In case he arrived early while she was in the surgery,' Georgia continued firmly, 'and then she ran back into the house to give full thought to the momentous news she'd just heard. Her father was in the surgery, so before she went to the dispensary to prepare the patients' medicines she flew to the telephone to confirm the news she'd been given.'

'She rang the Manor.'

'Yes.'

'Who answered the phone? The maid?'

'The odds are against it, or it should have come out in the evidence. It would have stuck in the maid's memory, and she might even have told Alice about it in later years. The fact she didn't isn't proof it didn't happen, of course. Anyway, the maid was going to the dance, the Bloomfield children would be in bed, she had probably put together a quick supper for Matthew and Isabel She-Wolf and Guy, and then been free to get ready for the dance. So it would have been Matthew or Isabel who took the call, or even Guy himself, though that would be unlikely.'

'So why didn't Matthew or Isabel give evidence to that effect?'

'Perhaps they did. It might have been in the statements collected at the time, but it wouldn't seem relevant to Ada's death from the police point of view, because the field by the wood where she was thought to have been killed was nothing to do with the Manor.'

'But didn't you say that that footpath through Crown Lea leads on through the woods past the denehole and past Wickenham Manor?'

'Yes. It runs to its rear, and then on to Wickenham Forstal.'

'A short cut to the Manor, in other words, if you don't want to go all the way through the village and up the drive.'

'Yes, but—'

'For a lady who didn't want to waste time.'

'Hang on a minute,' Georgia objected. 'She'd wasted over three hours by the time she set out.'

'Perhaps that was the time she'd been asked to come.'

'Odd time to choose. The evening would nearly be over.'

'True. Perhaps Guy Randolph, deserter, was anxious not to be seen.'

'He didn't have to be; he was in the Manor.'

'But where was he spending the night? And don't say in the denehole.'

'I wasn't going to. Perhaps he was planning to walk back to the station at that time, and suggested she accompany him.'

'Through fields in the winter darkness? Very lover-like. Anyway, the Manor would have cars at its disposal. Go on, Georgia, finish the story.'

'For some reason as yet unknown—'

'Shame!' Peter interrupted.

'As yet unknown,' she repeated with dignity, 'Ada met Guy somewhere along that footpath, or went to the Manor first and was walking back home. Eleven o'clock, rightly or wrongly, seems to have been taken as the deadline for when she died. It was probably wrong, but we have to go with it. So what was Ada doing for up to an hour between the time that Davy saw her through the window and the time of her death? We can only presume she was with Guy Randolph, either at the Manor or more likely in the woods, talking. Was it raining that night?'

'Don't know, but why would Guy kill her and then leap in the denehole?'

'Accident.'

'You can do better than that.'

'All right.' Georgia did her best. 'Let's say she does meet Guy, and is horrified – yes, that's it – when he confesses he was a deserter and even more—'

'When she discovers he is married with a family.'

'The upright respectable Ada is mortified and threatens . . .'

'Yes?' Peter prompted her, as she paused to think this out.

'. . . to tell his family, with whom she is still in touch, that he's still alive, where he lives and what he is.'

'Problem,' Peter immediately broke in. 'That's exactly why he came to Wickenham in the first place – to find his family.'

'True.' Then triumph. 'He wouldn't have told the Major about being a deserter. He'd say he'd had a loss of memory and so on.'

'Nope. Don't accept it. Why tell Ada the truth in that case?'

'Perhaps she guessed, knowing her Guy.'

'Were deserters still liable to court martial in 1929?'

'Don't know, but he might have thought so. Let's assume their row is about his desertion, and the fact he's married. Her threat to tell the Randolph family does not suit Guy's book at all. Ada is no longer the sweet forgiving lass she once was; she is a woman scorned. He curses the fact that she has discovered he was here. Then it occurs to him that no one knows he's meeting her, and all he has to do is silence her, and skip back to France.'

'How's that go?' Peter asked cynically.

'Well, it's probably true. He told Ada not to spread the word about his return, so he wouldn't expect her to tell anyone about their meeting. The name would mean nothing to the maid or to Rose Sadler, so only the Bloomfields would have recognized him. He had gone straight to the Manor from the train station.'

'But, darling daughter, he wouldn't have. Remember? He didn't know the family had moved.'

'The stationmaster could have told him,' Georgia replied mutinously. '"Well, well, look who it isn't. Master Guy returned from the war. Pity about the old folks selling up." "What?" Shock, horror. He'd have to go to the Manor to find out where they'd gone.'

'What about his dear little former girlfriend, Ada?'

Georgia thought rapidly. 'He's not ready to face her. In fact he wouldn't have faced her at all if it hadn't been for her finding out and ringing the Manor, and then he took care to ensure no one saw her with him. He didn't want to be seen, he's a deserter and meant to be dead.'

'I don't buy the stationmaster then. Guy would have leapt over a fence to avoid being recognized.'

'Accepted,' she agreed grudgingly. 'So he walks from the station to Hazelwood House and is told by the new occupiers that the Randolphs had left. He's a stranger to them, of course. He then takes the quickest way over the fields to the Manor, avoiding The Firs, to find out what's happened to his mum, dad and sister.'

'I am with you, daughter mine. So what does he do after he's realized that Ada is not taking his story at all well?'

'He strangles her to prevent her talking.'

'Yes. What then?'

'He realizes he's been a fool. He should just have rushed for the train and got back to France as quickly as possible. Instead, he's left with a dead body. He drags it into the field so it's not so obvious to the Bloomfields, who know about his visit, what has happened, then goes back to remove all traces and stumbles into the denehole by mistake.'

'Well done,' Peter said in genuine admiration. 'A few thin patches in it, such as being back with accident again, but feasible. However, let us assume for the moment that Randolph's death in the denehole was *not* an accident. It is after all unlikely, since you told me the denehole is ten yards from the path, and he would presumably have Ada's torch if not one of his own. There wasn't one in the denehole unless it hasn't been found yet.'

'Damn torches.'

'Which would suggest Guy was pushed or killed himself? Or are we back to a maniac, who killed both of them, or to some other lover – John Sadler creeping away from the dance.'

Georgia's memory suddenly stirred. It must be the whisky, she thought gratefully. 'Jean Atwater told us that Matthew Bloomfield fancied Ada – do you suppose *he* could have been the other lover?'

Peter grew interested. 'It might explain where the She-Wolf got her teeth. Okay, so produce a new story. And bear in mind you found no pathology report to help us support it either way.'

'It was scorned love,' Georgia decided. 'Ada turned Matthew down after the war when she was still mourning Guy, so Matthew stomped off and married the She-Wolf. He found out he'd made a big mistake, and went on silently lusting after Ada. Or maybe not so silently. Then to crown his unhappiness further, back comes Guy Randolph from the dead, just as much of a dislikable rogue as he always was. Hey, he says, Ada still around? Maybe I'll look her up. Matthew loses all control. Ada has heard the news, and rings the Manor. Matthew answers. Anguish, anguish, as he passes the phone to Guy and hears him make this appointment to meet her. He follows Guy and murders him to stop him getting Ada.'

'*Getting?*' Peter picked up. 'In what sense? Rape? Seduction? In October? And then Matthew goes and strangles Ada? What for?'

'Perhaps she'd seen him kill Guy.'

'I'm getting tired of this word "perhaps", and even more of "maybe",' Peter complained. 'Evidence comes next. Sorry, but nothing convinces me, though I admit we're a lot further along the road. We can agree up to the point where Ada sets off along the path to the Manor. After that, just like Ada, we're in the dark. Another whisky, if you please.'

Georgia trod every step from Crown Lea to Wickenham Manor at least twenty times during the night. She'd get to the point where Ada could have stopped, perhaps shining her torch on the path ahead. And whom did she see? Just as she seemed on the point of finding out, she would find herself back at the beginning of the footpath. She was relieved to get up and find that all that faced her downstairs was the dirty casserole dish from last night. That she could cope with, and a vigorous scrub eradicated the last traces of beef stew, even the lurking burnt gravy on the rim.

She drew back the curtains in her living room to see a

familiar unmarked police car outside Peter's door. What on earth was Mike doing here at eight thirty? Margaret came at eight, so Peter would scarcely be up. Uneasily, she decided to investigate, as soon as she had swallowed a bowlful of cereal and a mug of tea. She relaxed when she found Mike and Peter both at breakfast, Mike looking thoroughly at home, and Margaret looking after them both.

'Tea, Georgia?' Mike offered her.

'Just had some, thanks. So is this official or are you just dropping by?'

'Official,' he replied, to her surprise. 'The Darenth Super himself is now deeply hooked on the Randolphs. He wants all your input.'

Georgia was highly amused. This was unusual. Mostly the KCC did their best to keep him at arm's length. Nothing personal, they assured him, but they could cope without him.

'Good timing,' she observed. 'I'm sure Peter's told you our triumph over getting Guy Randolph's niece to have a buccal swab taken.'

'At length,' Mike agreed gloomily. 'But we're starting with Scraggs. Actually you kicked this off, Georgia,' he continued. 'Remember you asked me to suggest another check on his possessions for that war stuff the French folk talked about?'

'I do.' She had almost forgotten, in fact, since it seemed a forlorn hope that François had indeed walked off with anything interesting after the war, and that he would have passed it on to his grandson. In theory it sounded fine, but in practice it seemed a long shot.

'The Buckinghamshire police have reported back. Scraggs's parents had cleared the flat and taken his stuff back home, but were happy for the police to search the lot. No medals, your French chums were wrong there, but there were other little gems such as—'

'A picture of Ada?' she asked hopefully.

'Much better. An identity tag.'

Peter whooped with pleasure. 'The kind issued to soldiers in the war? They were usually in two halves, and both halves had basic info about you, number, name, etc. You took it with you into battle, and if you were killed one half stayed with you, the other went back to officially record the death.'

'*Right!*' Mike confirmed. 'This one was metal and its owner—'

'Guy Randolph,' crowed Peter. 'Hardly surprising, but it does confirm Georgia's story about the French connection. So, if the Frogs are right, Guy left the tag behind when he came a-seeking his fortune, presumably because it was unnecessary as his family would recognize him and he planned to go back to France anyway.'

'I suppose so.' It seemed odd to Georgia though. 'True, assuming Guy is Denehole Man, he would have come here to sort out whether he could lay his paws on any money from the family estate. His father must have been getting on, and Guy would want to get his oar in and establish his claim. Even though Hazelwood had been sold, Guy would have assumed that his parents had bought some other substantial property. Having tracked them down, he'd return to the lovely Rosanne to share his good fortune. Only he didn't, and François found the tag later.'

'Good,' Mike said without irony. 'Only what the Super is more interested in is Scraggs, with a view to his believing the skeleton to be Guy Randolph too, so I'm half back on the case to officially liaise with you.'

'Rather late,' Peter pointed out smugly. 'We've been talking about Denehole Man and Randolph's involvement all along.'

'But you haven't given me proof. The Super has,' Mike said incontrovertibly. 'Also he employs me. Right? Sometimes I think you're under the impression you do.'

'What more's happening over Terence Scraggs's case then?' Peter asked hastily.

'Remember those drawings we looked at, Georgia?' Mike

turned to her. 'I told the Super about the sketch of Wickenham Manor. Didn't you tell me Scraggs had been to see Bloomfield about a commission?'

'Do you think,' Peter broke in straight-faced, 'that Scraggs was on to the fact that Denehole Man was murdered by a Bloomfield?'

Not surprisingly Mike looked blank. 'What the hell are you on about now, Peter?'

Georgia explained, but Mike shook his head. 'Don't go with that. You're telling me that old Squire Matthew murdered Guy Randolph, if that's who it was, because he was casting an eye over Ada again. Nah. And if you're thinking Trevor Bloomfield then bumped off Scraggs to protect the family name, no again. The Bloomfields are out of it, anyway.'

'Out of what?' Georgia asked.

'Scraggs's murder. The SIO has a split-second timetable sorted out now. They reckon it all happened in a eight-minute period between 10.46 p.m. and the arrival of the police at 10.54. The team's compiled an analysis with evidence from Elgins, Todds and Bloomfields. It's like a blooming labyrinth. Want to see it?'

'I do. I also want a copy of it, right? Run me off one, will you, Mike? The copier's over there.'

'Certainly, sir,' Mike agreed sourly.

'*And* of that video?'

A pause. 'I'll try for you.'

'Good.' Peter held out his hand for the copy analysis and read it aloud for Georgia. '10.46: arrival of Todds at the Bloomfield house. Simultaneously the Bloomfield door opens and the three of them come out, father flanked by sons. They reach the Todd front line, with Scraggs far left, close into a huddle at 10.46 plus twenty, and the Elgins are sighted at 10.47; at plus ten the Elgin front line has reached the Todd/Bloomfield huddle. Scraggs by now has his back to the Elgins, wedged between the elder Bloomfield Junior, and Oliver Todd. The first lot of Elgins divides the group, with Bloomfield Senior and the younger Junior being thrust back to the outer flank, and their places filled by Todds surging forward from the rear. The other side of the group pushes Scraggs back towards the bushes, together with Bloomfield elder Junior, Oliver Todd and Lucy Todd – who scarpers. The right (from the Elgin viewpoint) flank of the Elgins is wheeling forward and round on them.

'At that point the two Bloomfields nearest the house turn and run for it, that's Trevor and Crispin. That's vouchsafed for by plenty of both Todds and Elgins, and by 10.50 the battle is in full progress. At that point, according to the general consensus, Scraggs still had his placard, which he was waving and shouting vigorously. At 10.51 (give or take a few seconds) the placard was whisked from his hands by Bloomfield Junior the Elder with the help of young Max White, who'd charged in to tackle Oliver or Scraggs, whichever came first, and the placard was thrown down on the ground. White picks up placard to wallop Mark Todd, Oliver's son, who's busy attacking White's brother Nigel. So far everyone's agreed.

'Then it gets murkier. Bloomfield Junior the Elder received a blow in the face from George Elgin, and promptly retreated from the fray. George White agrees that. At that point, front-line Elgins and Todds tentatively confirm Scraggs was still there, doing his best to ward off blows from another young Elgin, Paul White, grandson of Tom. At roughly 10.52 Paul was detached by a Todd, whose supporters closed round in front of Scraggs as the Elgins moved in to rescue their own – and presumably to duff Scraggs up some more. That was the last anyone remembers seeing Scraggs, until his body was found shortly after 10.54 by the police as the area began to clear.'

'So where does that leave you? Still sorting through Elgins and Todds?'

'The Super's going for the mass screen. Another reason I'm still with the Darenth Area. It's possible the hair we found under Scraggs's fingernail was sticking to one of those balaclavas in the Elgin gang, while Scraggs was defending himself against a punch or the knife. There's a trace of fibre too. Or perhaps he clutched at it as he went down.'

Georgia was silent for a moment, reliving the scene all too vividly, then quickly brought her thoughts back to what Mike had been saying.

She liked Mike's 'we found'. The idea of his large hands poring with tweezers and microscope in a forensic lab was a pleasant one. When the lab produced nothing, it was always 'them', of course, not 'we'. But then that was life.

The Medway was a peaceful sort of river, the kind that Ratty and Mole would like. *The Wind in the Willows* could have been written here. Even though it was wise enough to stay hidden in December, there was a powerful sense of animal and bird life thriving here. Distance was what she needed, Georgia had decided this Sunday, and Luke represented distance, as well as pleasure. Christmas was only eleven days away now, and the delicate subject of whether he spent it with them, or with his own parents or his newly married son, had either to be tackled or avoided through tacit understanding. A Sunday walk was just the answer. Georgia had plunged into ordering her turkey at the local butcher's a week ago, but if she and Peter spent Christmas with Luke she could tuck her turkey under her arm, à la Bob Crachit, and take it with her. Only Bob's was a goose, if she remembered her *Christmas Carol* correctly.

'God bless us, every one,' she observed to Luke. 'Especially those who deal with Peter every day.' At the moment her father was exceptionally morose. No, he would not be interested in going to Wickenham Manor or talking to the Bloomfields; no, he would not be interested in studying Guy Randolph's army record. He deserted from it, and that was all they needed to know, apart of course from the results of Jean's DNA. It hadn't been fast-tracked, so with the usual delay plus Christmas intervening, they wouldn't be hearing the result until the New Year. Until then, everything seemed to be on hold, leaving them with the usual routine of writing up notes, checking facts, and recording information received post-publication of their former books. Without yet knowing the basic thesis behind their Wickenham book, there was little point in even planning its structure.

'And especially bless you, my darling.' Luke put his arm round her as they fought the wind along the river bank.

Georgia laughed. 'And all publishers. How are sales going?' She realized that she was privileged that he had taken time off at the busiest time of his year, so far as sales were concerned. Weekend or not, work came first in the Christmas rush.

'Slacking off now that Christmas is nearly with us. The distributors are pleased. I've got the November reports in, and they're pretty good. Up on last year.'

'Must be *The Forest Gate Murder*,' Georgia said practically.

'Of course. Now you've sent in the 1940s murder script, I should be hounding you for the next one. I need a book a year.'

'Pretty soon we'll be committing the murders to keep up with your schedule.'

'How is dear Ada – and please, please don't tell me every single detail. I heard them all from Peter last night.'

'Stuck in a theory, but a tenable one. Everything's on hold at the moment. The trouble with theories is that invariably some details don't fit. It would be nice to think that the Randolphs, Proctors and Scraggses are all tied up together, but the Bloomfields are in the frame though they've been ruled out for the Scraggs murder. Moreover there's precious little, save hearsay, that Matthew was keen on Ada at one time, to link them with Ada Proctor's murder, even though we surmise she might have been on her way to the Manor when she died.'

'At least that's a wobble forward,' he agreed, ducking under a branch and holding it back for her.

'And the return of the Prodigal Son is still a favourite theory, with the probability that he wobbled into the dene-hole by mistake.'

'Don't like that,' he declared roundly. 'Not good for sales. This is a blame culture we live in. Can't you find someone to fix the murder on?'

She aimed a fist at him and he ducked.

'Seriously, how about this She-Wolf of Wickenham?' he asked. 'She sounds a formidable character. Suppose she strangled Ada out of jealousy and when Guy saw what she had done, she pushed him down the denehole?'

'How about reasons? We don't know anything about this lady save the recording we heard and her reputation as a formidable character. Flimsy evidence to fix two murders on her. Oh, and apparently she fancied the vicar too. Does that make her guilty?'

'The vicar who was rumoured to have been bumped off?'

'Yes. Do you think she did it? Fell for him and when, being a properly brought-up vicar, he rejected her advances, she killed him?'

'What was her husband Matthew like? A wimp?'

'From the number of times the doctor visited him – my only evidence – he wasn't exactly macho, and he died quite young.'

'Maybe she bumped him off too. When did the vicar die?'

'Goodness knows, but Matthew died in 1943.'

'Natural causes?'

'Don't know. Haven't looked into it.'

'Then why not, dearest Georgia, fill in your time while you're waiting for this DNA result, by doing some checking into these potentially interesting matters?'

'I am filling in my time, as you put it, by sorting out Christmas, in the traditional womanly fashion.'

'Ah. Could that Christmas include me? I'm seeing my parents on Boxing Day, but they'd love to see you and Peter if you want to join us, and Mark's going away to his in-laws in Yorkshire. So on Christmas Day . . .'

'I'd love you to come to us.' Christmas mysteriously assumed the magical quality that had been missing hitherto.

'One condition: not one word about Ada Proctor, Randolphs or Bloomfields. Understood?'

'Gratefully.'

Georgia drove home the next morning much restored, and even stopped to hurl herself into the supermarket to get some shopping en route. Presents, cards, crackers, food supplies, all had suddenly taken on a pleasantly traditional aura, and even the muzak carols blaring out had an appeal about them. She bought a small Christmas tree in the forecourt, pushed it happily into the boot of the car, and contemplated decorating it. Somewhere were the old decorations they'd used in her childhood; it would be fun to dig them out of her father's loft and put them up. They'd languished up there for some years after her mother left, as they were too painful a reminder of the absent two members of the family. Now, she felt she could even face the tin soldier that had been Rick's favourite, though that might be risking too much for Peter. Christmas was a difficult time, and Luke's presence would be a wonderful boost. Invite the neighbours in for a drink? Christmas morning church service? She was still filled with these pleasant thoughts as she unpacked the car, brought her newly acquired booty into the house, stood the Christmas tree outside in the rear garden for a few days, and went in to see her father to give him the good news about Luke.

One look at Peter's face and all thought of giving good news vanished. He was looking as dejected as she had ever seen him, huddled into himself.

'Dad, what's wrong?' She hurried to him. 'Are you ill?'

He shook his head impatiently. 'Bad news, that's all. I've had the DNA result. It was rushed through because Darenth

196

changed its mind and upgraded it to fast track two days ago. Whoever that poor skeleton in the mortuary was, it wasn't Guy Randolph.'

Chapter Twelve

T he evening stretched out dismally before them, and dinner had passed almost in silence.

'Shall we leave it until tomorrow?' Georgia suggested at last. 'The wine won't have done my thinking any good.'

'Let's have a go now, otherwise I'll be fuming all night,' Peter said practically.

She saw his point, so they returned to his study area after she had cleared away the dishes. Other parts of the house were in theory sacrosanct so far as work talk was concerned. Especially from unpleasant discussions such as this. Surrounded by Peter's books, computers and office clutter, she hoped her brain might be more willing to cope with this setback – though that word was understating the case.

Georgia blamed herself for getting carried away with the near certainty that the skeleton was Guy's. She could almost hear their friends in forensic science snorting with laughter, and reminding them there'd always be the possibility that the time dating for the skeleton had been tampered with. But that had seemed so unlikely in this case that it hadn't been worth taking seriously. Working from evidence up to a thesis was all very well in principle, but this skeleton had produced the French watch and coins, which surely could not have been popped in later and had been encouraging hints that their owner had come from France. In 1929 there couldn't have been many French tourists interested enough in Wickenham to come here. Or, looking at it another way, many casual workers who'd been to France or who made a specialty of examining deneholes. Fate had served Marsh & Daughter badly.

'If it wasn't Guy Randolph, who was it?' she began, and added quickly, 'Don't tell me it was a tramp.'

'It *was* a tramp,' Peter muttered viciously. 'Otherwise he'd have been on the missing persons' list in the Wickenham area.'

'And this tramp killed Ada?'

'No evidence whatsoever.' Peter remained deep in gloom. 'We can't tie the skeleton down to a precise time. We're back exactly where we started. We're agreed there seems or seemed to be unfinished business in Wickenham, and we assumed that concerned Ada Proctor and/or Davy Todd. We lost sight of the other possibility that the skeleton or some other problem, such as the feud, was the unfinished business, and that there *was* no unfinished business over Ada Proctor.'

'What does your sixth sense say about that?'

'I have to admit, Georgia, that my sixth sense is somewhat buried at the moment. It's difficult to go backwards and see things as we did at first.'

'I'm not so sure. We decided it was Mary Elgin who was causing those fingerprints and Mary Elgin is very definitely related to the Ada Proctor case. And,' Georgia reminded him, 'we can't let her down now. We have to go on prodding. She was very definite that Davy was with her, we know Ada made a phone call that night and informed the maid at The Firs that she was going out to meet someone, and we're sure she would not have dressed up in her best clothes for a badger hunt or even a dalliance with Davy Todd. No.' Georgia frowned. 'I still feel – is that allowed?'

'Tonight anything's allowed.'

'– that Guy Randolph was around that night. We've evidence of that too. He went to the Manor.'

'Slender evidence not tested in court, and based on hearsay.'

'True, but independent evidence it remains.'

'So the only tenable theory, for which as yet no evidence exists, is yours, that Guy Randolph murdered Ada to stop her talking, and then scarpered. Are we happy with this? I, for one, am not. Why didn't he murder the maid at the Manor too, to stop her gabbling to Rose Sadler and the like?'

'I don't know,' Georgia said crossly. 'What we'll have to do – ' the prospect stretched bleakly before her – 'is get on with the routine leads and see if anything pops up from that. Guy's war record, for instance. It might seem irrelevant, but you never know. We can check that if it still exists, and I can go to Kew. I can reread the local papers for 1929 and see if anything leaps out at me now we know a lot more. I can – oh hell.' She slumped mentally and physically in her chair. 'Perhaps tomorrow will look brighter.'

'It won't,' Peter observed. 'One of us has to ring Jean and give her the bad news.'

Georgia's heart sank even further. That was the trouble with cases that went wrong. Mud got stirred up for which they were responsible, and in their own setbacks it was all too easy to forget that other human beings had become involved. Someone had to smooth down the mud again. 'Do you want me to do it?'

'Good of you, but I was responsible for this daft theory about Guy Randolph. I sold it to you, so I should carry the can.'

'Shall we do the deed now?' she asked. 'It's only nine o clock, and it would get it over with.'

'Hold my hand, daughter dear, let's do it.'

From what Georgia could hear of Jean's voice at the other end of the line she was taking it rather well. Peter didn't overdo the apologies, nor did he underdo them. He spoke for some time explaining the pros and cons and what the situation was now, and there was no sign that Jean was trying to interrupt him.

At last she did, however, and what she said obviously flummoxed Peter. 'We'll be working on that, Jean,' he told her, sounding very confident, but Georgia knew his voice well enough to realize he'd been thrown off course. After assurances that they would keep in touch, and that the fact that the skeleton wasn't Guy's didn't mean he wouldn't have a role in the story (Peter tactfully didn't mention it might be that of murderer), he put the phone down. Then to her annoyance he began to laugh.

'What,' she asked crossly, 'is so funny?'

'Sometimes it takes an outsider to ask the obvious.'

'I rely on Luke for that.'

'Jean asked it. She said: "If it wasn't Guy in that dene-hole, but he was in Wickenham that day, what happened to him?" If he scarpered, Georgia, where did he scarper to?'

So much for getting work problems out of the way before bedtime. Now she would be dreaming all night about Guy Randolph. Georgia had mentally kicked herself hard several times for not following through her theory about his strangling Ada. In the knowledge (they had to assume) that Guy had been at the Manor that night, she had been so busy casting him in the role of Ada's killer that they had overlooked what happened next, apart from his 'scarpering'. If he'd killed Ada, she reasoned (and the coincidence of his presence there that day was an unlikely one otherwise), he had done it for the purpose of financial self-protection, and disappearance would put paid to that. He had had every intention of hunting down his family, so why hadn't he turned up at the new home? Answer, she supposed: the news would be out from the Bloomfields that he had been around, once Ada's body was discovered, and he couldn't have banked on the fact that a convenient scapegoat in the form of Davy Todd would appear.

Okay, he couldn't go to find his family right away, but there was no reason he couldn't skip back to France, and slip back into obscurity. He need not even have returned to Rosanne; he might just have temporarily vanished into the underworld of Europe. He would in due course have realized that the main players in the drama were dead and that he wasn't being hunted in connection with the Proctor case. So why was there never a word about Guy Randolph again? Possibly if he too were dead. He certainly would be by now.

She had been right, she thought confusedly as the night wore on, they needed to know more about Guy's background. Peter would be checking the National Archives/PRO site catalogue on line, and then – if the results were good – she would go to Kew. They needed this research for the book anyway, regardless of whether Guy proved to be Ada's killer or not. *Proved* to be? That was an inaccuracy by today's standards. Firstly, both were dead, which meant an official clearance was not possible since there'd been no trial. Secondly, only DNA could now unofficially prove guilt, and she recalled one recent rapist/murderer whose DNA profile matched that on the clothing of a victim nearly thirty years earlier. But there would be no chance of Ada's outer clothing or belongings still being around, so only an exhumation could possibly provide a DNA sample. And the chances of the police paying for that now were zilch. Marsh & Daughter's names were mud with the Darenth police.

Georgia got up early the next morning, suspecting that Peter would already be at his computer, pushing ahead with the job. Margaret regularly saw him out of bed and dressed at eight o'clock and officially he was supposed to have breakfast before he began work. If he protested loudly enough, however, she agreed to lose the battle once in a while, and he was permitted to go straight to the computer and return to breakfast in due course. Today was one of those days.

'Are we presuming our Guy was an officer?' he hurled over his shoulder to her, as she came in, bleary-eyed from disturbed sleep.

She did her best to concentrate. 'I'd say it was a near

certainty with a major for a father. He'd have been at public school and university, all set to follow Dad's path – in Dad's view at least. Then came the war, and every man expected to do his duty and volunteer; you bet he was an officer. And he must have done pretty well to survive three years.'

'Oh yeah? Survive how though? Desert? Dodge?'

'We can't prejudge. He might have been a brilliant leader of men before his nerve went.'

'Convince me.'

'I only said might have. So how are you doing?'

'Pretty well. Not all the PRO records survived the bombing in 1940, as you know, but officers' records are more complete than other ranks. There's a small bunch of Randolphs including a Lieutenant T.G. who was discharged in 1920. Not our chap, obviously. But there is a G.H. That's the one to go for. In file WO339. None of the others fit. I've written down the reference number for you. At the very least you'll get regiment and ID number.'

'I'm on my way.'

In fact it was the following day, Wednesday, that Georgia took the train and tube to Kew. Kew had happy connotations for her. She had loved Kew Gardens for many years, from the Chinese pagoda that had fascinated her as a child, to the steamy conservatories of tropical plants that conjured up images of a wider world than Britain more vividly than television, and the historic houses that spelt England. And then there were the gardens themselves, so large that peace and calm could be discovered in some corner at any time of the year. By connotation the PRO even under its new name of National Archives took on something of the same symbolism, plus the optimistic impression that if one burrowed deep enough truth could be distilled from all those facts.

An illusion, of course. Truth could by its nature elude even the most diligent researcher. The best stab one could make at it, she and Peter agreed, was to establish all the evidence possible and make a judgement. But then wasn't that what the courts were for? Yet, there too, truth could slip quietly through the window back to the Almighty, whose province it was.

This morning the PRO yielded up its treasure relatively easily, with no false starts of byways to divert her. Unlike the day she had come here to check the Ada Proctor records, this time the information was readily before her. Guy Henry Randolph had entered the First World War in 1914 as a second lieutenant, joining the Royal West Kent Regiment, and went missing on 26 October 1917 during the Third Battle of Ypres, by which time he was a full lieutenant with the 1st Battalion. Of course he was with a Kentish Regiment, she thought. The Buffs would have been a more natural choice but perhaps his father had been in the West Kents. That would figure, even if a progression over three years of only Second Lieutenant to Lieutenant did not suggest he was following in his father's more prestigious footsteps. Her next port of call was to the London Library, where again fate obliged her in the form of a weighty tome of regimental history, which she took into the reading room to study.

The Third Battle of Ypres, with the military front line bulging out in a salient round the town, had begun at the end of July 1917 over land already reduced to mud.

In October, the 1st Battalion of the Royal West Kents had been – oh yes, this fitted with Guy's story as they knew it so far – in a back area and it returned on the 24th to the front line near the village of Gheluvelt on the road from Ypres to Menin. Its next objective was not Gheluvelt itself, but to its north, and the village was the responsibility of Seventh Division. But there was a major problem for the West Kents.

Three weeks earlier the battalion had been fighting over this same ground and established a line that was not far behind the one they now held. In order to get a satisfactory preliminary barrage the battalion had to retreat to the earlier line, and the Germans, noting this, quickly nipped in and occupied the other one. This meant the battalion had to fight for it all over again, and this burden fell on two companies, who won it back at great cost.

By the time they reached it, they were exposed on their right and rear to the enemy. The division taking the village had been counterattacked and the survivors retreated to the old line; this left the two West Kent companies open to the enemy as they tried to push their advance forward to their new objective. Nearly all died since they were now too far from the line to be rescued by stretcher-bearers, and in any case mud was the chief enemy that day. It prevented the men from moving, it got into their guns and stopped communications. There was no ground won, and over two hundred were killed or missing from the battalion.

Georgia could not be sure which company Guy Randolph had been in, but it seemed likely that it was in one of the two that had been all but wiped out. They had been on their own, men disappeared for ever in the mud, and with so few landmarks left on land that had been bitterly fought over for three years, the survivors must have been disorientated. Guy Randolph probably didn't even know which direction he was walking in. From the map he might have been walking north-west to Polygon Wood or north to Polderhoek Château, or west to Glencorse Wood, but how could he have known? And how could she know whether at first he intended to be a deserter or whether he thought he was rejoining his regiment?

It was a chilling story no matter whether Guy was villain or hero. It was only a few months since men had been shot for desertion at Ypres. The news might not have been officially released then, but rumours spread and the purpose of the executions had been to deter others. But desertion could mean merely disorientation, followed by succumbing to temptation, overwhelmed with fatigue, fear and horror. On the other hand there would always be those who might consciously take the chance to escape and sweet-talk themselves into a new life.

So where did that leave them? Georgia returned home, feeling that one more piece had been fitted into their puzzle, but not one that helped Davy Todd. She had established where Guy had been and that the story he told the Berthès family was therefore probably true, especially as his identity number checked with the one Mike had given them. Nevertheless, this background was only an interesting sideline to Ada's story, unless they opted for the theory of Guy the unproven killer, and this brought Georgia back to what had happened to him. There would be no one alive now to bring forth evidence on whether he had murdered her, and then taken a train towards Chatham and Dover; no one to tell them they had picked up a hitchhiker that night, or had given casual labour to anyone. Moreover that watch and coin still tantalized. Christmas was only eight days away now, and Georgia had to force herself to concentrate at least a small part of her mind on the remaining essential preparations. At least, she consoled herself, they were an achievable goal.

'How long do we give it before we decide to write the story as we see it?' Peter asked her next morning, taking the practical approach for once. One glance was enough to tell her that after she had reported her discoveries last night, he had spent the evening with World War I books and maps, poring over pictures of Gheluvelt and the route Guy might have taken – they were still lying around. It was obvious he was still trying to salvage a tenable Guy Randolph theory. So was she, come to that.

'We have to check first if Luke reckons the book is still worth it, Peter. He might think a half-baked solution isn't good enough. Our story's all ends and no neat bows, which doesn't make for satisfactory reading. I know there are always question marks in our books, but here there are more questions than hard facts, which is getting distinctly dodgy.'

'It's also true to life.'

'Luke won't see it that way.'

'I suppose I agree.' Peter cast a glance at the file copies of their earlier books. 'Did we feel this way about any of our other cases?'

'I suppose we might have done.' One tended to forget too easily and the torments of research became lost in memory after publication. 'Remember how we couldn't tie up the blood groups in the Cornish case?'

'I do.'

'We could begin a new case,' Georgia said hopefully. 'Then perhaps inspiration will come out of the blue on this one.'

Peter cast her a scathing glance. 'Nothing comes by inspiration, only by hard work and a bit of luck.'

'Then we'll have to hope luck strolls along.'

'We had our dose – or so we thought – in Rose Sadler's granddaughter.'

'There could be some more.'

'Let's give it till the New Year. Then reconsider.'

'Agreed.' Nothing would happen, but it would be a relief to postpone the decision. Relief didn't last long, however, as the phone rang, and Peter picked up the receiver.

'What's new, Mike?'

Apparently quite a bit from Peter's attentive silence. He even gave Georgia a thumbs up.

At last he put the phone down. 'The good news is that the village is wholeheartedly co-operating in volunteering DNA samples.'

'And the bad?' Georgia asked resignedly.

'No matches so far with the famous alien hair DNA, including from those known to be anywhere near him, to the Bloomfields, Todds and Elgins.'

'Aaaaarrgh!'

'Very expressive. They're not finished yet, of course. Far from it.'

'But suppose Scraggs's killer was an outsider.'

'On the reasonable assumption any outsiders would be

207

professional protestors they're checking against the National DNA Database for a matching profile.'

'That could button it up,' Georgia said hopefully.

'With our luck I wouldn't count on it.'

'I presume Darenth Area told Mike the bad news about the skeleton.'

'Yes. He was not amused, but fortunately it appears that Lockhart at least is not so deterred as we feared. To him, Scraggs was a Randolph, and therefore probably had some mission in the village which wasn't fighting protests or painting pretty pictures. The skeleton was only one angle.'

'I'll give Mike a ring and tell him that the disk checked out with the PRO records.'

'And then what, Georgia?'

'I'll cook some mince pies.'

'Your mother was good at them.'

'Yes, I remember.' A silence, then she added, desperate to break it, 'I don't suppose she gets much chance to do it in France. They think our mincemeat and heavy puddings are a big joke.'

Peter laughed to her relief. 'They're welcome to confit of duck and foie gras. I'd rather have turkey and Christmas pud, wouldn't you?'

'Much,' Georgia agreed fervently. She caught his eye, and looked away. Times past were past. She couldn't bring Elena back – Peter wouldn't want her – but the hurt could never quite be put to rest. 'Plus a good bottle of Kentish white?'

'Burgundy,' roared Peter. 'English wine is a contradiction in terms.'

'Nonsense, you fuddy duddy. Get up to date. Try some.'

'Never.'

'Stick in a mud. Afraid to, eh?' Back on safe ground. Home and dry – for the moment. 'To answer your question properly,' she continued, 'my next job is to reread all about Ada Proctor in the local papers. I might have missed something.'

'That would be unlike you.'

'Thanks for the compliment, but I might overlooked the importance of something. I read them at the beginning of this quest, and one doesn't know the ins and outs at that stage.'

She almost begrudged the time at the reference library on the Friday, when she re-read the Ada Proctor trial case reports; they added little more to those of *The Times*. The death, the arrest of Davy Todd the following day, his appearance in court, his committal and the trial. Nothing new struck her. This was before the days of interviews with family members and witnesses. The most she could find to justify her visit was a short statement by Alfred Todd, Oliver's grandfather, that Davy had been innocent and that he would prove it, but she could find nothing more. *The Times* at least was indexed. Here one had to read every single issue. She studied the obituary of Ada's father again, then on impulse the obituary of the old Squire in 1929. Gerald Bloomfield had died in July that year. At the funeral mourners included, of course, Matthew and Isabel, and a couple from the US, presumably sister Anne and spouse. The service was taken by the Reverend Percy Standing. Poor chap. He only had fourteen years to go himself. On yet another impulse she decided to search through for his obituary. Not easy, for it took nearly an hour, but at last she found it.

The Reverend Percy had died suddenly on 18 November 1943 of gastroenteritis, aged sixty-nine. So that was how the rumours of poisoning must have begun. The She-Wolf surely couldn't have fancied him too much, even if he was described as 'much-loved vicar of Wickenham'. Moreover his widow and children were at the funeral, and the She-Wolf would have been in mourning for her own husband, who had also died in 1943. A busy year in Wickenham, Georgia thought. New Squire, new vicar, and the year François turned up. She turned back to check the funeral of poor old Matthew, the hen-pecked husband, and found he had died of heart failure in July. She didn't know what time of year François had come, but it was odds-on the vicar was still alive then, so wouldn't he have gone to call on him for information about the Randolph family if he got no joy at the Manor? Perhaps he did, but he obviously didn't get any or Jean would surely have known about the existence of the French family. For some reason, François seemed to have had made no more investigations however. If Guy didn't die here what happened to him? Jean's practical question still taunted her.

'Peter, what are you doing?' On her return Georgia found him at his computer, eating a late lunch with one hand and manoeuvring the mouse with the other.

'Going through our notes. We must have missed something.'

'Perhaps we have, but this is not the time. Bad for digestion.'

'So's this spaghetti. Guy Randolph *has* to be involved,' he continued without pause.

'Why?' She might as well give in and get it over quickly. If they didn't get rid of the Randolph story, perhaps they'd never see Ada Proctor clearly.

'He strangled her, and disappeared to start a new life just as he did at Gheluvelt.'

'Here we go again. Too many holes in the story.'

'Such as?'

'Holes such as if he strangled her on the spur of the moment, he forfeited his chance to make money out of his family – his main reason for coming.'

'Spur of the moment reaction to Ada's threats. What else?'

'Why didn't François Randolph go to the vicar, and if he did, why bother to go to see the maid?'

'Perhaps the vicar was out.'

'True. But why didn't François make another visit? The vicar could surely have put him in touch with the Randolphs.'

210

'Perhaps he did, but there was a war on, and François was on active service. Perhaps François decided to follow it up after the war.'

'But he *didn't*,' she almost shouted in frustration.

'We don't know that. Major and Mrs Randolph would probably be dead by then, and perhaps he couldn't trace the daughter.'

They were getting nowhere. Round and round the Randolph maypole, with no conclusion ever reached. Georgia knew her father was feeling as desperate as she was, especially when he grasped at a straw. 'At least we still agree Guy Randolph was at the Manor that evening.' Peter glared as Margaret came in, took one look at his half-empty plate on the corner of the desk, and bristled with disapproval.

'Leaving good food,' she muttered.

'I'm not leaving it. I'm relishing every mouthful, damn you,' Peter informed her. 'I'm just busy.'

'So,' declared Margaret, 'am I. I'm leaving in fifteen minutes. I am washing up now. All right by you?'

'Understood.' Peter shoved another mouthful in. 'I still say Randolph is the key.' He waved his fork at Georgia. 'He turns up at the Manor and, hey presto, a few hours later his ex-fiancée is strangled. These are incontrovertible facts.'

'So's your spaghetti,' Margaret warned him.

'Just a minute. This is important, Georgia. They *are* facts, aren't they?'

Before she could answer, Margaret intervened. 'No, Peter, they are not.'

'I beg your pardon?'

'Stands to reason, doesn't it?' Margaret snorted. 'I could go up to the Manor myself and say I was Guy Randolph. Doesn't mean to say I am.'

Chapter Thirteen

'Margaret's right, you know.'

'Why?' Georgia couldn't see the wood from the trees any longer, particularly where Wickenham Manor was concerned. They'd been thrashing it out over the weekend, but getting nowhere. 'Why,' she tried again, 'should he not be Guy Randolph? Did Rose Sadler get it wrong?'

'Possible. Unlikely though. They didn't know Guy, and I doubt if you mentioned Randolph in your initial letter to the Sadler family.'

'No. So –' Georgia battled with yet more theories – 'the visitor lied about his name or the Bloomfields lied, or some other mistake was made. An older Randolph perhaps. His father – that would explain quite simply how they stayed in for the evening.' At the moment this explanation appeared like heaven, to be grasped and cherished.

'And when Ada rang up, eager for a lover's tryst, this simple fact wasn't given to her, and the elderly Major Randolph then strangled her. You're not following through, Georgia.'

She had the grace to laugh. 'I'm doing my best.'

'Getting lost in the wood though. If the old major landed up in the denehole, firstly, he'd be missed, and secondly, we're back with the DNA problem again. He'd be even closer to Jean than Guy.'

'No. They only checked the maternal line.'

'Care to suggest to Darenth they do more tests?'

'No thanks, the idea's stupid. Anyway, it's like that old round you use to sing to me,' Georgia said viciously.

'There's a hole in my bucket, dear Charlie, dear Charlie . . . Round and round, and back we come to where we began. But there's a hole in my bucket.' She took a deep breath and tried again. 'Ada would have realized as soon as she saw him, if Margaret's thesis, unlike Charlie's bucket, holds water, that this wasn't her beloved Guy. Shock, horror, devastating disappointment.'

'Reason for murder?'

'Could be. Neither the maid nor the Sadlers would know this wasn't Guy Randolph, since they came to the village after the end of the war. But Matthew Bloomfield would, even if the She-Wolf didn't, and so would Ada.'

'But the coins, and the watch,' wailed Peter. 'And Guy Randolph of the farm *was* the real Guy Randolph. No doubt about that now. So the Scraggs connection tied in.'

'And yet Terence Scraggs died, perhaps coming to investigate it. It's interesting, you must admit. This chap comes in 1929 and says he's Guy Randolph, he disappears, probably murdered. Ada comes to see Guy Randolph, probably murdered for her pains. François comes to find out about Randolph – not murdered, but inquiries seem to end there, and Terence Scraggs comes to ask about the Randolphs and, blow me, he dies too.' A pause. 'Not to mention the vicar!' An idea began to form in her mind.

A howl from Peter. 'What about the vicar?'

'Died of gastroenteritis not long after François's visit, and, if rumour is correct, a close association with the She-Wolf Bloomfield.'

'What possible connection . . . ?' Peter stopped.

'What do vicars do?' Georgia promoted him encouragingly.

'They marry, baptize, bury. People confide in them or they might listen to confessions.'

'Like that of the old Squire Gerald, who died in July 1943.' She produced her plum from the pie.

Peter was cautious. 'Another leap in the dark.'

'Maybe I landed safely on the other side this time.'

213

'Maybe you fell in a denehole.'

'It's a thesis,' she said defensively.

'Go away, Georgia, and come back to me when you have supporting evidence.' And as she went out of the door he hurled after her, 'And remember the Bloomfields are clear so far as Terence Scraggs is concerned.'

There was only one place she could go, and that was Wickenham. She had no plan, nothing but a vague hope that something might emerge – either in fact or in her mind. She was sorely tempted to ask Luke if he were free to come with her, but decided against. Her antennae needed all her concentration, and never were they more necessary than now. She salved her conscience for coming to Wickenham without specific purpose, by persuading herself she could throw herself into a supermarket for the final round of the hell of Christmas shopping. On Christmas Eve this was not to be welcomed, and she blessed on-line shopping and the obliging village stores, which between them had already taken care of most of the chores. Christmas cards had gone and presents had been bought, only awaiting wrapping. Somehow she'd managed it, by letting Wickenham lie in the back of her mind.

Now she was here again, and decided to let her instinct guide her as to where to go. It was a grey day and she parked the car and wandered round the Green. Everyone seemed so intent on their own business, she wasn't, to her relief, greeted with any hostility. She pondered between the Green Man and the Forge, and decided on the latter.

Jim Hardbent was in, fortunately, and seemed reasonably pleased to see her though it could hardly have been welcome so close to Christmas. 'Thought you'd deserted us,' he said, leading the way to his beloved workroom.

'You and Wickenham are always in my mind,' Georgia said truthfully.

'Anyone throw rotten tomatoes at you?'

'No. What's the general feeling now?'

'It's moved on, I reckon.'

Janet produced coffee and they chatted for a while.

'Funny how things work out,' Jim observed. 'Having been at each other's throats, the village is getting together now because they're volunteering for DNA profiling.'

'That doesn't mean they'll welcome me again.'

'You're safe enough, to my way of thinking. No one now is connecting Ada Proctor to poor old Terence Scraggs. Except us, of course.'

'*You* do?' Georgia was surprised. She didn't think Jim knew about the Randolph link. She should have known better. Jim liked keeping a few surprises up his sleeve.

'Of course. Scraggs came here, asking me about it. He'd been to the Bloomfields, who couldn't or wouldn't help him, so he came here. While he was painting, he asked me if I knew what had happened to them. He reckoned he was descended from them, and his great-grandfather owned this big estate here. No big estates here, except Wickenham Manor, I told him. Hazelwood House only had a few acres. Would fetch a few bob now, but compared with Wickenham it was nothing. He started asking me all about the Broomfields and I lost patience. You find them and ask them, I said. That's their family history, not mine. If you ask me, Georgia, it's a good thing they've gone.'

'*Gone?*'

'Moved out last week.'

'The police must know where they are.' Georgia was surprised they'd put their plan into practice so quickly, but once they'd been cleared, she supposed the police couldn't stop them even if they wanted to.

'I'm sure they do. Why?' Jim eyed her keenly. 'Think they're mixed up in this affair, do you?'

'I'm beginning to think that they're mixed up in *every* affair.'

'That's the Manor for you.'

So the Bloomfields had left. Could that be part of the reason that the mood of Wickenham seemed much lighter?

Certainly Alice White, whom she ran into outside the Green Man, greeted her as cheerfully as if nothing had happened.

'I heard Mary wasn't too good, you might go and see her,' Alice mentioned.

'I planned to. What's happened to the sports fields by the way?'

'Nothing yet. There's a rumour that our Trevor's going to do the honourable thing, though, and turn them into a trust for the village.'

'Good for him. Though your family will miss out.'

'No, they won't. The supermarket's bought Dickens Field instead.'

Georgia tried not to laugh. 'Far enough away not to be a threat to the Todds,' she ventured to say.

'Want to bet? They'll object to anything.'

Things were moving on rapidly in Wickenham. It had only been three weeks since she was last here, yet the Bloomfields had vanished, and the waters had closed over the Todd–Elgin feud – for the time being. Happy Christmas, Wickenham.

Even so, as she walked around the village, there still seemed a sense of marking time. Perhaps it was just the inevitable one of waiting for Christmas. It was hard to tell, for the atmosphere she and Peter had picked up not only when they had first come here but when they began this project had been polluted by what had happened. It was easy enough to make a secure area, free of trampling footsteps and contamination, in an official police crime scene, but their own variation of that, full of fingerprints and impressions from the past, could not be so easily maintained.

Troubled at what she might find when she arrived at Four Winds, she was relieved to see Mary was well enough to be in her chair rather than in bed.

'Morning,' she grunted, as Georgia came into the room. She had been looking out over the gardens below, and Georgia wondered what she was seeing. Perhaps it was the cottage garden her mother had tended so carefully, that later became hers when she was married to Bill Beaumont.

'I'm glad to see you up,' Georgia greeted her, laying a Christmas gift on the bed. She had pondered for some time on what to buy.

'Thought you'd be coming. What's that?' She looked suspiciously at the parcel. 'Not toffees, is it?'

'No.' It was another shawl, the brightest and gaudiest she had been able to find, and she'd arranged for flowers to be delivered later today.

'Something's happened, hasn't it? You've got a bit further.'

If only. Still, there was no need to disillusion her. 'You're a miracle worker, Mary, as well having as the sight,' Georgia joked.

Mistake. 'No joking matter, young woman. 'Course I can't work miracles, but I know when they're about to happen. I knew it that last time I saw you, when you brought Miss Gwendolen's daughter. 'Ello, I said, to myself, things are moving at last. And with my bowels I know *that* feeling well.' She cackled. 'There now, there's a joke for you.'

Georgia dutifully laughed. For once Mary's 'sight' must be letting her down. No miracles had appeared on the horizon yet, or showed any indications of doing so.

'So what is it? Tell me,' Mary demanded.

'That's the odd thing,' Georgia began, scrabbling to make truth sound positive. 'Nothing really. We thought we'd inched forward when we learnt that Guy Randolph, Miss Gwendolen's brother, had been at the Manor that evening, and we were almost sure he would turn out to be the skeleton in the denehole. But her daughter's DNA didn't show any matches.' She wondered if Mary knew what DNA was, but she didn't comment. 'So we're sniffing around the Manor again, because it seems mixed up in some kind of mystery, not to mention the murder of this young man over the sports fields protest. I don't mean they did it, of course,' she added, 'but there's something there we can't quite get at.'

'Bad blood in them Bloomfields,' was all Mary commented. 'You sure the old Squire didn't do Ada in?'

'It's a theory,' Georgia admitted cautiously. 'Or his visitor that evening, whether it was Guy Randolph or not.'

'Poor old Ada, eh? Thought she was going to meet her dead lover – can't think who else she'd traipse over the fields for in the dark. And to think my Davy saw her. I can see him now, as plain as anything, peering out of those curtains. We'd only just finished doing you know what, see, and he was still buttoning himself up with one hand. Come back from those windows, I said. I was giggling, but he just stood there looking out. It's Miss Ada, he said. Funny thing, that is. And he stayed there watching till she disappeared.'

'But he didn't go out to see where she was going?'

'I wouldn't let him. Pretended I was jealous. Don't be daft, he said, and we were just about to go at it again when me Dad came back early. Davy would have liked to go out then I can tell you. Caught with his pants down. We both were.' She caught her breath. 'Oh my Davy. Look here, you know that old song "Georgia on My Mind". Makes me think of you.'

Did she know it? Of course she did. Zac was forever twitting her about it. Even in bed. No, Georgia, *no*. She pulled herself back to the present.

'You've been on my mind too,' Mary continued happily. 'I reckon you're going to do it, you're sniffing around the right quarters if you ask me. Go on, girl. Give me and Davy a Christmas present.'

'I'll try but—'

'I'll make a pact. I won't die before New Year – give you till then, I could die easy anyway, now I know you're getting somewhere.'

'But Mary, we *don't* know that!' Georgia was divided as to whether Mary was deliberately winding her up, or whether she meant it. Perhaps some of both, a thought that alarmed Georgia even more.

'That's because you're out there batting for England and I'm stuck in a chair with nothing to do but think. You try thinking, instead of batting, eh? See you in the New Year. And on your way out, tell that girl I need a pee.' And as Georgia moved to help her herself, 'Not you. You've got better things to do. The clock's ticking fast.'

The clock's ticking fast. What did that remind her of? Georgia thought as she drove back to Haden Shaw. That French watch that could have belonged to anyone, probably to the skeleton, but perhaps not. Perhaps there was a hoard down there of stolen goods. No, the police would have found it by now. Let's assume the skeleton did own that Bréguet. Ticking away . . .

As she walked in her front door, she bent down to pick up the pile of Christmas cards on the mat. She'd open them this evening, she decided. Then a sudden impulse made her look through the addresses now, just in case there were any with handwriting she didn't instantly recognize, or recognized only too well and remembered she'd forgotten to include it on her list.

She saw the stamp first – Italian. Then she saw the handwriting, and was instantly in shock. It was Zac's. Why on earth did this have to happen? He *never* sent Christmas cards, it was one of his pet phobias, albeit because of sheer laziness. He had never sent her one before, so why now? She had no doubt about its source, even though there was no address on the back of the envelope.

This couldn't be left until this evening. She had to brace herself to open it now. Georgia tore open the envelope and saw a guileless Madonna and child picture, but she knew that when she opened the card she would see his familiar scrawl: 'Zac with love'. Whenever Peter or someone had nudged him into remembering it was her birthday, or he wrote the occasional note to friend or family, it was never 'With love from Zac', but always: 'Zac with love'. Till he let them down, of course.

She opened the card, feeling her stomach churn, as she

saw the words she expected: 'Zac with love'. Plus 'Say hello to the old man'. That was Peter, the 'old man' who had put him in prison. Great. This time, however, there was a longer message too, which she forced herself to read, though she wanted to chuck the thing away as soon as possible and forget about it. 'My gorgeous. All hail to thee. Living here with a delightful Botticelli of a lady, but Sweet Georgia always on my mind. The Tichborne Claimant will pop up one of these days.'

You bet he would. Why couldn't Zac just disappear with his Botticelli Venus and stay that way? He had *no* claim on her, his former wife, nor any more cause to see her than the false claimant had on the Tichborne estate in the nineteenth-century cause célèbre.

Her stomach churned again. It was Christmas Eve, why did this have to happen *now*, when her mind was already spinning so much it couldn't tell turkey from goose or sprouts from cabbage? The stuffing had to be prepared. Why hadn't she brought the frozen variety? The pudding had to be thought about. The bread sauce. And Luke was coming tonight. What to eat then? And on top of it all, *Zac*.

Half an hour later she managed the strength to visit her father. She had packed a lot into those thirty minutes, and the glimmerings of the – preposterous? – idea that had come to her had mercifully pushed Zac into the background. She'd take it steadily though, suppressing excitement.

She found Margaret there, though she wasn't due for another hour or two. It was immediately clear why she'd come. She'd decided to serve his Christmas Eve meal – a special one – herself.

'Georgia,' Peter demanded, 'kindly tell this woman she shouldn't come in tomorrow. We can manage without her. Not wanted.' He glared at Margaret.

'Tomorrow?' Georgia said, horrified. 'Oh Margaret, you mustn't. You've your own Christmas, and family.'

Margaret went slightly pink. 'You're part of it,' she muttered. 'What's Christmas all about if you can't help

220

family? You'll be cooking, Georgia, and rushing around, and Luke will be helping you. It won't take me a moment to pop in. When I'm too old to work you can put me out to pasture. Until then I'm coming. Is that understood?'

'I shall take Christmas Day off,' Peter said grandly, after Margaret had left. 'I thought I'd read the new Dalziel and Pascoe. Oh, maybe an Allingham too. Haven't read *Tiger in the Smoke* for some time.'

'Father, have I got news for you,' Georgia said as calmly as she could.

'Don't tell me. Trevor Bloomfield's confessed to murder.' He looked at her sharply.

'If only. Look.' She thrust Zac's card in his hand.

'Don't get upset—' Peter stopped, as he read the complete message, took a second or two to ponder it, and then realized why she'd shown it to him. Then: 'Is your conclusion the same as mine?'

'Yes, it was some threat to the Bloomfield inheritance that caused the deaths of Denehole Man and/or Guy Randolph from Berthès Farm, and probably Terence Scraggs too. What else could have kept them so wary over the years?' So far so good. She could see Peter was with her.

'How's Ada mixed up with that?' There was no challenge in Peter's question. He, like she, was thinking fast and furiously. 'I see. She isn't the main player after all. Your theory is that it's been always been Wickenham Manor causing problems in this village, in 1929, 1943 and today. A wide sweep, isn't it? Have you a scenario, Georgia?'

'Yes. Guy Randolph from Berthès Farm had a claim on Wickenham Manor.'

'How can that be?' Peter's question was rhetorical, now that they both realized the probable answer.

'Because he wasn't Guy Randolph. He was Jack Bloomfield.'

The truth had been there before them all the time, but they had been looking in the wrong direction. They chewed it over for an hour, until finally Peter nodded. 'Okay, Georgia, convincing scenario, please.'

She took a moment to think herself back in the Wickenham of the early twentieth century. 'There were the six of them, Guy and Gwendolen, Ada and Anne, Jack and Matthew,' she began, 'who were the core of the social life at the Manor before the First World War. Guy and Ada were an item, whether formally engaged or not. The war claimed Jack and Guy, and after it Anne married and Gwendolen left the village, leaving only Matthew and Ada in Wickenham in 1929. Matthew married Isabel, the She-Wolf, in the early twenties, and a new chapter opened at Wickenham Manor. Jack had officially died in the war, and Guy was missing. I need to go to the PRO again to check this, but it's probable that Jack and Guy, being great chums, were in the same regiment, even the same battalion.

'However it happened, they were both in the same engagement in which Jack Bloomfield officially died, and from which Guy deserted. But it was in fact Guy who died, and Jack Bloomfield, much the same sort of character as Guy, according to what we've been told, who deserted, having neatly switched identity tags with Guy's corpse. He is now, he tells himself, Guy Randolph, and we know how he set himself up nicely in France with first Farmer Berthès' daughter and then Rosanne. Unfortunately he doesn't like farming or indeed any hard work. He is, he tells his family, heir to a big estate in England. Not Hazelwood House, as we'd thought, but Wickenham Manor. Perhaps he read the notice of his father's death in *The Times*. With his preferred lifestyle, he no doubt kept in touch with events in England. The problem is that he knows he can't go back there.'

'Why?'

Georgia's mind raced. She was slightly surprised Peter hadn't stopped her before, since she was conscious of more speculation here than usual. 'Firstly he's a deserter, and for all he knows, he could still be arrested as Guy Randolph. Secondly, perhaps he didn't want to knuckle down to the responsibilities of running the estate, and thirdly, there would be a major legal battle with brother Matthew over who was the real heir to Wickenham. True, he was officially dead, but he had only to show his face in Wickenham for the whole village to recognize him.'

'So why come, and, as he did, why the need for secrecy?'

He'd trapped her, Georgia thought furiously. No, he hadn't. 'As I said, he didn't want the responsibility of running Wickenham. He wanted *money*, though. So he set out to blackmail brother Matthew and his wife, the She-Wolf. He came straight to the Manor incognito, announcing himself as Guy Randolph. The maid fortunately didn't recognize him, though he took a chance there. It must have been somewhat of a shock for Matthew, especially since I doubt whether he had the kind of money brother Jack had in mind. Furthermore, no doubt brother Jack pointed out that he had legitimate children of his own, who would be all too interested to know of their heritage. There was an even worse shock when in the midst of their discussions, Ada Proctor rings up in great excitement. All of them are in a quandary now. The Bloomfields can't risk her seeing Jack's face, nor can Jack himself if he's going to get his cash. So . . .'

'Go on,' Peter prompted as she broke off.

'I can't. I'm stuck.'

'How about this?' Peter took up the story for her. 'Jack/Guy makes an arrangement to meet Ada later on either at the Manor or somewhere along that footpath. Perhaps it was a spot they once knew well and did their courting there. Jack could have known all about that. What more splendid tool than Ada to get his way over the blackmail, Jack thinks. The Bloomfields are trapped. If they don't agree, Ada will spread the news of Jack's Return Home in a flash. They have to come to some financial arrangement by say, ten o'clock, or earlier if Jack had to walk to the meeting place. When Ada turned up, she had to find "Guy" had gone.'

223

'Accepted,' Georgia agreed. 'Just one problem in Jack's plan. There was no money at Wickenham to pay him off. So Matthew and Isabel see their whole livelihood threatened, and their kids' legacy at risk. It would take Jack time to disentangle the official death verdict, but it could be done. His face was evidence enough, coupled with his undoubted grasp of every pre-war family detail. There was only one answer, as they saw it. Jack had to disappear before Ada arrived, and this time for good.'

'Into the denehole,' Peter murmured.

'Yes. Matthew or he and the She-Wolf between them murder Jack and Ada.'

'Hang on, Georgia. Why Ada? They could time it so they would miss her arrival. They must have known she was coming some time around ten p.m., according to our scenario, and they wouldn't have wanted to strangle her too, especially Matthew. Far too risky.'

'The She-Wolf wouldn't have been so picky,' Georgia said.

'Slander.'

'This is only a scenario.'

'Go ahead then, but take it easy. I'm not altogether happy.'

'Nor am I. Perhaps they mistimed it . . .' Georgia was foxed. 'Perhaps they killed Jack but it took longer than expected to get him into the denehole. They're unlikely to have run it so close though. I'm stuck. The timing just doesn't work.'

'Timing,' repeated Peter meditatively. '*Timing.* Now that watch he was wearing. . .could it have been set to a different time, since he'd come from France?'

'No, I'm pretty sure French time was the same as Greenwich in 1929. Wrong path, Peter.'

'Time could well come into it somehow,' he persisted. 'Otherwise there seems no explanation for Ada's death. As I see it, Ada must have arrived all bright-eyed and bushy-tailed at ten o'clock, just in time to see them either killing the man she thinks is her lover, or throwing him in the denehole. But then, as you said, why did the Bloomfields leave the murder so near to the time when they knew Ada might be around.'

'Perhaps –' Georgia thought this through logically – 'they *didn't* know that she'd be around. If the maid or even Jack himself took the call – it had been his home after all – only he would know what arrangement he'd made with Ada. Perhaps –' her hopes grew – 'he kept this back as a fail-safe bargaining point with the Bloomfields. They won't see things his way, so he gets up from his chair and announces he's off to catch the last train to London and – incidentally – he's meeting Guy's former sweetheart on the way there. She might not have recognized Jack's voice on the telephone but she certainly would recognize face to face that this was Jack, not her beloved Guy.'

'Good,' Peter said approvingly. 'But, darling Georgia, if, say, he was due to meet her at ten fifteen or ten thirty, and he made his dramatic announcement between nine thirty and nine forty-five, the Boomfields would make sure that they kept Jack well out of Ada's path. Checkmate, I think.'

'Not yet.' Georgia grappled with this last stumbling block. What was it Peter had said earlier? Bright-eyed and bushy-tailed. *That* was it. 'Of course, Peter. Ada was a woman,' she cried out triumphantly.

'I always said you were a great detective, Watson.'

'Quiet please. Ada hasn't seen Guy for at least twelve years. She doesn't want to waste a second of this reunion. He must surely feel the same. He might arrive early. *And so would she.* She does so, and catches the Bloomfields in the last stages of pushing Jack down the denehole.'

'Possible. In fact, probable,' Peter graciously allowed after a seeming never-ending silence. 'I note however that we're both referring to *them,* not just Matthew Bloomfield.'

'I assume that where Matthew went the She-Wolf was not far behind.'

'Lady Macbeth soiling her hands. They strangled Ada?'

Georgia nodded, on safer ground now. 'She'd either run

for her life or walked with them to the edge of the wood, where she was killed, and then they dragged or carried her back to Crown Lea.'

'Why not push her into the denehole too?'

'She'd be missed.'

'Why the field?'

'The need to distance the body from the denehole and the Wickenham estate. There was no torch listed in the exhibits at the trial and, though that isn't conclusive, it could have been because her torch was left where she was killed, and Lord or Lady Macbeth scooped it up later. Ada's handbag had to go with her, though, or it would be missed.'

'Agreed. Done. Theoretical scenario very provisionally accepted.' Peter leant back with satisfaction and Georgia began to think longingly of escape. 'Now, about the She-Wolf . . .' Peter began.

Georgia could see where this was going. Ah well, better to get it over with. She thought for a moment. Then: 'The She-Wolf and the Vicar. This scenario runs: by 1943 Matthew is frail, he realizes he hasn't long to live, and the murder of his brother hangs heavily on him. He needs to confess. So he does, to the vicar. The She-Wolf is furious when Matthew tells her, or she finds out, but assumes the vicar won't split on them for the usual reasons, after Matthew's death.

'However, along comes François and the vicar is in a dilemma. If Matthew has explained about the Randolph connection, then he knows that François is actually Jack Bloomfield's son, and François and his brothers have a claim on Wickenham. What should he do? Direct François to the Randolph family or the Bloomfields? Either course seems wrong. He takes François's address, and tells Isabel she must tell François the truth, but he dies as a result.'

'So far, so good,' Peter said approvingly. 'But what if Matthew just told the vicar that he'd murdered his brother and Ada, without any mention of the Randolph connection? There'd be no reason for Matthew to mention it.'

'Ah.' Georgia was checkmated. Or was she? 'The vicar would have given François the Randolph address if he had it. *But –*' thinking furiously – 'when François got no joy at the Manor, he had told the She-Wolf innocently that he would go to see the vicar. And so he does, but the vicar either doesn't have the address or smells a sufficient rat when François begins to talk dates and background for Guy Randolph to be cagey. So he sends François to see the Manor maid.'

'Why?' Peter asked politely.

Sinking heart time. 'Offloading responsibilities,' she tried hopefully. 'Guy Randolph came over here in 1929, and Jack Bloomfield and Ada were murdered. Surely no coincidence, he thinks. He can't say a word, but why not give François a sporting chance to look into it? He sends him to see the Manor maid, but says if he comes across the Randolphs' address he'll send it on. Manor maid doesn't have the Randolphs' address. End of story.' She glanced nervously at Peter, but to her relief he did not comment.

'And then,' she concluded, 'the vicar goes to see Isabel She-Wolf after François' visit. He is torn in his duty, he says. Matthew has not implicated his wife, but the vicar feels a duty to the Randolphs too.'

'Both possibilities accepted,' Peter said. 'Go on.'

'Thanks very much. The vicar is a loose cannon, thinks the She-Wolf. He's getting on and goodness knows what he might say. The She-Wolf has her son's future to think of. So the vicar has to go. Easy enough to invite him to lunch, and slip the rat poison into the pie. She stops short of murdering his whole family—'

'I'm relieved.'

'So that's it,' Georgia concluded.

'What about Terence Scraggs?' came the inevitable question.

One more river to cross . . . She made a huge effort.

'Okay. Here goes. Terence is a Randolph. He has been told by Grandpa François this legend of the great estate and

François's own fruitless errand, so he comes to Wickenham to chat with Trevor Bloomfield. He's also heard about the body in the denehole. He makes a plan of the estate and begins to put two and two together, but unfortunately only made three. He still believes it was Guy Randolph who had come here in 1929, and had been the skeleton in that denehole, and innocently assumed Trevor would like to know. Or,' she amended hastily, seeing Peter's expression and interpreting it correctly, 'not so innocent. Maybe he saw the chance of a bit of blackmail too.'

'And where, dear daughter, does that leave us?'

'Back on the Bloomfield doorstep.'

'Their DNA profiles weren't a match with the alien hair.'

'Perhaps the hair was nothing to do with it.'

'Trevor Bloomfield is a businessman. He wouldn't lose his nerve at a blackmail threat from the likes of Terence, and, after all, blackmail over what? That for some reason his grandfather bumped off Guy Randolph? So what? It was over seventy years ago. If Trevor Bloomfield wanted to stop Scraggs from talking, it would be over a threat to his pocket, not his ethics. Where's your evidence? he'd ask.'

'Some kind of shadow must have lingered over the Bloomfields,' Georgia maintained obstinately, 'and it's flared up again now. They could all have known, or at least the heirs, that Jack was passing himself off as Randolph and that he had a family. They *wouldn't* know what evidence that family might still have that Guy Randolph was actually Jack Bloomfield. Suppose the message came down to Trevor that there could be a major threat to their ownership from anyone called Randolph.'

'Possible. I'll buy that,' Peter graciously agreed. 'But not to the extent of his murdering Scraggs. I'll see you in court, would be Trevor's reaction.'

'Doesn't it depend on what Terence said to him? He wasn't exactly sophisticated, but he had a lot of intelligence and could have worked out the Bloomfield–Randolph connection.' She warmed to this. 'After all, François could have told him all about his visits to the Manor and, if we're right, the vicar. Suppose Terence barged in to see Trevor with a definite claim. Hey, I'm a Randolph, but I've evidence I'm really a Bloomfield and heir to Wickenham. The deal for the sale was just going through, and considering the jittery state the Bloomfields were in over the sports fields protest, it could have been the last straw. Delay might have put paid to the sale in the case of the hotel. No one wants a lawsuit hanging over them, whether it's likely to succeed or not. Terence would have had no hesitation airing his claim to all and sundry.'

'Possibly, but do I have to remind you *again*, Georgia, that there is no DNA evidence that the Bloomfields were involved in Scraggs's murder? They and just about every blinking member of Wickenham village has had a sample taken. You're turning into a bit of a She-Wolf yourself about the Bloomfields. I'm with you up to and including Isabel's drastic methods of silence, but today murder is a far less effective weapon than the courts. Especially when one side has money and the other hasn't.'

Georgia had only been half listening. 'That's it,' she said slowly.

'That's what?' Peter asked extremely crossly.

'You said the Bloomfields had all given DNA samples. You meant father, son Jacob and son who were visible at the protest. How about the She-Wolf in lamb's clothing, Julia? The Bloomfields have upped and left Wickenham. Did she volunteer a buccal swab before they left? I doubt it. And she wouldn't stomach any threat to the sale. Or to her financial security. Trevor might have brazened it out with Scraggs, but his own She-Wolf could have been all for direct action, given such a splendid opportunity. Julia was interested enough to help me when I first met her, but my mention of the name Randolph put the heebie-jeebies into Trevor; he probably gave her hell after I left, and told her exactly why the Randolph name was so unpopular.

Knowing Julia, I think she'd have seen the message right away. *And* acted on it.'

He frowned. 'Going out on a limb, aren't you?'

'Am I?' She seized the evidence file and rummaged to find the police breakdown Mike had given them. 'Here,' she said in triumph. 'The Bloomfields came out and father and younger son retreated. Jacob remained, and went later, but Terence was still alive then. No mention of Julia Bloomfield at all. According to her husband, she was in the house. Anything to stop her from donning a balaclava, coming round from the rear of the house and joining the Elgin gang?'

'No, Georgia, there isn't. But this is here and now, not fantasy land.'

'Here and now things *happen*. Isn't it worth asking Mike casually, just *very* casually, if Julia Bloomfield has given a DNA sample to see if it matches that hair caught under Terence Scraggs' fingernail?'

Late that evening she let herself into her house to find Luke there, a fire in the grate and, from the smell of it, dinner in the oven. The Christmas lights were on, her slippers were waiting by the sofa. Luke turned round at her entry and came to meet her.

'Well, sweetheart? Progress?'

'We think you may have your book.'

'Based on what?'

Georgia smiled. 'What Peter always hoped for. Jack's Return Home.'

Epilogue

'How do you feel about Wickenham now?' Luke asked. It was New Year's Day, and the village presented only its fair image, children out with parents, strolling over the Green, or marching towards the sports fields. A Todd talked to an Elgin, the Green Man had a festive air.

'Delightful,' Georgia answered. It was. She could swear there were no fingerprints here now. A whole week without the Ada Proctor case, a week of bliss. Then yesterday morning Mike had called to tell them that the skeleton's DNA sample had sufficient in common with that of Trevor Bloomfield to convince the police that it was worth pursuing Julia Bloomfield's DNA. If it matched that of Terence Scraggs that would put her in the frame for his murder.

Peter had grunted. He had already, Georgia suspected, erased Wickenham's fingerprints from his mind, and he'd long forgotten about the East Anglian case. He seemed more interested in an out-of-the-way pub they'd visited over the holiday period. Friday Street was the name of the hamlet, and even Georgia had been bound to agree there was a weird atmosphere about it. Then she had forgotten it as Morris men arrived to dance their Christmas special, and she and her father had fiercely debated the pros and cons of reviving ancient customs.

One duty and pleasure remained in Wickenham, however, and she, Peter and Luke were here to fulfil it: Mary Elgin.

Somehow they had managed to get Peter's wheelchair into the small lift at Four Winds. He was not, he insisted, going to be left out of this, and since Mary was in bed again, the staff refused to allow her downstairs. She was very weak, Georgia could see, but still, to her relief, alert. The gaudy new shawl was draped over the bedcover, which was a good sign.

'Three of you, eh? So it's all right at last.' Mary looked hopefully at each of them in turn.

'Yes, Mary. We think we've done it.'

'It were those Bloomfields, weren't it?'

'Yes.'

'Always trouble at that Manor, Mum said. Nasty lot. Wickenham would be better off without them, the way she saw it.'

'And now it is.'

'That's all right then. So Davy's clear.'

'Yes,' Peter told her gravely. 'The problem is, Mary, that it can't be official now. Even though they've found the dead body of Jack Bloomfield, who also died that night, no one can ever prove up to court of law standard that what we are sure happened is true. We can try for an official clearance of Davy Todd, but that's doubtful, not because the police don't believe it, but for technical reasons.'

Mary made not a sound or move. She just watched him.

'What we can do,' he continued, 'is publish our book. We can make sure that everyone who reads it will know Davy was innocent.'

Here came the sticky part, as Georgia knew very well. They'd discussed it endlessly not only with this case, but previous ones. 'We can publish our book and Davy is theoretically cleared,' she had said to her father yesterday, 'but the innocent in the Bloomfield family will suffer without proof. There's no libel problem, but there's a moral one.'

'We can't judge that,' he had answered. 'We can only present our evidence, draw our conclusion and make it clear there's a difference between the two.'

Now Mary looked in disgust from one to the other. 'Who in Wickenham is going to read a whole blessed book? Anyway, you've done what you said. I knew he was innocent, and you've told me what happened, so I can pop up there and say hello, Davy, I'm here to stay, any time I choose.'

Mary's eyes closed, and, frightened, Georgia realized they hadn't said the right thing. She was still set on death. What more could they offer? Perhaps after all they had been wrong to expect to satisfy the crabby old lady of the teashop.

'Who's going to read a blinking book?' Mary repeated faintly, eyes still closed.

'Quite a lot of people,' Luke said firmly, 'and we can spread the word further with reviews of the book in the paper and television interviews—'

Mary's eyes flew open. 'You mean I might be on telly? Now you're talking.' Slowly she heaved herself up on the pillows. 'Tell you what, Davy,' she croaked, 'I'll only be a jiff, but I'm going to hang on for them telly folks first.'`